A MATTER OF TRUST

A MATTER OF TRUST

Maxine Barry

CHIVERS

British Library Cataloguing in Publication Data available

This Large Print edition published by AudioGO Ltd, Bath, 2012.
Published by arrangement with the author.

U.K. Hardcover   ISBN   978 1 4458 4473 2
U.K. Softcover   ISBN   978 1 4458 4474 9

Printed and bound in Great Britain by
MPG Books Group Limited

CHAPTER ONE

Nesta Aldernay saw the first road signs indicating that Oxford lay just ahead of her, and felt the tension already tightening her shoulder blades intensify. Deliberately, she forced her muscles to relax, and took a deep, relaxing breath.

She got in line at a busy T-junction, still a little nervous of driving, having passed her driving test only a short time ago. Naturally, a big lorry promptly started tooting angrily behind her. She refused to let herself be bullied, however, and waited until she felt safe to move off.

It was a fine late September morning when her rather ancient Beetle finally entered the city limits, but the leaves were turning early this year, she noted, with a faint sigh of regret. A freak frost had nipped the chrysanthemums and Michaelmas daisies in the gardens lining the streets, and a few copper-coloured leaves were already beginning to litter the pavements as she carefully negotiated the big and busy roundabout at the head of Banbury Road.

She kept a sharp look out for taxis and the ubiquitous bicycles in this strange new city and told herself not to be such a mouse. She had enough worries to think about, without getting a phobia about driving!

On the passenger seat beside her lay a map of Oxford. In her boot was a large, tatty suitcase, packed with a variety of clothes, mostly culled from second-hand shops and closing-down sales. She had, at that point, no idea how long she would be staying in Oxford. Nor had she any illusions about the kind of reception that she might soon be facing.

And it definitely wouldn't be the red-carpet treatment.

Nobody who came to rock the boat could expect to be greeted with open arms. Things, Nesta thought grimly to herself as she carefully overtook a cyclist, could get very nasty, very fast.

Of course, a lot depended on the attitude of one Sir Vivian Dalrymple, and what she herself would be able to uncover in the next few weeks or months. And be willing to pursue, to its ultimate, grim conclusion.

She slowed down as she checked out the name of the road leading off on her right. Sir Vivian, she knew, lived in an area off the Banbury Road called Park Town. According to the map, this was located in the up-market and leafy suburb called Summertown.

A few more hundred yards up ahead she found it, indicated with care, and slowed the old, mint-green VW Beetle into a crawl. The area was a wealthy one all right. Private schools and very desirable residences smugly beamed at her from behind neatly trimmed privet hedges and freshly-painted black iron railings.

It was a far cry from her street back home in Durham. But then, she was the daughter of working-class parents who'd been raised on a council estate, and not Sir Vivian Dalrymple, Peer of the realm, Oxford Don, and noted psychologist.

She found the house she was looking for tucked away in a small round cul-de-sac, and pulled to a halt outside a set of large, intricately patterned wrought iron gates. She'd bought the VW Beetle with the proceeds of her mother's meagre inheritance just last year, and the new found freedom her beloved little car had given her was much appreciated.

After the death of her father when she'd been barely five years old, she and her mother had naturally become very close, and her loss had hit Nesta hard. But attending university at the time of her death, and being surrounded as she was by her friends and living in a crowded, cheerful student dorm, it had helped her get over the worst of the shock and the accompanying feeling of acute loneliness. And having to concentrate on getting her degree and sitting her final exams had also aided her with the grieving process. It gave her something to concentrate her mind on other than just the unfairness of life, and of a woman dying at just forty-six years of age due to a heart attack.

3

Her mother's small council house, that she'd scrimped and saved to buy back in the eighties, had, of course, been left to her only child in her will. And it was during the long vacation that Nesta had decided it needed a thorough 'do out'. Which was when she'd discovered her father's old papers in the attic.

Until that day, she'd thought that life had already thrown at her the worst that it possibly could. Now she was learning that there was no limit to the number of blows that life could deal to you . . .

Nesta caught herself up abruptly and angrily shook her head. First things first. She might have been ignorantly blissful before, but now she was armed with knowledge. And determined to use it. Come what may.

She retrieved her briefcase from the back seat, and carefully locked her car before glancing around. Then she pushed open the iron gates and walked, tight-lipped, up a well kept and weed-free gravel path. Her chin was set at a firm angle. Her shoulders were back. She looked like what she was—a woman prepared to do battle.

Even so, she glanced around her curiously. The house was a simple, two-storey Cotswold stone house with big bay windows, and a lovely creeper, now turning a deep red, which climbed the height of its walls. The garden wasn't huge, but it was very well tended. Neatly clipped bushes, now turning a little brown

4

about the edges, had probably given loads of lovely colour during the summer months. Over to the left was a small rose garden, still bearing several yellow and pink blooms.

She stopped suddenly as she noticed an old man, busily dead-heading a bush. She paused to reflect for a few moments, then abandoned the path to the front door and headed towards him instead. One part of her wondered if she was just being cowardly and postponing the inevitable for a few minutes, whilst a second part of her assured her that it was only good tactics to spy out the lie of the land first.

'Excuse me?' she said softly, and watched the old man give a start, and spin around.

He was one of those old men who looked wonderfully rounded and pink-cheeked. The kind of man, for instance, who could easily play Father Christmas at the local orphanage. Even the blue eyes sweeping over her so speculatively had a nice twinkle in them.

'Hello,' he said, straightening up with just a wince, and a pronounced breathlessness. Noticing her sympathetic look, he explained cheerfully, 'Touch of lumbago. And the old ticker's giving me jip. Can I help you. young lady?'

The courtly expression somehow suited the man. It was impossible to get any feminist feathers ruffled by his old-fashioned courtesy, and Nesta smiled at him widely.

'I was wondering if Sir Vivian Dalrymple

5

was home?'

The blue eyes twinkled some more as the old man slowly removed one of his gardening gloves. 'At your service,' he said politely, even half-bowing his head as he did so. Then he moved closer and held out his hand.

She was a pretty little thing, Sir Vivian thought, intrigued by the sudden flush of hot colour that diffused her cheeks, then just as suddenly disappeared, leaving her looking distinctly unnerved. And the psychologist in him instantly became alert. He noted the interesting body language as her small figure suddenly tensed. She was, he guessed, about five feet two in height, but at that moment she was mentally projecting an image of a six-footer. Her deep red hair was cut in a becoming bell shape, framing her face and coming to two sharp little points either side of her jaw. Like most natural redheads, her skin was very fair, but now it looked positively ghostly.

He watched her give herself a little mental shake as she realised he was still holding his hand out, ready for it to be shaken. Her eyes, a lovely emerald green, became abruptly sharp and focused as she too, took a step forward.

Sir Vivian gave her an encouraging smile. There was definitely something in the air. He only hoped that she didn't want to consult him privately. He hadn't taken on private patients since he'd first earned his doctorate.

Nowadays, he was strictly a lecturer. And a soon to be retired one at that. His doctor had made it very clear that it was high time he took things easy.

'How do you do, Sir Vivian. My name is Nesta Aldernay.' The voice was cool, polite, and had a touch of the north-country in the accent.

'Nesta. What a charming name!' he beamed, and realised how cold her hand felt in his. 'Would you like to come in for a cup of tea, Miss Aldernay? I was about to take a short break, anyway. There's a difference between a little gentle exercise, and overdoing it. At least, so my doctor says.'

Nesta smiled. 'Thank you. I'd love to,' she murmured. Well, so far, things were looking good. Sir Vivian seemed like a very nice man. But it was early days yet.

Sir Vivian nodded, took off his other gardening glove, and led the way across the gravel to the front door.

'I must say, we're certainly getting the early frosts this year, don't you. . .' Th . . . umph!

Sir Vivian's pleasantries came to an abrupt end as he went to open the door and started to go through it before it was actually open. Consequently his shoulder hit the firm wooden barrier a glancing blow. He stood back, ruefully rubbed the top of his arm, and tried the handle again. Evidently, it refused to budge, and he shook his head exasperatedly.

7

'The catch must have slipped down again. The dratted thing does that all the time. I keep meaning to get it fixed . . . Oh well, follow me.' The old man gave a half-amused, half-annoyed chuckle and turned around.

Nesta, hiding a grin, followed the noted psychologist back through the rose garden to a small garden shed set well back by the rear wall. He briefly stepped inside, then emerged a few moments later, triumphantly waving a big silver key.

'Always keep a spare kitchen door key in here,' he beamed, and shuffled around the back of the house.

Nesta, thinking of her rather crime-ridden estate back home, wondered ruefully just how long her DVD player and television would remain in her house if she did the same.

What it was to live in the rarefied and safe atmosphere of academe! Not that Sir Vivian seemed to be the sort of man who needed to flaunt his wealth and status. At that precise moment in time, he was wearing a pair of rather disreputable trousers, and a thick jersey with holes at the elbows.

He really was a poppet. Already, Nesta began to feel some of her tension dripping away. She had chosen her champion well. Whatever happened next, at least she wouldn't be denigrated, threatened or angrily dismissed as a little air-head.

But she mustn't ever forget that this was

a very influential man. For all his 'favourite uncle' appearance, he'd been a Fellow of St Bede's College for over thirty years. He still lectured regularly for the university, and was the author of numerous, well-received books. She had no doubt that he'd retained the brain of a very, very sharp man indeed. Which was why she'd picked him in the first place, of course. She needed someone with an impeccable reputation on her side if she was ever to get justice for what had been done to her father.

A man she could now barely remember.

'Ah, that's better,' Sir Vivian said, as the key turned in the lock and he pushed open the door triumphantly. Then they walked into a wonderfully warm, cheerfully yellow kitchen.

'Right then,' Sir Vivian rubbed his hands briskly. 'Tea. China, Indian, or something dreadful and herbal?' he offered hospitably.

Nesta laughed. 'Whatever you're having, Sir Vivian.'

The old man nodded with satisfaction. That was better. She had a bit of colour back in her cheeks now, and that aura of dreadful tension had lifted.

And something had long-since told him that this was no prospective patient, either. In spite of her obvious nervousness, there was also a feeling of competency about her. An aura of what he'd always secretly labelled HSOR (head-screwed-on-right). It was a very un-doctor like expression, and he'd die before ever admitting to having used it, but there was no doubt that, at times, it described people very accurately indeed.

Now he put on the kettle and indicated a chair. 'Unless you'd like to go into the living room, my dear?' he added hastily as an afterthought, hiding a twinge of embarrassment as he recalled the state of that room.

He made a mental note to clear it up before his wife came home from the hospital.

Nesta quickly shook her head. 'No thank you, I'm fine,' she assured him. The kitchen had that lived-in look that all good kitchens had. The rectangular wooden table in the centre was scratched but big and well used, and the chairs around it were round-backed, well padded and looked comfortable.

They were.

She sat down gratefully, then deliberately put her briefcase on the table in front of her. This business-like gesture was definitely not lost on Sir Vivian, but he nevertheless kept up a pleasant line in chit-chat as he set about preparing the tea.

'Are you an Oxfordian, Miss Aldernay?' he fished for information gently.

'No. I come from Durham. I've just finished getting my B.A. there.'

'Oh? What subject?'

'psychology.'

Sir Vivian paused momentarily, frozen in the act of extracting a spoonful of tea from the tea caddy. 'Oh? I do hope, you're not under the impression, er . . .' he broke off, looking a little embarrassed.

But Nesta was already ahead of him. 'No, I'm not here to try and wangle a graduate place at Oxford, Sir Vivian. This is strictly personal.'

Sir Vivian shot her a quick look. She looked very composed, sitting there in her plain black slacks and grey and lavender coloured pullover. The tones suited her, without making any particular statement. They were casual, but smart.

Sir Vivian smiled. Interestinger and Interestinger, as Alice might have said during her sojourn into Wonderland.

The kettle boiled and he made the tea, bringing it to the table on a battered tray. He took a milk bottle from the fridge and set it down beside the teapot, much to Nesta's relief. After watching him spoon in the old-fashioned loose tea leaves, she'd half expected him to bring out a hideously expensive Royal Dalton tea-set and silver creamer. And she wouldn't have felt comfortable using either!

She helped herself to a spoonful of sugar and good splash of milk.

Sir Vivian instantly noticed that the tension was back in her shoulders. Of course. They were about to get down to the nitty gritty.

11

Although he was on the verge of retiring from academic life, and was very worried about his wife June, currently in the John Radcliffe Hospital undergoing tests on a suspicious lump in her breast, he found himself, for the first time in months, actively intrigued and excited about something.

It was a new sensation for a Don who'd thought he'd seen everything, and he was somewhat amused by his own anticipation as the pretty redhead opened her case and brought out a surprisingly large stack of papers.

Nesta lay them on the table in front of him, rather like a conjurer displaying a pack of cards and inviting him to take his pick. For some reason, the old man had an image of a ticking time bomb . . .

Sir Vivian raised one voluminous silver eyebrow. 'That's an awful lot of paperwork, my dear. Am I supposed to read it?' he asked mildly.

'Yes,' Nesta said softly. Something in her tone, a hint of iron perhaps, but wrapped in something softer—sadness maybe—made Sir Vivian lower the eyebrow again. She looked so serious. Both resolute and angry.

'Can you give me a brief summary?' he asked softly, a hopeful note in his voice. 'There's an awful lot of reading in there.' He tapped the pile of papers significantly.

Slowly, carefully, Nesta took a deep breath

and told him why she was in Oxford.

When she'd finished, Sir Vivian was as pale as she had once been, out in the rose garden. His breathlessness, she noticed with some alarm, had come back. For a long, long while, he didn't speak.

Thoughts raced through Sir Vivian's head. She couldn't be right. It was unthinkable. It was horrendous. Perhaps, after all, he was mistaken about her. She could be delusional. What, after all, did he really know about her?

'Tell me about Durham, Nesta,' he finally said, his voice gentle but firm.

Nesta, who was now feeling emotionally drained after such a catharsis, looked puzzled for a moment. Then, suddenly, she understood. Sir Vivian was wondering if she was lying. Or worse—if she was paranoid.

For a second her emerald eyes flashed a vivid, warning green. Sir Vivian noticed it, but continued to hold her gaze steadily.

And once again, Nesta was forced to take a deep breath. Losing her temper was definitely out of the question. She hadn't just spent four years studying the intricacies of the human mind not to understand the importance of self-control.

Besides, looking at it logically, she could appreciate Sir Vivian's point of view. What she'd just told him must have come as a considerable shock. Given his well publicised

13

love of Oxford, and of the university in particular, it was only to be expected that it would take some persuading for him to take her accusations seriously. Especially since she was asking him to do something that would bring pain and shame to the institution he loved so well.

Well, all right, she thought grimly. He wants to be convinced that I'm not hysterical, delusional, or downright vicious. So be it.

'You can, of course, check out my credentials with Durham University with a single phone call,' she began quietly. 'However, in the interests of saving time, I can tell you that I've studied everything from J.P. Guildforda's claim . . .'

'Which was?' Sir Vivan interjected quietly, watching her carefully.

Nesta smiled grimly. 'That intelligence was made up of a hundred and twenty different factors, and that an I.Q. is only an "operational definition" of intelligence. I also studied Philip Vernon's type "C" intelligence. In my final year I specialised in the effects of "maternal deprivation". It's the field I'm most interested in. I've always found affectionless psychopathy very intriguing. I did the usual study of the Arapesh tribe, the Mundugumor tribe, and of course, I can tell you exactly what significance to sociological . . .'

She trailed off as Sir Vivian held up his hand. 'Enough, Nesta. You obviously are who you say you are.'

'Thank you,' she acknowledged, somewhat dryly.

'Now don't get defensive, my dear,' her companion rebuked her gently. 'I had to make sure. You must admit that this . . .' Sir Vivian once again tapped the slightly yellowed and dusty-smelling papers gingerly, 'is something that cannot be taken as sacrosanct, merely on your word alone.'

Nesta sighed tremulously. 'I know that, Sir Vivian.' She leaned forward earnestly, twisting her hands together in her lap. 'Don't you see, that's why I came to you?'

Her green eyes were brightened now by held-back tears. 'I need someone independent, respected, *believable*, to . . . well . . . champion me, if you like. Oh, I can do the research myself,' she assured him, with perhaps just a hint of threat that she would do so, should it prove necessary, 'but unlike you, I don't have ready access to such things as the Bodleian. And I don't have anywhere near the knowledge of the university that you have, nor the contacts,' she admitted honestly. 'What would take me weeks, even months, you could do in hours. Besides . . .'

Her voice lost some of its passion, and her green eyes ceased to glow like those of a cat.

'Besides,' Sir Vivian finished for her gravely, 'people won't want to believe you.'

'No,' she predicted simply and quietly. 'They

15

won't, will they?'

For a moment or two, Sir Vivian looked at the bent, red head. He could almost feel the waves of misery emanating from her.

'I'm very much afraid that they won't want to believe me either, my dear,' he warned her sadly.

Nesta sighed and looked up. She looked perfectly composed. 'No, I realise that,' she admitted. As she spoke, she noticed how much older Sir Vivian was suddenly looking. His hand was pressed to his chest as if he were in pain, but she had a fair idea that his torment was more mental than physical.

He looked less like Father Christmas now, and more like Ebenezer Scrooge. His face had a pinched, tight look, and he was frowning. But it was not miserliness, but rather misery, that had effected the change in him. As if sensing her thoughts, Sir Vivian stirred in his chair.

'You must understand one thing,' he began gravely. 'At the moment, all you have is a theory. Backed up by hear-say and a few tentative notes of research.'

Nesta nodded meekly. 'I know,' she admitted softly.

But her theory was right. She knew it. And she suspected that Sir Vivian knew it too. Otherwise, why hadn't he told her to take her 'evidence' and go?

For the last time that day she took a deep shaky breath. 'Will you help me?' she asked

16

solemnly.

Although it would be a blow if he were to refuse, she would by no means be beaten by it. There were others she could ask. And if they all refused, she'd do it herself. On her own. If it took her years. She would meet with nothing but hostility, and no doubt the academic world would curl up on itself like a prickly hedgehog, to try to keep her shut out. But she wouldn't give up. No matter what it took.

'Of course I'll help you,' Sir Vivian said, his voice rife with weariness now, and all sense of his previous excitement having vanished. But it had been replaced by an implacable resolve, Nesta was sure. Proof of it was there, in his eyes. Above all, Sir Vivian Dalrymple was that rare thing these days—an honourable man.

'If things are as you say they are, then . . . yes. It must be brought out into the open. But,' he leaned forward suddenly, fixing Nesta with gimlet blue eyes. 'I must, in return, have a promise from you, young lady. And when I say a promise, I mean a *real* promise. Something you mean. Something that you intend to honour, so help you God. I realise that to most people that might seem like a hopelessly outdated concept nowadays. But I think I'm right when I say that you, perhaps, understand its true worth.'

Nesta went from wilting relief to instant wariness. He sounded so vehement.

'*If* I can make you a promise, I will,' she said

17

slowly. 'And you're right. I believe in keeping my word. That's why I've always been careful when and how to give it.'

'Very commendable,' Sir Vivian said with a brief and somewhat dry smile. He hadn't missed the fact that she'd put so much emphasis on the word 'if' in her previous statement.

'So just what is it you want me to swear to?' she asked warily.

Sir Vivian looked at the beautiful young redheaded woman a little sadly. So much passion. So much youth. He wished, suddenly, that June was here. She'd like this Nesta Aldernay. He wished, too, that he were a decade younger and still fired with just a little of her zeal. He wished . . .

He sighed and pulled the papers towards him. 'I want you to promise me that you'll do nothing, and say nothing to anyone, anyone at all, under any circumstances whatsoever, until I've had a chance to do the proper amount of investigating about this matter.'

As Nesta opened her mouth to angrily contend with him, Sir Vivian imperiously held up a hand. It was a blue-veined hand, slightly scratched by the rose-thorns despite the protection of gloves, and right at that moment it was shaking slightly, no doubt a reaction to the shock she had just given him. Nevertheless, such was the man's innate authority, the raising of that hand totally silenced her,

18

'No, Nesta, listen to me,' Sir Vivian said, his voice deep, almost hypnotic now. 'This is a very serious matter. You've made a very serious accusation, against a very well liked and respected member of this university. Until we have proof, anything you say is legally slanderous, and morally reprehensible.'

Sir Vivian ran a shaky hand across his forehead. 'Let me see if I can explain to you why I must have this promise from you. In Oxford, my dear, academic and personal reputations are exceedingly fragile—far more so than in any other walk of life or indeed in business. In London, a city stockbroker or a politician can easily pick himself up and dust himself off and still get on with things after almost any amount of scandal. And no doubt many do so! But here? Just a rumour about any wrong-doing can utterly ruin a career or a reputation of decades' standing.'

His shoulders slumped slightly. Was he getting through to her?

Nesta took a long, slow breath. Even though she still had many years more training to do if she wanted to work in the field of psychology, she knew enough about the ways of universities to know that what Sir Vivian was saying was no more than the harsh truth.

'I hate to say it of my fellow academics, my dear,' Sir Vivian carried on wearily, 'but professional jealousy is rife in this city. Now you must see, or at least acknowledge, that until I've been able to check this out thoroughly,' and again he tapped her father's papers, 'we must keep it quiet. Just in case things are not as they seem. Yes, I know . . .' he again raised his hand as Nesta looked set to interrupt him hotly, 'I know how cut-and-dried it seems. But the fact is, we're *not sure of our facts yet.* And until we are, and if I'm to help you, I must have your promise on this. You'll discuss your case with *no-one.'*

Sir Vivian watched her expressive face closely as Nesta forced back the immediate sense of frustration and denial that coursed through her.

She realised what she was experiencing, of course. She would one day be a practising psychologist herself, so she should! And right now she was giving in to a mild feeling of paranoia. But her own instincts and common sense told her that Sir Vivian was not closing ranks. He was not trying to con her (or her father) out of their due rights. He was not scheming to destroy the precious papers, or keep her dangling on a string until he could think of a way of silencing her.

He was a well-respected and decent man. And, for her own mental health, she had to begin trusting in people again. And what he said, really, only made sense. And she certainly didn't want to lay herself open to counter-charges of libel or defamation of character. Things would be tough enough without that.

20

Besides, she hadn't any money with which to pay a barrister to defend her in a court case.

No. In these circumstances, Sir Vivian was right. The only ethical and moral thing to do was get irrefutable proof first. And although she had no doubt about the guilt of the Don they were discussing, would it really hurt her to agree to say nothing, until Sir Vivian was as convinced as she was?

Slowly she leaned back against her chair. 'Very well, Sir Vivian,' she said quietly. 'I promise I won't tell anyone about these papers until I've got undeniable proof of my claims.'

She didn't know, then, just how very much that promise was going to cost her.

*   *   *

Nesta left a while later, feeling a little easier in her mind. The psychology Don had had a photocopier in his private study, and had been more than amenable to her taking a copy of everything she had, and retaining only the photocopies for himself, whilst she held on to the originals.

He'd also gone over with her a list of things he was to do next—most of which included interviewing Dons and students who'd been around when her father had been up at Oxford.

He'd promised to start right away, and she believed he would. For now she had other, more immediate and practical things to concern her—like where to find some cheap lodgings.

Inside his house, Sir Vivian rose slowly and stiffly from his seat and made himself another cup of tea, watching from his window as her mint-green VW Beetle drove away. He was left with a feeling of acute depression.

Then he began to read Brian Aldernay's papers. The originals had had a dusty feel to them, further evidence that Nesta's claim to have found them in the attic of her house was probably a truthful one. And even though he had only photocopies now, some of the strength of character in the man's handwritten notes in the margins still came through.

Sir Vivian had an academic's skill at reading. He read quickly, able to skip and skim until he came to really pertinent passages, all without losing the thread of what he was reading.

As the hours ticked past, he forgot to eat lunch, but the pile of notes he was making began to overflow his notepad. At just after three o'clock, he turned the last page of the manuscript, and leaned slowly back in his chair.

He looked grey.

Nesta had not lied about any of the pertinent facts. The documents were exactly as she'd described them. Already he had a feeling in the pit of his stomach that tasted like melting iron. Bitter. Acrid. Destructive . . .

But he still had a lot of work to do.

He'd practically have to camp out at the Bodleian for the next few days. Perhaps he'd take the material down to his country cottage, where he would be free of phone calls and friends popping around, and could get some really serious studying done. His findings would have to be meticulous, scrupulous and unarguable. It would take time and patience.

But he was not looking forward to it.

Normally, whenever he thought of the Bodleian, he did so with pride. The famous library, over the centuries, had retained a copy of every thesis written by a graduate in Oxford. It was also given a copy of every book ever published. The Bodleian, that vast reservoir of research and academic publication; it had always been his own private paradise.

But now, amid its tomes and silent places, he might just find evidence of a deep, dark, ugly secret.

But, in all fairness, he was not yet *that* well acquainted with the Don concerned, or with the D.Phil thesis in question, to judge whether or not plagiarism had taken place.

Plagiarism. Or something much, much worse?

Sir Vivian slowly leaned forward, resting his head in his hands. If it was true, it would rock Oxford University like a bomb. It would mean catastrophe for one college in particular.

And for one currently well-respected Experimental psychology Fellow it would mean ruin. Disgrace. Perhaps, even, prosecution.

Suddenly Sir Vivian began to wish that he'd never set eyes on the pretty, clever, determined Nesta Aldernay.

CHAPTER TWO

Nesta Aldernay was not the only young woman entering Oxford for the first time that morning, but the arrival of Markie Kendall couldn't have been more different.

Whilst Nesta searched for cheap accommodation in a second-hand VW Beetle, Markie Kendall made her way down the Banbury Road in a low-slung silver Ferrari convertible, with personalised number plates. With the top down, and her long trademark waist-length black hair flying out behind her in the breeze, many heads turned to watch her progress into the city of dreaming spires.

And clustered outside the famous Randolph hotel, situated opposite one of Oxford's many stately museums, a gaggle of paparazzi awaited her arrival—news of which had been carefully leaked by her publicist.

As she pulled into the narrow hotel entrance and flashed a smile at the sudden flurry of flash photography, she surreptitiously checked her appearance in the driver's mirror. She needn't have worried. Her make-up—which she'd applied that morning in her London penthouse apartment overlooking the Thames—still looked good.

She parked her car in a VIP slot and got out, making her way back to the front entrance. She could have chosen to slip into the back of the hotel, but Markie Kendall rarely made anything other than a major entrance. Especially when she was working.

'Marcheta, over here,' a voice shouted from the journalistic crowd the moment she appeared, and a brief noisy barrage met her as she stepped out onto Broad Street. 'Marcheta, are you in Oxford for long?'

Markie vaguely recognised the second voice as belonging to one of the bigger daily papers, and she paused in front of the middle aged man who was waving a mini-cassette recorder in front of her famous face.

'Hello, boys,' Markie waved generally at the group and stood, one hip slightly thrust forward, and flipped a hand through her hair. It was the pose that had first made her famous when she'd achieved supermodel status at the age of only seventeen, and she still used it occasionally even now. As expected, the photographers went wild.

She was dressed in a modest knee-length fitted dress of mint-green, black and white, with a high collar and full-length sleeves. It was the work of a new designer to the fashion scene, but she was wise enough to know that showing hardly any flesh made her look, paradoxically, even more sexy. Not that she'd ever posed in the nude, of course. And even when she did photo shoots for lingerie ads, she never wore any of the really revealing items, preferring to leave that to the newer, hungrier girls coming up through the ranks.

At nearly thirty, her days at the very top of the tree were numbered, and she knew it. But the thought didn't fill her with dismay, as it did some of her fellow models. She had long-since made her plans to diversify, and that was partly why she was in Oxford now.

'Yes, darlings, I'm here for a little while,' she cooed to the crowd in general. 'I'm launching a new fragrance this Valentine's Day, and the laboratories creating it for me here in Oxford have invited me to check on their progress. Isn't that sweet of them?' she asked archly, and sighed theatrically. 'But I really can't imagine why any of those nice, clever, boffin-type scientists would want to ask me to visit them in their lab, can you?'

She did a way-over-the-top puzzled pout, and they all erupted into laughter. Even several of the older hacks had to smile. Everyone in the business knew that Markie Kendall was hardly just another dumb model. For all of her career she'd handled her own money, and her investment portfolio alone was the envy of many people in the city. Since her father was a well-known financier, and she herself had been educated in top schools all her life, it was, perhaps, only to be expected.

'What's the perfume called?' one female voice called from behind a press of photographers, who'd leapt forward to catch that pretty pout for their editors back home.

'Why, Marcheta of course,' Markie said, batting her eyelashes frantically. 'What else?'

Like a few of her contemporaries, she was known by the single name. Never Miss Kendall, or even Marcheta Kendall. Just and only Marcheta.

Her deeply romantic mother had indeed and truly given Markie Kendall the name of Marcheta (pronounced Mar-keet-hah). As a child though, her family and friends had always called her Markie. But when it became clear, just after hitting puberty, how truly and astonishingly beautiful she was going to become and she decided to try her hand at modelling, it made sense to make the most of her unusual and pretty name.

And from the moment she'd walked into a top modelling agency at the tender age of fourteen, and the company's leading photographer had taken her picture and told the owner to sign her up on the spot, the modelling phenomenon known as Marcheta had been born.

27

Now, fifteen years later, hers was one of the most photographed faces in the country if not the world. At nearly five feet eleven inches tall, and with the lithe willowy grace of a black swan, her figure had modelled and sold everything from the top designer one-off dresses worth tens of thousands, to high-end chain-store ranges. And with her perfect pale oval face and large blue eyes, her image regularly promoted cosmetics and jewellery ranges.

Now she'd decided that it was time to start promoting her own products. The fragrance was only the first in a planned long list. She was already in talks with biochemists lured from a big Parisian cosmetics giant to make her own range of lipsticks, mascara, eye shadow and face creams. Within ten years she fully intended to have her own range of fashion lines as well. Which was another reason she was in Oxford—she wanted to see if she could spot the next big thing straight out of University and snaffle him or her for herself.

'Is that the only reason you're here, Markie? Or is there a man?' a young lad shouted.

Markie Kendall laughed, a genuinely amused gurgle of merriment. 'Oh you lot! You're always trying to pair me off with someone! How many times do I have to tell you? I'm currently foot-loose and fancy free. Honest! Cross my heart,' she said cheekily, and did just that. Of course, the flash photography went wild again as she made the provocative gesture over her left breast.

And she was in fact, telling the truth. She'd never been married, and had in fact dated relatively little so far. Most of the times when she was seen out and about with this film star at a premiere, or with that pop star at a rock concert, or eating with a television presenter at a top restaurant, they'd been 'dates' arranged by her publicist and the PR people of the other parties concerned.

It was far harder to meet a genuine 'normal' man when you always had to drag around 'Marcheta' with you than most people would imagine, Markie mused a trifle sadly. Some men found her fame too much to bear and quickly ran a mile when the media began to sniff around their personal lives. And the ones who liked the limelight tended to be jealous when she, inevitably, was always the biggest star. All of which meant that her love-life to date had hardly been anything to write home about.

The truth was, Markie Kendall led a much more sedate and scandal-free existence than any of her fans would be willing to believe!

'Actually, I'm here to give a party. Well, not me personally, but Oxford University. My late grandfather, as you know, attended here back in the thirties, at St Bede's College, and when he died, he endowed the University with the

Kendall Prize.'

Several of the journalists nodded their heads, marking them out as locals, whilst the majority merely looked bored or disinterested. Markie gave a mental sigh. That was the trouble with the media—they went wild for the shallow and meaningless, but give them anything genuinely interesting to listen to and they didn't want to know!

Nevertheless, she was determined to do a good job. 'The Kendall Prize is given every five years, and is awarded to a psychology Fellow of the University. It's a substantial amount that funds the winner for a five-year period in their area of research. It's hotly contended. This year, my father asked me to attend the award Dinner and present the Prize. But don't ask me who's won it, because even I won't know until the Dinner!'

That last was rather a fib, but she'd been sworn to secrecy.

'What're you going to wear, Marcheta?' a voice demanded, and Markie bit back a groan of annoyance. What on earth did it matter what she was going to wear, she thought crossly. Didn't they understand that a five-year research grant was heaven to an academic? Every time the Kendall Prize became available, the Oxford University psychology Department fairly boiled with excitement!

But as she looked around at the crowd of bored or eager journalists, the seasoned hacks and the still-keen newcomers, she realised that it was pointless trying to tell them how really proud she was to be here on behalf of her family to award the prestigious Prize. None of the rest of Markie's family had followed her illustrious grandfather into the academic world, but her father especially was proud to uphold the family's heritage. And she'd been genuinely touched and proud when he'd asked her to award the Prize, for the first time.

But if fluff was what they wanted, fluff was what she'd give them. 'Oh nothing too see-through,' she said, with an exaggerated sigh. 'I don't want to give any of the older College Dons a coronary.'

There was an explosion of laughter as she turned pertly on her pretty Jimmy Choos and with that parting and daring riposte disappeared into the hotel. A professional doorman kept the media from pursuing her inside, and once she was booked in and shown to her room, 'Marcheta' could disappear, and Markie Kendall could once more take her place.

She took a quick shower and changed into a simple beige pants suit with an orange blouse. She competently rolled up her long tresses into a loose chignon, and tied it up with matching orange scarf, and donning a pair of sunglasses went outside to explore the city.

Unusually, she'd arranged her calendar so that she had no work scheduled for the next two months.

It had been ages since she'd had any proper time off, and the idea of autumn in a new city, killing several birds with one stone, had appealed to her.

She would oversee and give final approval on her choice of perfume, give the Prize, find her future fashion designer for the Marcheta Casual range, and take a holiday, all at the same time.

For Markie Kendall, that relatively leisurely schedule would be a walk in the park!

Or so she thought.

*　　*　　*

On the first day of October, Sir Vivian left the Bodleian library with a weary sigh, shivering as a cool autumnal breeze teased the flaps of his raincoat and sent chills across his legs.

As he waited in the queue for the Summertown bus, he transferred the heavy briefcase from his left hand to his right, and wished that his arms and legs didn't feel quite so weak and tremulous. He stumbled as he mounted the bus, and all but fell into his seat. He closed his eyes briefly as the shops and pedestrians of Cornmarket Street sped by the bus windows.

It had been six days since Nesta Aldernay had come to visit him, but it felt like so many years.

Tonight, he would go to the hospital to speak to his wife. He badly needed her right at that moment. His whole world felt as if it was crumbling around him. Her tumour had turned out to be malignant, and was to be operated on as soon as she was strong enough to withstand surgery. He didn't know what he'd do if the worst came to the worst and he had to live life without her.

But he knew, no matter how black things looked now, just the sight of her face and brave smile would make life worth while again. Even when he told her about Nesta Aldernay, and her father's thesis.

For there was no doubt now—none at all.

And soon now he was going to have to take the first step on a very unpleasant journey.

He looked across the green expanse of a small churchyard, and picked out the rooftops of his college—St Bede's—towering over Little Clarendon Street. He still kept his room there, and tomorrow, or perhaps the day after, he would take in all his papers and related research. Keeping them on college premises would be better in the long run, of that he was sure. If he was to have the backing of his college before going to the Vice-Chancellor, it was only fair that Lord St John James, the Principal of St Bede's, had the opportunity to bring in other, independent eyes, to run over his findings.

In truth, it would be a relief to hand over

the whole mess to other, younger, more robust hands.

Sir Vivian sighed and leaned his tired head against the window. An old lady, who knew him and his stop, nudged him awake helpfully when the bus reached Park Town.

*　　　*　　　*

Dr Rosemary Naismith smiled at the two undergraduates who were gathering their things together. 'Don't forget, I want those essays by the end of the month,' she warned them.

Her two students mock-groaned but nodded, and when she walked with them to the door and opened it, she glanced at her watch and her heartbeat picked up pleasantly.

He was almost certainly going to be on time. He always was. That was one of the many things she remembered about him from her time as his tutor. He would be a challenge, and she liked challenges. Especially when they looked like Dr Callum Fielding.

She left the door ajar for him and went back inside to run a comb through her hair, and touch up her lipstick. She squirted some of Dior's 'Poison' behind her ears and hastily turned around when she heard a tap at the door.

She checked that her white slacks were wrinkle-free at her curving hips and moved forward to throw the door open wide. Immediately her whole vision was filled with him. He was so damned big. Six feet six easily, with white-blonde hair and sea-green eyes that could turn a cold stormy grey, on occasion. Classically square-jawed, with a not-quite aquiline nose, he looked like the ex-rugby and rowing blue that he was.

'Callum, thanks for coming.'

'Dr Naismith.'

Rosemary hid a wince, and stood aside to beckon him inside. 'Oh come on, Callum. It's been three years now since you were my student. Surely you can call me Rosemary?'

Dr Callum Fielding smiled dryly. 'Of course. Rosemary. I was surprised to get your message.'

Rosemary shut the door behind him, and gestured to one of three large leather armchairs grouped around a coffee table. Oxford prided itself on its tutorial system. Most Dons had a room at college (or a suite of rooms, since some of the unmarried ones preferred to live in.) Here they gave tutorials to one or two students at a time, in a relaxed, homely setting. Rosemary Naismith had found this system very beneficial over the years. It had meant she had her pick of handsome young male students, for she had a voracious sexual appetite.

Unfortunately for her, the gorgeous Callum Fielding had always been the one who

35

got away.

'But not an unpleasant surprise, I hope?' she teased, raising an eyebrow.

Rosemary was now forty-two years old, but she looked younger, with long honey-blonde hair, brown eyes and a trim figure. She'd married and divorced young, had no children, and had been tutoring for her college, Truman Hall, for the last fifteen years. To all outward appearances she was a hard-working but possibly unspectacular academic.

Callum smiled briefly. 'Of course not. I was just a little puzzled, that's all.'

He'd always felt a little wary around Rosemary Naismith, and the fact that he was now a Doctor in his own right and a Fellow of St Bede's didn't make him feel any less cautious.

He knew that, when he'd been working for his D.Phil, several of his friends had been envious that one of his tutors had been Rosemary, whose repuation had a habit of going before her. But Callum had never found her particularly helpful as a tutor, and he certainly didn't want to become just another notch on her bedpost. All of which meant that he'd been relieved to earn his doctorate and move on out of her orbit.

'Yes, I dare say you were,' Rosemary said, her eyes moving over his large, powerful frame. 'Still keeping up with the rowing?' she asked, but she could see from his powerful arm muscles and the impressive width of his chest, that he was.

'Some,' Callum said briefly. 'But my glory days in the Boat Race are far behind me nowadays.'

Rosemary could have told him differently. As a young twenty-something, Callum had been quite a sight to behold, but now into his thirties, Callum Fielding had matured into a truly heart-stoppingly masculine presence.

'I was just hoping to have a quiet word. Since you left Truman for that rabble over at St Bede's I hardly ever see you.' Her college was one of the newer ones (only three centuries old) and the high-ceilinged, square, elegant room overlooked a quad and velvet-soft green lawn. She saw him glance down briefly, but St Bede's was even older, and had far more extensive grounds.

Callum said nothing. The truth was, he'd taken the offer of Experimental psychology Fellow at St Bede's, rather than a similar post being offered to him by Truman Hall, simply because he didn't want to work or live in the same College as this woman.

Not that she'd actually stalked him or anything, but Callum had always felt like a tasty worm being eyed by a particularly hungry starling, whenever he'd gone to her for a tutorial. And since he'd always intended to make Oxford, and academe, both his career and lifestyle choice, he'd been determined to find another college in which to put down his roots.

And he'd never regretted his choice. St Bede's had been good to him, and for him, over the years.

'Tea? Coffee?' she offered.

'Thank you—coffee would be fine,' he said, folding his large, powerful form into one of the—thankfully—strong and sturdy armchairs.

Rosemary disappeared into a small kitchenette and, once the drinks were made, came back and took the chair opposite him. Beside her on the coffee table was the photograph of a handsome, dark-haired man dressed in the athletic garb of Great Britain's Olympic team. He was holding up three silver medals to the camera, and smiling widely.

She noticed his gaze on it, and smiled. 'That's my partner. Well, about to be ex, I think,' she sighed. 'I have the feeling he's about to leave for pastures new.' In fact, she knew he was, the rat. 'He's an archer. He won three silvers at the last big show, and is hoping for better things next time. One gold at least. He's about to leave for the States to do some serious training with a coach there that he's been raving about.'

Callum smiled. 'I'm impressed.'

'Oh you don't need to be impressed by anyone, Callum,' Rosemary said, her voice caressing.

Callum blinked and took a sip of his coffee.

'So, Rosemary, why am I here?' he asked calmly.

Rosemary smiled. That was another thing she remembered about Callum Fielding His sometimes unnerving habit of coming right to the point.

'It's about the Kendall Prize,' she said.

'I'm sorry?' he said, puzzled. 'I'm not quite sure . . .?'

'Please, Callum, you know we're both in the running for it this time.'

'I thought it was always kept very hush-hush. You know, nobody but the Chancellor knows who's won it until the Kendall family representative hands over an engraved crystal bowl at the party.'

'Together with that lovely enormous cheque, yes I know,' Rosemary laughed. 'But I know people who vote on the committee, and between you, me and the bedpost, I've seen the short list. You're on it, and so am I. Then there's Dr Ngabe, and Felicity Ollenback of all people.' Nervously she began to twirl a tress of hair around and around her middle finger. She shifted in her chair, crossing one leg at the knee, and hugging onto her shin with the other hand.

Callum felt a bolt of excitement lance through him. Was he really in with a chance to win the Kendall Prize? The thought was a heady one indeed. For the next five years he could do any research he chose, and be fully

39

funded. His college would even be happy to reduce his teaching commitments, because it would be a feather in their cap for any college to have a Kendall Prize winner on their prospectus. He could travel the world in his chosen field, and the Kendall name, a well-respected one in all circles of psychology, would open the doors to give him access to private libraries and collections that he would otherwise only be able to dream about.

Then he abruptly came back down to earth. Even if he was short-listed, there was no saying he would win it. Dr Ngabe was doing very interesting research right now, and would have to be one of the major contenders. Of course, his own D.Phil thesis had been a spectacular success, and had been the reason he'd had his choice of several posts with Oxford University. But that had been over eight years ago now, and he couldn't rest on those laurels for ever.

He'd had two books published since then though, both very well received and lauded.

On the other hand, perhaps Rosemary Naismith was up to something. He wouldn't put it past her—she'd always been a woman with a plan, as he recalled.

'What's going on, Rosemary?' he asked bluntly. For although he could understand why Ngabe, Ollenback and himself might be Short listed, he couldn't quite see why Dr Naismith was. He'd never found her a particularly inspiring teacher and she hadn't been

40

published for years. And apart from producing a blinding D.Phil thesis of her own, she'd done very little since to merit catching the attention of the Kendall Prize Committee.

Her big brown eyes became abruptly shuttered and she stiffened in her chair. 'Nothing!' Rosemary shrugged casually, but her eyes darted about the room, unable to settle.

The truth was, she'd been bedding one of the adjudicators on the Kendall Committee, and he'd let it slip that she wasn't on the short list at all. But since it was never published, and only the winner of the Prize was announced at the Dinner, nobody was to know that. Of course, her indiscreet bedmate had, with a little persuasion, given up the names of those who *were* on the short list, and as usual she'd come up with a plan to profit by such hotly-guarded knowledge. 'But I had this great idea.'

She leaned forward in her chair and put her hand on his. Callum watched her, coolly amused. 'What if you and I were to strike up a deal?'

Callum's grey-green eyes flickered. 'Such as?' he asked, his voice neutral. Trying to disguise his distaste, he very gently moved his hand out from under hers.

Rosemary's eyes flashed dangerously, and then she laughed. 'Oh come on, Callum! Live a little for once. You always were so straight-laced. I'm not proposing anything scandalous.

It's just that I thought we could maximise our chances of getting something good out of this. Now, either one of us could win the Prize,' she lied, 'which would be nice, or both of us could miss out. But we could double our chances, by agreeing to share it, if one of us wins it. What do you think?'

Callum felt like laughing. Trust Rosemary to try and beat the system. She'd always been something of a rebel, and this was another reason why her colourful ways made him the envy of his friends. But Callum had always been aware of a touch of cruelty in her breezy way with the truth, and the way she had of trampling over anyone or anything in her pursuit of having fun, and, rather than attracting him, it had always repelled him.

Now he said flatly, 'I think you haven't changed, Rosemary.'

He saw her lips thin. 'No, I don't suppose I have,' she said boldly. 'And you're still standing in judgement on us lesser mortals, aren't you, Callum?' she taunted. 'I was hoping you'd have loosened up a little by now!'

Callum felt himself wince. Once or twice before he'd heard similar things from other people. His own mother was openly despairing of him ever marrying and producing children, warning him he was in dire peril of becoming a curmudgeon of an old bachelor in the worst Oxford style, if he wasn't careful.

He shrugged the thought off uneasily and

finished his coffee. Carefully placing the mug on the table he rose from the chair. 'It's been nice to see you again, Rosemary,' he said politely, if less than thruthfully.

She grimaced as he rose to his feet, a big Adonis of a man, and felt her rage build. 'You're such a cold fish, Callum, did you know that?' she said mockingly. 'We could have had such a good time together, but no, you were all hands off. And even now, you're giving off waves of haughty disdain as if you were somebody's maiden aunt being shown something nasty in the woodpile. Why don't you grow up and get a life?'

Callum smiled grimly. 'Thanks for the coffee, Rosemary,' he said and walked to the door. But when he looked back at her, he suddenly felt a shaft of pity for her wash over him.

She looked lonely, and just a little beleaguered.

'Are you all right?' he asked softly. 'You have someone to talk to?'

Rosemary shot him a furious look. 'Of course! And of course!' But if she was openly showing how vulnerable she felt to Callum Fielding of all people, she'd have to be careful!

When her temporary bedmate had told her who'd been short listed for the Prize, she'd known instantly that Ngabe and Fielding had to be the front runners. She didn't know Ngabe well, but had decided there might be something to gain by trying to con Callum Fielding. After all, if he could be persuaded to split even half the prize money with her, it would fund her own research project for another couple of years. It wasn't going very well, and already there were rumblings at Truman's that she might have to cut it short.

But she should have known that Callum Fielding would have a knight-in-shining-armour attitude when it came to personal honour and integrity. Damn him.

For a long, long while after he left, Rosemary Naismith stared at the wall in front of her, her face outwardly blank, her inner mind churning.

Callum had been born into a staid, reasonably well-to-do upper middle class family. He'd always been able to take his privileges and his first-rate education for granted. What did he know of self-doubt?

But she, Rosemary Naismith, had been the daughter of a small-town provincial solicitor. Her mother, when she wasn't secretly drinking, had done nothing more civic-minded than chair the odd church committee. She'd been educated in a run-down, clapped out grammar school. She'd earned her undergraduate place at Oxford by sheer force of her own self-discipline, her grim and dogged willingness to study after school in the public library, and had even then only succeeded in gaining a place by the very skin of her teeth.

44

There'd been no old-school tie sponsor in her background, smoothing the way. But she'd got her place. And even, again through sheer and unremitting slog, had managed to gain an upper second. Even so, she had to watch and burn with envy as others, far less hard-working students than herself, had somehow breezed their way to a first class degree and a guaranteed graduate place.

She knew that, by comparison, she'd only been allowed to go on to get her B.Sc., because her tutors had backed her corner. Knowing that she didn't have a first-class academic mind, they argued that her drive and hard work would make up for it.

But she'd shown them all, and had got the B.Sc., and then scraped a two-year Research Fellowship on the basis of it. Enough to allow her to at least start on a D.Phil. thesis of her own. Nobody, though, had believed she'd get it. Not even, in the deepest, darkest part of her, herself. But if she'd wanted to stay in Oxford, if she was to become a full-fledged Oxford Don, she needed that D.Phil.

Needed it badly.

And Rosemary was determined not to leave Oxford. From the very first day she'd arrived to begin her undergraduate studies, the city had captivated her. Enthralled her. Boosted her. Back home, in that dull little Midlands town, she was a nothing and a nobody. But here, in Oxford, she was one of the elite. And as a Don, rather than a student, she could be one of the super-elite.

Dining at High Table. Being invited to ceremonies at the Sheldonian Theatre. Striding to Schools, in the lush rich gown of full academic dress, seeing the sightseers watching her, having her picture taken by the tourists. Somebody noteworthy. Somebody important. Somebody other people in the street pointed to with admiration and respect.

It was not surprising then, when she'd been assigned as Brian Aldernay's supervisor, she'd been thrown into despair by the quickness and quality of his work. He'd made her feel totally inadequate, as she compared his progress towards earning a D.Phil. degree, and her own. Because her B.Sc. was in the same area as his own research, she'd been able to follow his line of thought faultlessly. And quickly realised that it was vastly superior to her own.

Rosemary leaned forward in her chair now, rocking back and forth, her arms folded across her chest in a mute attempt at self-comfort. Her mind, however, sped back over the years.

Brian had been a shy, uncommunicative sort of man, a typical academic, living in his own narrow world. She'd encouraged him not to discuss his work with others, mainly because she couldn't bear to have others know how bright he was, in comparison with herself.

As his supervisor, she'd made encouraging reports on his progress and work, without going into detail about it. So when, her own Research Fellowship having run out only a month before, Brian Aldernay had died before being assigned another supervisor, the plan had leapt straight into her head.

She'd contacted his widow and learned that she was going back north with their young daughter. So there would be no opposition there, and no awkward questions coming from that quarter.

She'd very cleverly represented herself to Brian's widow as both his tutor and the university's representative. Thus, acting as a go-between, she'd managed to make sure that nobody else from the university would ever have the opportunity to read Brian's work.

It was during that time that she'd copied down all of Brian's work before handing it back to the grieving widow. Even then, Rosemary hadn't been sure she would go through with it.

And yet she'd found herself finishing his research, bringing it to a conclusive, clever resolution, something that was easy to do, since he'd already done all the hard work and thinking for her. And because their fields were so similar, and she'd been so purposely vague with her own supervisor about her work over the months, she was able to gradually incorporate Brian Aldernay's work into her own and represent it as totally her own thinking.

47

When she'd finally submitted the thesis, she'd half expected the heavens to open. For somebody—Brian Aldernay's ghost, his widow maybe or the university authorities— *somebody*, to expose the sham, ruin her life and have her drummed out of Oxford in disgrace.

But it had never happened.

She'd been awarded the D.Phil, and been accepted by her own College as junior tutor in Experimental psychology.

And if those in the know had, in private, expressed some surprise that the rather mediocre Rosemary should come up with such a brilliant thesis, most had put it down to her being a late-achiever.

And over the years, she'd settled down, thinking about Brian Aldernay less and less, until his memory bothered her not at all. She rarely thought about the young man, killed when knocked off his bicycle by a drunk driver. Writing minor, thesis-related articles that were at least regularly published, she'd managed to weave her life into the fabric of Oxford, until she'd almost forgotten that she'd ever stolen someone else's work in the first place.

But things had not been going well for her for some time. She did not have an original mind. She needed to do something to put her back on top, which was why she'd been hoping to muscle in, through the back door, by getting her hands on some of the Kendal Prize money.

And she still wasn't finished with Callum Fielding yet. There was something about his aloofness that made her itch to shatter his armour of invulnerability.

*   *   *

Nesta Aldernay paced restlessly about the small bedsit she'd rented for herself in the suburb of Holywell, trying not to feel so helpless.

It had been over a week since she'd first introduced herself, and her problem, to Sir Vivian, and the waiting was torture. But he was the kind of man who needed time to do his research well and thoroughly, and only then would he act.

He would simply have to. Dr Naismith had robbed her father of the credit for his life's work and then cynically climbed to prominence off his back—she'd stolen his very thoughts, his brilliant conceptions and had blatantly plagiarised his theories, no doubt thinking that it would be safe for her to do so.

As it had been, for so many years.

Nesta knew that her father must have been barely months away from presenting his thesis when he died so suddenly and tragically. And with that degree under his belt he could have done anything he desired. Private practice. Teaching. Pure research. A glittering career could have stretched before him. How different all their lives would have been if only fate had been kinder. But instead of a life of promise, Brian Aldernay had died, and his family had ended up with no money, no home, and no prospects.

After all, what did Brian Aldernay's widow know about her husband's brilliant theory in Experimental psychology? Nothing. Mavis Aldernay had been the daughter of a coal miner, perfectly content to do a dead-end job and be the family bread-winner, safe in the knowledge that eventually a glittering, professional lifestyle lay just around the corner for all of them.

She'd been happy with her baby daughter, and working in the local branch of Mothercare until such time as Brian had finished his studies. It wasn't hard to understand, then, that when he'd died so senselessly and catastrophically, she'd wanted to do nothing more than return to her home in Durham to lick her wounds, where her own mother and family could give her the support and loving care she had so desperately needed.

Even if she'd given her husband's papers a passing thought, she'd never have been able to understand them. Much less realise their true value and worth.

But somebody else had understood them. And had stolen them. And only Nesta, uncannily following in her father's footsteps in pursuing a career in psychology, had been qualified to understand what she was reading, when she'd stumbled on his academic papers in the attic all those years later.

Nesta jumped as she heard a door slam just along the passage. One of her fellow tenants, no doubt, just on the way out for the evening.

She was glad that she'd made some plans for the evening.

Her lodgings were in the converted attics of a rabbit warren of a house, and came complete with a garrulous landlady and extremely bad plumbing. Although reassuringly cheap, it wasn't the sort of place you hung around in when you could be somewhere else.

Now she walked determinedly to her wardrobe (the doors of which didn't quite meet in the centre) and pulled out her one good dress—a black satiny-looking creation with a square, lace-filled neckline and long, black lace sleeves. It fell to knee length in a no-nonsense cut, but with her bell-shaped red hair and large green eyes, the colour suited her perfectly.

She was looking forward to this evening. Her father still had friends who remembered him in Oxford, and when she'd tentatively approached two of them, a married couple who'd both roomed with Brian way back when, they'd instantly invited her to Dinner. She hoped they'd remember something of what her father had been working on. When the monkey wrench was thrown into the works, she wanted to know that she had people who would stand by her.

And more importantly, stand by her father.

Not that she could tell them the whole story now, of course. Not after her promise to Sir Vivian. But she could feel out the lie of the land. In this town, she was sure, she was going to need all the friends she could get.

She sighed and collected her bag, then switched off the light. The time was just gone seven o'clock when she let herself out of the building and got into her VW Beetle. As she turned on the rather noisy engine and indicated to pull out, she wondered what Dr Rosemary Naismith was doing right now. Had Sir Vivian approached her yet? And if he had, what had been her reaction?

Unaccountably, she found herself shivering, just as if someone had just walked over her grave. A feeling of foreboding sent her hands trembling.

'Damn it, Nesta, get a grip,' she muttered angrily to herself. 'Nothing *that bad's* going to happen.'

But she was wrong.

CHAPTER THREE

Callum Fielding checked his appearance in the mirror briefly. Normally on a Thursday night, he'd be dining at High Table, where a dark suit and tie would make him amongst the better dressed. But tonight was hardly any other Thursday night.

The Kendall Prize Dinner started at eight, and he couldn't afford to be late. The Prize was always held at St Bede's, of course, since it had been George Kendall's old college, but this was the first year for many a decade that a member of St Bede's itself might also be in with a chance of winning it. With around forty colleges comprising the university though, Callum wasn't holding his breath. No matter what Rosemary Naismith might have to say.

Rosemary. Just what was she up to? He'd heard the rumours circulating around the university that her latest research wasn't going well. Theirs was a small world, and filled with gossip, after all. But did she really think he'd collude with her to cheat the Kendall Foundation?

He sighed, and checked his tie.

He was wearing a black tuxedo with a pale electric-blue silk bow tie. He'd had the suit hand-tailored for him at one of Oxford's best gentleman's outfitters, simply because, being his height and impressive width, buying anything off the peg was all but impossible. With his silver-white hair and the colour of his tie making his eyes seem more sky-blue than sea-grey, he thought he looked passable.

When he walked into the Dining Hall a few minutes later, however, the way all female eyes gravitated towards him could have told him that he looked downright spectacular, but Callum barely registered the interest.

Instead, his eyes ran over the room, and with a brief smile he acknowledged both friends and colleagues, before reaching for a glass of red wine from one of the college's scouts, who was walking around with a loaded tray.

As he moved further into the room, he noticed a gaggle of men surrounding a female figure in the centre of the room, but his eyes were on a short woman in a bright orange and yellow African gown, with a matching turban. He'd never been much good at socialising, and preferred to use any occasion as a chance to talk psychology—especially in his own field.

'Dr Ngabe, hello again. I read your paper . . .' He began to converse with his colleague, and within minutes was listening intently to her reply. Hers was an astute mind, and the two of them had often spent hours discussing their various theories. He felt a presence hover at his elbow and turned to find Sir Vivian Dalrymple beside him.

54

His face creased into a genuine smile of pleasure. 'Vivian!'

The old man had been his primary tutor during his undergraduate years, and he'd often felt he'd learned more from the great man than most of his other tutors put together.

In the centre of the room, and surrounded by men, Markie Kendall found her eyes tracking a giant of a man as he walked into the room. The light hitting his ultra-fair hair caught her eye first, and then she'd felt her heartbeat pick up a beat as she took in the tall, muscled length of him. He might have been almost too handsome if he hadn't also been very interesting to look at as well. He moved like an athlete, and seemed to be hardly aware that he was in the midst of a party. Something about his aloofness sparked a defiant challenge deep in her feminine psyche.

His face as he listened to his companion talk was tight with concentration, and Markie knew she had to meet him, to have him look at her like that, and she gently eased herself from her circle of admirers and began to gravitate in his direction.

Unfortunately, as she did so she got waylaid by the party bore. There was always one at every event, and this night it was Professor Michael Porter, a forty-something Fellow of Truman Hall, who obviously thought of himself as the university Casanova. He'd been trying to gawp down her dress from the moment they'd been introduced.

'Marcheta, let me get you a fresh drink.'

Markie sighed, and glanced at her watch. In just a few minutes they'd be going in to dine and then she'd be limited to interact with whoever was in her immediate radius. If she was to inspect the intriguing fair giant close up, she'd better get cracking.

She waited until Professor Porter turned to retrieve a fresh glass for her, and then slipped away towards her quarry. As she did so, an older, distinguished man joined the intently talking pair, and she wondered just what her opening gambit should be. In a room full of academics, she was feeling—most unusually for her—just a little bit intimidated.

She heard the blond giant say, 'Vivian,' and then felt her elbow clamped by Professor Porter. She bit back a sigh of annoyance, and smiled.

'Here you are. Old Sin Jun can usually be relied upon to provide some decent plonk. You've met the Principal, I expect?' Professor Porter said smoothly.

Markie nodded. 'I've met Lord St John, yes.' She had contacted the current Principal of her grandfather's old college not long after arriving in Oxford, when they'd gone through the protocol for the Dinner and prize-giving.

'Who's that distinguished-looking old man?' she asked craftily, pointing just beyond her. Surely, the Professor would then give her a

56

run down on all three of them. The blond giant had his back to her and hadn't yet seen her, and as she spoke, she noticed that the woman in the eye-catching African garb looked up at him with an expression of concern on her face.

Callum returned Dr Ngabe's look with one of his own. For it was now apparent to both of them that Sir Vivian Dalrymple was slightly the worse for drink. And in all the years that Callum had known him—which were many— he'd never seen the eminent man even mildly intoxicated before.

'Are you feeling well, SirVivian?' Dr Ngabe asked gently.

Just beyond them, Professor Porter said, 'Oh, that's the great man himself. Well, one of them. Oxford is full of them. But this one won your family Prize many years ago now. Sir Vivian Dalrymple.'

'Oh yes, I remember Father mentioning him,' Markie said. 'I'd love to meet him. Who's that with him?'

Michael Porter beamed at her, and held out his arm, giving her little other choice but to slip her hand through the loop made by his elbow. 'Then allow me,' he said, without answering her question.

Sir Vivian smiled faintly at the question just asked of him. 'Well, I am feeling a little disturbed, actually,' Sir Vivian admitted. He liked and trusted both Callum Fielding and Dr Ngabe, and ever since his invitation to

57

the Dinner had arrived, he'd been dreading this night. Because he knew that Rosemary Naismith would be here, and he simply didn't want to see her. Consequently, when he'd arrived, he'd quickly consumed a glass of wine for courage. Now he had the feeling that he may have had a second one as well. And now here he was with a third glass. The wine was strong, and he'd never had much of a head for alcohol. He was feeling just a bit light-headed.

'You see, there's someone here tonight who shouldn't be here,' he said, and then blinked. 'Perhaps I shouldn't have said that. But the proof is there. I know it is.'

Callum shot Julia Ngabe a quick look to see if she was following this, but she looked as nonplussed as he did.

'Someone shouldn't be here?' she echoed, watching her colleague with concern. He seemed to be swaying a little on his feet.

'Yes. Actually, they've no right to be here at all—in Oxford I mean. Let alone at a Dinner as important as this one.' He leaned forward towards the small African woman and said quietly, 'A cheat. A plagiarist.'

Both of the other two instantly tensed. Such an accusation, coming from such a source, rocked them both.

'What do you mean, Vivian?' Callum asked sharply, and caught the genuinely distressed and horrified look in his old friend's eyes.

'I mean what I say,' Vivian said angriliy,

then, appalled at his sudden lack of discretion, clamped his lips shut. Good grief, he'd definitely had too much to drink! This was most certainly not the way he'd meant to broach the subject of what Nesta Aldernay had uncovered.

'I have the evidence . . .' he began and then jumped as they were smoothly interrupted.

'Hello there, I thought you might like to meet the guest of hon . . .' Professor Michael Porter chorused cheerfully, and Callum turned quickly to him.

'Not now, Michael,' he said curtly. What had Sir Vivian been about to say? That he had evidence?

'I must excuse myself,' Sir Vivian said in dismay. 'Er . . . bathroom, you know. Had a bit too much to drink, I think,' he said, flushing painfully.

'Vivian!' Callum said with sharp concern, his eyes narrowing now on the older man's sudden pallor. 'Let me take you home.' His old friend obviously wanted to discuss a very serious matter, and the middle of a party was hardly the venue for it.

'Oh no, I just need to splash some cold water on my face, that's all,' Sir Vivian demurred, pulling himself together with an effort. He turned and saw Markie, and his mouth all but fell open.

Callum, seeing his stunned look, also turned around and saw Markie Kendall for the first time. The vision hit him like a punch, and he felt his lungs contract in surprise, dragging in a huge breath. Her image seemed to burn itself into his retina, and would remain with him for the rest of his life.

What he saw was a tall woman dressed in silver-shot emerald green. She must have been nearly six feet tall, because he didn't have to look far down at her, as he did most women. She had a mass of ebony black hair, held up and around her head in a mass of waves and curls, and shot through with sparkling diamond and emerald hair pins. Her blue eyes were lined with matching green, and her low cut gown, which clung to her curves, shimmered as she moved. A single emerald pendant gleamed at her throat, pointing the way down to the swell of her breasts, which displayed a cleavage that made him blink.

She smiled, showing a flash of white teeth, and Callum blinked again.

'Hello, I'm Mar . . .'

Sir Vivian Dalrymple staggered a step backwards, and Callum's hand shot out to steady him. He knew that he needed to do something fast. Sir Vivian would be hideously embarrassed to make a scene at such a high-profile event as this.

'Come on, let's get you a seat, old chap,' he said, with a curt and dismissive glance at Porter, who was looking spitefully pleased. He knew that Porter was the biggest gossip in the university, and spiteful with it. And whilst he had nothing in particular against Sir Vivian, who was universally well-liked, Callum knew he wouldn't hesitate to spread his bile given the chance.

The beautiful woman he ignored completely.

'Sir Vivian's wife is very ill,' Callum said, who knew about June's condition. 'She's currently in the hospital, and I think the strain is getting to him.' He said this with a glare at Porter, who had the grace to at least look a little shame-faced.

'I'll be fine,' Vivian said weakly.

'I noticed a bench just outside,' Markie said firmly, handing her unwanted glass over to Professor Porter, who took it without thinking. 'Come on, Sir Vivian, how would you like to escort a lady out into the moonlight?' she asked with a ravishing smile, taking the old man's arm firmly.

Markie shot the giant a telling look, and seeing those cool blue eyes turn his way, Callum quickly took the old man's other arm, and together the two of them walked Sir Vivian gently out into the fresh air.

Callum, taking most of his weight, steered him to a garden bench near the entrance to Hall, where the rose gardens, still rife with late blooms, scented the air.

'Thank you, Miss . . . er . . . ?' Callum said briskly. He wanted to get Sir Vivian alone so that he could talk to him properly.

'Markie,' Markie Kendall said, not liking the dismissive note in his voice. The man sounded as if he positively wanted to get rid of her! And she was definitely not used to men barely noticing her!

'Markie,' Callum repeated, trying not to notice the way the moonlight was shining down on her, making the silver strands in her dress sparkle and shine. Or the way the fabric clung to her as it did so. Or the way the moonlight caught the jewels in the black velvet of her hair, and reflected the light into her eyes.

'I'm sure your date is missing you,' he prompted curtly. Trust Michael Porter to come to the Dinner with a stunning woman like this, he thought sourly. The man had no sense of decorum at all.

'My date?' Markie echoed with a puzzled frown and a dangerous edge to her voice. Anyone who knew her well could have warned Callum Fielding that when she went quiet and succinct in just that way, you needed to watch out.

'Porter,' Callum said dismissively.

'Professor Porter is not my date,' Markie said, still in that calm and reasonable voice. 'I met him less than an hour ago.'

'Oh,' Callum said, trying to pretend that he didn't feel his pulse quicken in delight to hear it.

'You should both of you get back to the

party,' Sir Vivian spoke up suddenly. 'This night air is clearing my head wonderfully, and I don't need baby sitters. Please, you young people go back and enjoy yourselves. Callum, I insist.'

Callum, Markie thought. His name is Callum. It suits him, somehow. Unusual and haunting, but sort of macho at the same time. Then she frowned. Wait a minute. Dr Fielding, the winner of the Prize, wasn't his first name Callum too? Could this be the same man?

She opened her mouth to ask him, then closed it with a snap again as she saw that he was looking at her with an expression that hovered somewhere between grim and impatient.

'I think you and I need to discuss something, Vivian, don't you?' Callum began, then swore very softly under his breath as they were interrupted yet again.

This time by Porter.

'Come on you lot, they're calling us in to dinner.'

'You go, I'll stay out here and get some more air,' Vivian said firmly. 'I'll come along in later.'

Left with no choice but to comply, Callum strode frustratedly ahead, trying not to notice when Michael Porter reached out to take the stunning woman by her elbow. Or that he bent down to whisper something in her ear.

Markie barely heard what it was, but she

noticed with a shaft of savage satisfaction that the blond giant's shoulders tightened when he saw the gesture. She made herself laugh provocatively. Good. So he wasn't as indifferent as he pretended.

With a toss of her beautiful head, Markie let the university Casanova walk her back into St Bede's under the nose of Callum Fielding.

*   *   *

Nesta walked into her dark and deserted room, and fumbled for the light switch. Walking to the tiny sink, she filled the kettle and made some tea, rubbing her eyes tiredly.

She hadn't been sleeping well lately, but something told her that tonight she'd sleep like a log. Perhaps because it had been such a therapeutic evening.

Her father's friends had once again taken her out, this time also inviting three others over for dinner who'd known Brian Aldernay, and all of them had talked about him with both fondness and respect. Unfortunately, none of them had known enough about his work to become suspicious when that other, plagiarised work had been published. But if they had been, she was convinced they would have acted.

She was sure now that everyone who mattered would heartily endorse her pursuit of the truth. And that was the reassurance she'd subconsciously been seeking ever since coming to this city. She was *not* being vindictive, nor was she being unduly harsh—the two things that had most worried her, when she'd set out to see Sir Vivian. This was not about a vendetta. This was about justice.

She took her mug of tea and climbed onto the bed, finding that it sagged in the middle and rolled her determinedly into the centre. Giggling and wriggling into a more comfortable position on the wayward mattress, she leaned back against the headboard with a sigh. And found herself, unexpectedly, thinking of Rob.

Rob Gingridge, a music graduate from her year at Durham. The tall, golden-haired, golden boy. They'd met in their first year at college, and had gone steady ever since. All her friends had envied her, for everyone agreed that Rob was going to be the next Simon Rattle. His good looks, personality and drive had made him stand out from the common herd, and his contacts in the media (his father worked for the BBC) would no doubt stand him in good stead for the future.

Too bad, really, Nesta mused now, with a wry twist of her lips. With so much going for him, she had always suspected that the time would come when he would cheat on her.

For Nesta had no illusions about men. Some, a very rare few, might have the ability to be faithful to one woman for the rest of his life, of that she was sure. But she'd never truly believed that Rob was one of them. Not even at the beginning, when everything was all rose-tinted glasses and champagne. Even then, there'd been tiny warning bells in the back of her mind every time she caught him eyeing up a curvaceous figure.

Nevertheless, when it had been merely a suspicion on her part, she'd been able to live with it. She might, after all, be doing him an injustice, and she'd been determined never to let jealousy, that most destructive of emotions, hold sway over her.

But actually catching him in bed with a beautiful brunette had been quite another matter. The funny thing was, that although it had hurt at the time, now, barely three months later, she could look back on it and, not laugh, exactly, but at least smile ruefully. It had all been so predictable. Ever so slightly tawdry. And so deeply pathetic.

Of course, Rob had tried to woo her back. Had spent, in fact, nearly a whole month on the attempt. Flowers, entreaties, rash promises. He'd done the lot. Nesta, though, had simply been too sick at heart to give him a second chance. More because of herself, and her cowardly actions, than because of Rob's behaviour. If she'd really mistrusted him so much, why hadn't she ended their relationship before? It was a question that still plagued her to this day. Oh, she'd rationalised it all very well at the time, of course. She wasn't a psychology graduate for nothing!

She'd very rationally and logically reminded herself that she had no *proof* that Rob had been cheating on her, so what could she have done? Hire a private investigator to follow him? Drill her friends for any gossip about him? Drill *his* friends? Kept on demanding reassurances from him, that she was the only one in his life, thus driving him further and further away?

What would that have said about her state of mind then?

Nesta sighed and sipped her tea.

Instead she'd done nothing, except wait for the other shoe to drop. And was that any better?

'Oh damn,' Nesta said softly. Why didn't she just admit it? For it to have hurt her so relatively little, it had to mean that Rob had never meant as much to her as she'd assumed. Or tried to make out? Ruthlessly examining her own psyche, Nesta forced herself to face some very hard facts.

True, Rob had been her first lover. He'd been surprised (and full of masculine-like smugness) to find her, at eighteen, still untouched. No doubt he'd gone out of his way to make their time together something special. And at first, it had been wonderful. But now, looking back, Nesta was able to acknowledge to herself that she'd probably, like a lot of teenagers, been more in love with the *idea* of being in love. She'd been so pleased with herself, and her supposed newly found maturity, in taking a lover at last. She'd been so eager to make the leap from childhood to independence that she hadn't really ever stopped to ask herself, exactly, what she wanted from life.

Well, from now on, trust was going to be further up on her personal list of 'must haves' than ever before. If the debacle of her affair with Rob had taught her one thing, it had taught her that any relationship without trust wasn't worth a damn.

Nesta's lips twisted into a rather bittersweet smile. Well, they say you lived and learned.

She placed her now empty mug on the rickety bedside table and slipped off her shoes. Within minutes she was undressed and back in bed, shivering slightly beneath the covers. Her mind, however, kept replaying the events of the night, and a small, glad smile curved her lips.

It had done her good to do something positive for a change.

*   *   *

Markie rose to her feet and smiled around at the table of expectant faces turned her way.

The evening was now well advanced, and a delicious dinner had been consumed, and the

Principal of the college had made his speech. Now it was her moment in the spotlight.

She was seated at Lord St John's right, with a lady Professor of Physiological Sciences on her left, and Callum Fielding directly opposite her. To his right was Dr Ngabe, and to his left, Felicity Ollenback, a rather loud but pleasant American woman who'd tried to explain something to her about rats and mazes.

All night long, she'd been very careful to talk to everyone but Callum Fielding. She'd flirted outrageously with the Principal, who'd told her to call him Sin Jun, just like everyone else did, and both of them had thoroughly enjoyed the game. She'd sparkled for the men in her immediate range, and been friendly with the women.

To the blond giant, however, she'd said barely a word, something that the others had probably noticed, but been too polite to mention.

And Callum was now seething.

It hadn't taken him long to realise that 'Markie' was actually the Kendall family member here to present the Prize, and he was feeling all kinds of a fool for mistaking her for Porter's latest feminine accessory. Even worse, Sir Vivian had not reappeared to take his place at the Dinner, and he suspected the old man had gone home early, which meant he wouldn't be able to talk to him about what was obviously troubling him until tomorrow.

And for the last hour, he'd had to endure the cold shoulder treatment from the high-and-mighty Miss Kendall, who couldn't make her displeasure more obvious. Much to Michael Porter's glee.

And it didn't help that Callum couldn't help but feel that he deserved it. He'd been desperate to be left alone with Sir Vivian so that he could question him more closely, and he was uncomfortably aware that he must have made that plain. For all that the raven-haired beauty had stunned him, he'd wanted her to go. And it was obvious that a woman as rich, as well-connected and beautiful as Markie Kendall, wasn't used to being dismissed so cavalierly.

Now as she rose to her feet, and smiled around at them, he tried to pretend that he was immune to the beauty of that smile and the caress of those stunning blue eyes.

He reached for a glass of wine, which he'd barely touched all evening, and took a sip. What with the shock Sir Vivian had given him, and then the consternation that the arrival of Markie Kendall had stirred in him, he was barely aware that the Prize was about to be awarded. Something that had once been so exciting, now barely seemed to matter.

If he could just get her alone for a moment, and explain and apologise, he'd feel a whole lot better.

The Lalique crystal bowl, a traditional gift

given with the Prize, sparkled in her hands as Markie lifted it into the air. As she did so, she noticed a blonde woman in the sea of tables in the main body of the room lean forward avidly.

Rosemary Naismith eyed the crystal bowl with a pang of envy. It was not the intrinsic value of the thing that mattered, of course, although it was beautiful and expensive, and would adorn any room. It was what it represented.

What she wouldn't have given to be in line to be awarded it!

'It gives me great pleasure,' Markie said, with a somewhat wry smile, 'to award the Kendall Prize to Dr Callum Fielding.'

She was watching him closely, of course. All night long she'd been punishing him for his boorish behaviour, and now she was intrigued to see how he reacted.

Callum heard her say his name, and he slowly put down the glass of wine in his hand. His eyes rose to meet hers—mocking blue, meeting shuttered, cautious sea-green.

Again his breath caught. She was so damned beautiful! He found his thought processes stalling, as if he'd just run into quicksand. For a man who'd always delighted in his quick, astute brain, feeling like a lovesick calf made him feel angry.

Markie saw his eyes flash, and felt a jolt of electricity flash through her.

The sudden loud applause released their

71

mutual feelings of paralysis, and Callum rose to his feet, rising up as Markie tracked his progress, and her smile flashed bright and challenging.

'Dr Fielding, congratulations,' she said, handing over the bowl and then the long, flat brown envelope that came with it. The mega-cheque that ensured his research for the next five years. A Prize, for an academic, above all others.

And yet, as Callum Fielding took it from her, and saw her turn coolly away from him, he suddenly realised that the Kendall Prize was a mere shadow of what he wanted from this woman.

He wanted her to want him.

And the knowledge made him burn with unprecedented desire, whilst at the same time, his innate sense of caution made a cold, hard warning shiver run up the length of his spine.

*   *   *

It was now gone midnight.

Back in her room at Truman Hall, Rosemary Naismith poured herself a huge glass of brandy and stood by the drinks cabinet, gulping it noisily. Every now and then her teeth hit the glass, making a chattering sound, but she didn't stop until all the liquor was gone. Then she poured a second bulbous glass and took it to the settee. She sat down

72

carefully, on legs that felt made of nothing more substantial than air and water.

Her stomach churned, and she had to make a sudden dash for the bathroom.

Five minutes later, white and shaking, she returned to the living area that comprised the bulk of her rooms, and walked to the gas fire. But even though there was warmth, there was little comfort to be had from it. She gazed up from the fireplace and around the room, her face blank with shock.

She'd lived in these rooms in college for nearly fifteen years, yet everything, tonight, looked strange to her. As if she'd never seen it before. The Oxford skyline pen and ink drawing she'd bought from a flea market in Woodstock. The Oriental rug an ex-lover had given her as a present, on his return from a conference in Turkey. A highly polished bureau with very fine carving on the legs. None of it seemed familiar, somehow.

She knew, with one detached part of her mind, that she was in shock. She forced herself to take a hot shower, then climbed into bed. There she stared at the ceiling. Things were bad. Very bad.

But she'd think about that in the morning.

*　　　*　　　*

Tom Jenkins, the porter of St Bede's, checked that everything was all squared away in the

73

lodge for the final time, and that the kettle was unplugged. The main gates were already locked (college policy demanded that they be locked at ten-thirty p.m. every night) and he was just about to do the same for the lodge itself.

He turned out the lights and locked the door behind him, then hesitated as he glanced upwards and saw the lights still on in the upper rooms. No doubt his wife was waiting up for him with a cup of cocoa. They'd been living in the small but cosy flat for the past thirty years now, and had their routine down pat. Grace did the early morning shift from seven a.m. until three p.m., and then he took over from then until eleven at night.

It had been a good job, and a good life, living in St Bede's. The flat had been a bit cramped when they'd had the two boys, of course, but they had both long-since moved out. One to go to work in London, and the other to live in Australia.

He was looking forward to visiting the one in Australia next year.

It had turned into a cool but not particularly cold night, and Tom decided to do a quick 'rounds' of the college before heading upstairs. Just to re-check that the side gates leading into Little Clarendon Street and Walton Street were locked and make sure nothing was amiss after the big party. All the students had their own pass keys, of course, but sometimes

74

vagrants or the homeless made their way into the grounds and curled up on or under the garden benches, and it was part of his 'unofficial' duties to do a bit of security work.

He flicked on his torch and set off, noting that a few lights were still on in Webster. Some students regularly burned the midnight oil, of course, and he paid no attention to this. There were similar lights on in the other two residences, Walton and Wolsey.

His torch beam turned the foliage lime-green as it passed over the rose gardens and herbaceous borders, and once, in one of the two college car parks, he accidentally kicked a discarded tin. Muttering, he picked it up and put it in one of the rubbish bins.

He checked the bench in the Fellows garden first, but it was free of anything other than a startled hedgehog, which scurried for cover under a bush as he swept the torch beam over it.

Above him, the weeping silver birches, famous to St Bede's, sighed and swayed in an evening breeze. The porter turned and checked the Little Clarendon Street entrance, then retraced his steps.

He was passing Wolsey and looking towards the pretty Becket Arch, and so almost missed a strange shape at the base of the wall. Then he spotted it, and the porter quickly swung the torch back, then clicked his tongue in annoyance.

Sure enough, lying close to the wall, no doubt to keep out of the wind, lay the unmistakable shape of a human body. Face down, which was unusual, his head turned towards the wall.

'All right, come on, Sir, you know you can't sleep here,' Tom said, habitually polite, and moving forward. He was already crouching down, and about to put his hand on the tramp's shoulder to wake him up, when something stopped him. Something was out of place. Something was not quite right.

He couldn't figure out at first what it was. Then he realised. The clothes. All the homeless that he occasionally saw on the streets of Oxford were dressed similarly—in layers of clothing, tatty and ill-fitting, and nearly always topped off with a waterproof raincoat or mackintosh. But this man was dressed in a suit. Black, or maybe dark blue by the look of it.

Tom Jenkins felt his mouth go dry and he slowly pulled his outstretched hand back.

'Sir?' he said again, loudly.

The body didn't move.

Kneeling down now, Tom angled his torch down and around, trying to illuminate the man's face—but it was not easy. Sparse white hair moved in the breeze and made Tom shiver.

He was dead. Tom just knew that he was. The body was not that of a young man either.

Apart from the white hair, his skin was wrinkled. And Tom knew him. He knew that he was a Don. But not one that he saw around the college all that often, and certainly not one who lived in.

Should he move him? The old gent must have had a heart attack or something. Slowly he reached out and took the man's wrist, but his skin was already cold and he didn't even bother trying to find a pulse. He stood up slowly and looked around helplessly. He didn't want to leave the body, but he had to get help. Trouble was—he didn't want a student, perhaps one a little the worse for drink, stumbling over the old man and kicking up a fuss.

Tom Jenkins was as loyal as any other member of St Bede's—and the college came first. Dignity for its Dons. Discretion from the staff. Above all, decorum. That was what St Bede's stood for.

Tom, after a moment's hesitation, took his coat off and lay it over the prone body, then walked rapidly towards Webster.

This was a job for Lord St John James, the college's redoubtable Principal.

* * *

St John James, known to one and all simply as Sin Jun, wasn't in bed. An ex-military man, he'd become used to rising early and retiring late. Besides, he was still buzzing after the party. Not only had a St Bede's Fellow won the Prize, that gorgeous creature Marcheta had flirted and flattered him outrageously. He was still glowing from the memory of it, and was certainly in no mood to go to sleep.

So he was sitting contentedly in his study, reading an autobiography of Winston Churchill, when the tap came on his door. He was surprised, but didn't show it. A quick glance at his watch told him it was nearly a quarter past eleven. Hardly a suitable time for visitors.

He was even more surprised when he opened his door to find the porter there.

'Jenkins,' he said crisply, but with no hint of impatience. Sin Jun was the kind of man who inspired confidence in almost everybody—be it a cocky first-year student, a humble scout, a long-standing Fellow or a lost tourist.

'Sir,' Jenkins said flatly. 'I think you'd better come. I've found someone dead, lying outside Wolsey.'

Sin Jun blinked, then nodded. 'Let me get a coat.' He collected it on the way out and followed Jenkins without another word.

The porter took him to the spot, trained his torch on the body, and waited.

'Your coat, is it?' Sin Jun asked, nodding at the covered corpse, and Jenkins nodded.

'Yes, sir. I thought it best to cover the gentleman up.'

78

Sin Jun said nothing, but removed the coat and handed it back to Jenkins, who didn't quite like to put it back on again.

'Lying at a funny angle, ain't he?' Sin Jun said, more to himself than anyone else, and stood back a little, stepping out on to the croquet lawn and peering up.

Wolsey was a three-storey stone building, with rows of high sash windows. On the top floor, he could see a white lace curtain being blown in, then out, of an open window. Which could be significant, or could mean precisely nothing. Sin Jun frowned and looked down again. It was hard to tell in the dark, but he could see no bloodstains. He crouched and very carefully pulled back on the man's shoulder to see his face. He drew in his breath sharply.

'It's Sir Vivian Dalrymple,' he said quietly.

Tom Jenkins sighed heavily. 'That's bad, Sir,' he muttered, in massive understatement.

Sir Vivan had always been a well-liked man. Known tio have a first class brain, he'd also been approachable and charming. More or less retired now, of course. And getting on a bit. But still . . . Tom sighed heavily. This was no way to go.

'Yes,' Sin Jun acknowledged briefly. 'Stay here. If any student stumbles by, send him to bed with a flea in his ear.'

'Yes, Sir.'

'Is the lodge unlocked?'

'No, Sir. You want the keys?'

'Please.' Sin Jun held out his hand for them, gave Sir Vivian a final, thoughtful look, and headed back to the lodge.

There he phoned first for an ambulance, and then, after a pause, looked up the number of the Thames Valley Police Headquarters in Kidlington. His old friend, Fishers, was the chap to speak to now. He could, of course, simply have dialled 999, but he didn't want to do that. Things had to be handled quietly. Discreetly. That was the way things were done in Oxford.

Or at least, they were in St Bede's.

*   *   *

Nesta was having a nightmare. She was running through the streets of Durham, a dark, cold, cobble-stoned landscape that she barely recognised. Rob was chasing her, swearing undying loyalty. She turned a corner and abruptly found herself in a pretty town square. It was now broad daylight, and a cafe had just opened for business. It was one of those that had tables and chairs spilling out onto the pavement, and sitting at one table was Sir Vivian. He was sipping a cup of coffee, the bright sunshine beaming down on his bent head.

She called to him but he didn't hear her, or look up.

Behind her, Rob was gaining. He was waving her father's papers in the air and accusing her of never having loved him. She ran towards Sir Vivian, calling to him again and again but still he didn't look up. Neither, she noticed, did anyone else. It was as if she were invisible. She ran on, into a dark alley, and it was night time again. A few street lamps burned, casting ominous pools of murky light that only served to make the rest of the darkness seem all the more intense.

At the end of the alley stood a man.

Nesta couldn't see who it was. He was in shadow—with the light illuminating just the plane of one cheek and the line of his jaw and nose. He looked solid. Powerful. Masculine.

She skidded to a halt, her heart thumping. Although she couldn't see his eyes, couldn't, for instance, tell what colour they were, she knew he was watching her intently. Looking into her heart. Reading her soul. She wanted him to stop. But never to stop.

Behind her, she turned to see Rob fading away. Soon he was gone, as if he'd never existed.

She turned around again, half expecting the phantom stranger to be gone also, but he was still there. Although she'd never met him, and had no idea who he was, had never so much as heard his voice or touched his hand, he felt ten, twenty, a hundred times more *real* to her than Rob ever would.

Or ever had. 'Who are you?' she said.

The man dropped a piece of paper. It fluttered to the ground, and was picked up by a playful breeze that skittered it towards her. She bent down and picked it up, and began to unfold it. She knew what the message contained was the most important thing in the world.

She began to look down, got a fleeting impression of individual letters . . . and woke up. She sat up in bed, her heart pounding. She reached for the light and switched it on, her eyes going automatically to the clock. But it was not the middle of the night, as she'd expected it to be.

It wasn't even yet midnight. Two things struck her at once. The first, for some reason, was the image of Sir Vivian, sitting in the bright daylight at the pretty cafe table, drinking coffee and not being able to see or hear her. He had seemed so far away.

And then, more urgently, the man in the shadows. Who was he? Nesta shook her head. It was only a dream. And easy, in a way, to interpret.

Rob disappearing was the most simple to explain of all. He was out of her life for good. And the fact that he'd been waving her father's papers at her and accusing her of having more interest in them than in him was also child's play for a psychology student. She did have other priorities in her life right now.

But the stranger was an enigma. The shadowy figure that she'd felt she'd known, or would know, for the rest of her life. Where had that feeling come from? And what did it mean?

If she'd been superstitious, she might have put it down to that old chestnut about women dreaming of their one true love. Hadn't her grandmother on her mother's side once told her that her own great-grandmother had had the second sight? It was all rubbish, of course. Appealing rubbish, but nothing to lose sleep over.

Nesta determinedly shut off the light and lay staring up at the ceiling. She found herself trying to recall the stranger's face, but couldn't. Annoyed, she tried to turn her mind to other things, only to think about the piece of paper he'd dropped for her, that the breeze had so obligingly brought right to her feet. Carrying a message that was so important.

If only she'd read it before she woke up. But the subconscious did things like that to you. It teased and tormented you, sometimes mercilessly.

Nesta turned over and thumped her pillow angrily.

This was the brave new millennium. Women married and divorced regularly. They could have surrogate children as surrogate mothers, have lesbian relationships, and rear children without the long-term presence of any man.

Flit from relationship to relationship like a butterfly if they chose.

They certainly didn't dream of their one true love anymore. It was stupid. Nesta determinedly closed her eyes.

And wondered if her dream lover would come back to her.

CHAPTER FOUR

Detective Inspector Lisle Jarvis rubbed a weary hand across his broad forehead and stifled a yawn. He'd had a hard day, and had climbed into bed at just gone nine o'clock, foolish enough to believe that he might actually be allowed to catch up on some much needed sleep.

It was now just gone midnight, and here he was, being driven to St Bede's where a dead body awaited him in one of its quads. After being given the victim's name, he'd been ordered by his Superintendent to investigate the matter quickly, thoroughly and quietly. His boss had gone on to say that it would most probably turn out to be a case of death by natural causes, but given the eminence of the victim and the institute in which he'd been found, he wanted a senior officer on the spot.

And Lisle was it, whether he liked it or not.

The sergeant who was driving looked

equally tired, but also reluctantly excited. Jim Neill, unlike Lisle, had not investigated many suspicious deaths before. (In the world of the police, any death was deemed 'suspicious' until proven otherwise.) Lisle could have told him to save his enthusiasm—however the case turned out, it meant a long, long night lay ahead of them, with probably very little reward at the end of it.

'The college is just up ahead, Jim, but don't turn off down the alley. I want the car park checked for any unknown vehicles. It's a long shot, but one we'd better carry out, if only for form's sake. Get some uniforms onto it. You'll have to park out front,' Lisle instructed quietly.

'There's double yellow lines on this part of the Woodstock Road, Sir,' Jim pointed out prosaically.

'Well, if we get a ticket, Jim, it'll come out of your wages,' Lisle said dryly. Then, at his sergeant's aghast look, said quickly, 'Joke, Jim. Joke.'

'Sir.'

Jim, who'd worked with Lisle for over two years, still wasn't quite sure how to take his superior officer. It was a problem a lot of the men and women at the local police station shared.

For Lisle Jarvis had a somewhat unusual background for a high flying, up-and-rising detective inspector.

Lisle, as everyone knew, had been raised in the rough area of Blackbird Leys, one of Oxford's grimmest suburbs. Not only that, but as a juvenile, in common with all his friends, Lisle had had a record. Joy riding. Shoplifting. Petty vandalism.

And all before the age of fourteen.

And then it had all changed one afternoon, when he'd lifted some tape cassettes from his local branch of Woolworths. It had been done, as usual, on a dare from his mates. They'd hit the shop just the day before, and knew the floor walkers were bound to be alert, so they'd teased him that he wouldn't be able to get away with it twice. And neither had he. One sharp-eyed off duty constable had seen to that.

One instant, the cocky thirteen year old Lisle had grabbed a handful of tapes (embarassingly, as it was to turn out, all Des O'Connor offerings) and the next instant, as he was headed for the door and his jeering, sniggering mates, he'd felt himself being lifted off the floor, his collar having been well and truly felt by the massive hands of one PC Vince Moreland.

Vince had been a policeman for nearly thirty years on the afternoon that he'd collared the young tearaway.

The rest, as the local force now knew, was history, and had developed into a kind of modern folklore. Simply put, Lisle had been 'straightened out' by a good, honest copper.

86

But exactly how Vince had managed this minor miracle not even Lisle, to this day, was quite sure.

Perhaps it had been a combination of his guilt and terror.

The young Lisle had always known that his widowed mother worried her heart out over him, and even at the tender age of thirteen, he'd understood that she was terrified that he'd influence his younger brother, Davy, into a life of similar crime.

And Vince, with his knowledge of Blackbird Leys families, had played on his guilt ruthlessly. Add to that the fact that Vince was built like a brick outhouse, and had hinted, without saying one word, that Lisle was due to get the hiding of his life if he erred again, and you had all the ingredients ready mixed to instil a rapid change of heart in any wayward schoolboy.

Lisle couldn't remember his father, who'd walked out on them when he was four, and then died a year later, drunk behind the wheel of a stolen car. So he'd never had the discipline he'd so badly needed, and had never before met a man who, instead of giving him a good hiding, had given him golden advice instead.

For the next three years, Vince had become a surrogate father to him, before he died of a heart attack two months short of retiring from the force. And in those three years, against all the odds, Lisle had become a son for both

Vince and his mother to be proud of. But it had not been easy.

Years of truancy had left him barely literate, and his teachers at the hard-pressed, local run-down comprehensive school could have been forgiven for being suspicious of his sudden yen to learn. But they had not let him down. Extra hours of tuition, private reading and writing lessons, and all the encouragement they could give him had him passing his O-levels at sixteen, much to his own astonishment, and the delight of his mother and Vince.

His juvenile record, according to the laws of the land, was wiped clean, since his crimes were committed before the age of fourteen. In due course he sat his A-levels and then, (unbelievable to many), joined the police force two days after his eighteenth birthday. By then, of course, he was anathema to all his old school friends, most of whom he'd since had to arrest for drink-driving, vandalism, gbh, burglary and other assorted crimes.

It would have been a transformation impossible for most men. But Lisle Jarvis had never been like most men.

Inevitably though, he still had problems, even to this day. It was hard for him to accept authority, for a start, and there were several 'superior' officers that he felt were anything but, and for whom he had no respect whatsoever, either for their non-existent brains or for their tactics. But, with a bit of teeth grinding, he'd managed to swallow his defiance and rise to the rank, at only thirty, of Detective Inspector. What's more, he was tipped for promotion in the near future.

Known as a bit of a maverick, but one who could play the game and—more importantly— constantly achieve good results, he held a unique place in both the rank and file, and with the powers that be.

Now, feeling bone-weary and totally unaware of the kind of awe in which both his sergeant and most of the local nick held him, he yawned widely as Jim Neill pulled up the unmarked police Rover to a halt outside the main gates of St Bede's.

Lisle got out of the car and stood on the pavement, looking at the golden stone facade with a disgruntled expression on his face.

Most of Oxford now slept, and there was no passing foot traffic at all; only a few cars cruising the night streets at a steady thirty miles an hour. A street lamp away to his left cast light down onto the pavement and across the plane of one of his cheeks, illuminating the hard line of his jaw. He looked solid, powerful and fundamentally masculine as he stood there, calling on his reserves of stamina and contemplating the case ahead of him.

In the lodge of St Bede's, lights shone from almost every window. The massive and ancient double oak doors, like those of most colleges, had a smaller door inset inside one of them, and this now opened. A tall, erect figure walked through it.

For an instant, Lisle thought it must be the porter, who was bound to be expecting them. But as the man approached, stepping into the pool of light shining from the porter's window, the policeman quickly changed his mind. For this man was dressed in a dark suit, and had a thick wave of white hair, a pair of piercing blue eyes, and a manner that fairly screamed 'establishment'.

'Good evening, Inspector. You are from the local constabulary, I take it?'

The cut-glass vowels and upper class accents automatically set Lisle's spine stiffening, and he forced himself to relax, with something of an effort. You might take the boy out of the gutter, but the gutter had a nasty habit of staying with the boy, Lisle thought, with a wry internal smile.

Lisle took a swift breath and firmly held out his hand. 'Detective Inspector Lisle Jarvis. Sergeant Neill. And you are . . .?'

'Lord Roland St John James. The Principal.'

Lisle hid a smile. Great. Now what, out of that whole lot, was he supposed to call him?

'Well, er, Sir Roland,' he hazarded with a confidence that concealed all hints of his unease, 'perhaps you could fill me in on the events of tonight? I understand there's been an unexplained death?'

'That's right. Our porter found the body of

90

one of our Fellows lying near his residence.'

'I hope the uniformed branch have already sealed off the area?' Lisle asked sharply, but the older man nodded quickly.

'Oh yes, yes indeed. Yellow police tape everywhere. Please, step this way.'

Sin Jun led them through the gate and into the gloomy shadow of St Agatha Quad. To their right was the porters lodge and residence, to their left, the vast, ancient chapel, where world-famous choirs came to give concerts. Ahead were the rising walls of Webster, and, straight on, access to Wallace quad, with its war memorial and college clock. In the distance he could see a pretty stone arch, set in a dry-stone wall.

As they walked across the noisy gravel of the first car park, the Principal was very much aware of several more lights coming on in Webster and the other residences.

It was inevitable that the students would be awoken by all the activity, but he knew that a constable had been stationed by the body, and would turn back any curious undergraduates.

Lisle gloomily took in all the trappings of an ancient Oxford College, and felt deeply uncomfortable.

He was very much 'town', who had stumbled, very decidedly, into the territory of 'gown'. His O-levels and few A-levels suddenly felt very paltry compared to the might of all this academe, and the sudden feeling he had of guilty inadequacy angered him. Especially when he knew that he'd done well with his life, given the circumstances.

Damn it, if he wasn't careful, he was going to get an inferiority complex about all of this. And wouldn't that make his Superintendent laugh and choke on his cigar? Again, Lisle indulged an inner smile at his own expense.

But although he managed to suppress all traces of these negative thoughts, the wealth, prestige, and academic worship oozing from these ancient walls made him itch all over. This was going to be a pig of a case. He just knew it. Shrugging off his pessimism, he sighed heavily.

'The er . . . body . . . is just up ahead,' Sin Jun said quietly, trying, and for the moment failing, to get a line on this big, tough-looking and unusually silent copper.

Sin Jun had managed to get hold of Fishers, of course, who'd promised to put their best man on to it. So the Principal knew that DI Lisle Jarvis would soon get to the bottom of this affair. His old friend had also promised to handle the press, and generally keep a beady eye on how things progressed.

So although Sin Jun had no doubt that this man was up to the job, something instinctively told him that if Fishers tried to rein in *this* subordinate, he was going to be given very short shrift indeed. And it worried him, somewhat. Although Sin Jun could not quite put his finger on it, something about Sir Vivian's death struck him as being not quite right.

Unaware of the Principal's unease, Lisle walked slowly towards the crime scene—if crime scene it was.

He'd surmised (quite rightly, as it turned out) that this was most definitely an example of a powerful college applying a little pressure to his superiors.

Why else assign a DI to a case that, on the face of it, might turn out to be nothing more than death due to natural causes?

As the Principal led him through Becket Arch, Lisle saw that the uniformed branch, called in a good half hour before he himself had been roused out of bed, had already set up a large set of lights. He was glad to note that they'd been careful not to trample all over the scene.

But the lights meant that the three men now looked down at a grimly surreal scene. For Sir Vivian Dalrymple now lay like a spotlighted piece of macabre art, a grisly study in black and silver, lying awkwardly on a grassy green carpet.

Lisle carefully approached, looking at the ground around the body. 'People have been walking around here,' he said flatly.

Sin Jun, in spite of himself, was impressed. 'I dare say that would be Tom Jenkins, the porter. He discovered the body, and of course, checked to see if, well, he could do anything.'

Lisle looked at him quickly. 'Does he usually do a nightly patrol?'

Sin Jun blinked. 'I have no idea. You'll have to ask him that yourself.'

Lisle sighed. 'So I will. I take it a doctor has seen him, or is on the way?'

'Yes. I mean, one is due. Fishers said he'd send someone,' Sin Jun clarified, not missing the quick, hard, and sardonically knowing look that Lisle gave him.

'You're a friend of Chief Constable Fishers Sir?' he asked, at last, with deceptive lightness.

Sin Jun, most unusually, felt as if he'd been wrong-footed. He cleared his throat loudly. 'Yes. A great pal. Golf, you know,' he added. What was it about this policeman that made him feel so uncomfortable?

'You must understand, er, Inspector Jarvis, that the college can't afford any, well, adverse gossip. So naturally, when we found poor Sir Vivian this way . . .' He trailed off helplessly.

Lisle Jarvis nodded. 'Yes, Sir. Quite so,' he said, his voice flat but somehow managing to sound sardonic at the same time.

Sin Jun almost flushed. But, in spite of the man making him feel like a first class heel, shamelessly playing the old public school tie game, his estimation of the policeman sky-rocketed.

After all, it was not many men, Sin Jun thought, who can put the wind up me!

94

'And on tonight of all nights too,' Sin Jun sighed, and when Lisle looked at him sharply, explained about the Dinner, and the Kendall Prize.

Lisle sighed. Great. That meant they had fifty or more guests to contend with, he thought, disgruntled. Just what he needed!

'All the guests have long since departed, I take it?' he asked flatly.

'Yes of course. We had no idea anything was wrong, you see.'

Lisle nodded again. 'I take it the college gates are locked at a certain time?' he pressed on with the routine questioning doggedly.

'Yes, Inspector. But Tom Jenkins, the porter, is the best man to talk to about the specifics of that. I know the postern gates and everything else gets locked at ten—but he'll be able to tell you if anything had been amiss tonight. But surely . . . I mean, Sir Vivian was in his seventies, and I know for a fact that he had heart trouble. This is going to turn out to be a simple case of heart failure, don't you think?' Sin Jun asked quickly.

Lisle looked at him sharply. Was he imagining it, or did the Principal sound a little too hopeful just then?

Lisle had summed up Sin Jun very rapidly. He already had him pegged as an old soldier, one whom the college had elected as their Principal in the hope of strong leadership and common-sense practicality. He was not,

Lisle felt sure, a man to make mountains out of molehills, or indulge in hysterics. So if something about this death worried him, Lisle knew he should be worried too.

On the other hand, he might just be so tired he was reading things into nothing.

'Well, we won't know for sure about that until after the doctor has had his say, will we sir?' he answered Sin Jun's question with deliberate pragmatism. 'And a post mortem will tell us for sure, one way or another.'

Sin Jun sighed. 'I was hoping that wouldn't prove necessary,' Sin Jun said sadly. 'His wife is in hospital, and I had hoped to spare her that.'

Lisle sighed heavily. 'I'm sorry to hear that, Sir Roland. But it's not up to me, and I think the coroner will almost certainly ask for some kind of examination to be carried out.' He hesitated for a moment, and looked down at the back of his hand thoughtfully. 'Especially if there should prove to be any signs of trauma on the body,' he added smoothly, and quickly looked up.

It was a technique he'd used often in the past, when questioning witnesses. When they thought you weren't looking at them, Lisle had often caught expressions on their faces that they'd have given anything to hide.

The Principal's face, however, was simply blank.

'Trauma?' Sin Jun echoed questioningly.

'From a fall. At the moment it's too dark to see, and we can't examine the body properly until it's been seen by a medical man. So we have no idea what injuries Sir Vivian may have sustained. And you had noticed there's a window open up above, hadn't you, Sir?' Lisle asked calmly.

Sin Jun actually flushed, and hoped the darkness would hide it. 'Yes. I had, as a matter of fact.'

'Did Sir Vivian, in fact, have rooms in this building?' Lisle pressed, unaware that Jim Neill was listening avidly, an open look of admiration on his face.

Lisle had certainly caught the old feller napping there!

'Wolsey—this building is named after the famous cardinal. And yes, he did. On the third floor,' Sin Jun, having been caught out once, now felt the need to over-compensate. 'When we heard of his heart trouble, we were going to move his rooms to the ground floor, but he was more or less retired, and hardly ever came to his rooms here, so he insisted that we were not to bother. I'd hate to think that climbing the flights of stairs brought on an attack,' Sin Jun said, perfectly genuinely. 'But I suppose it might have been like that. If he'd felt breathless, he'd almost certainly have gone to the window to get some air. Perhaps he leaned forward to breathe deeply, had a dizzy spell and fell. But I hope not.'

Lisle ignored all this very convenient guesswork, and glanced around. So far, no inquisitive student had appeared on the scene, and the grounds remained deserted. But they wouldn't have been so earlier on.

'Did anyone see him come in, do you know?' he asked. 'Did he attend this party of yours?'

'Oh he must have done. He was certainly invited, and I can't think what else he'd be doing in College otherwise. But I don't remember talking to him—but then, I was mostly taken up with the guest of honour. A famous fashion model, and all that,' Sin Jun said, realising he was suddenly waffling, and lapsing into an embarrassed silence.

'I don't think we need to go into all of that at the moment, Sir,' Lisle said, hiding a smile.

Sin Jun could appreciate the economy of the inspector's questioning, and even admire the ruthlessness of his reasoning. And under any other circumstances, he'd be gratified and fascinated with the DI's performance. As it was, he shuffled uncomfortably under the younger man's gimlet eye.

Lisle sighed. Until the doctor had been and gone it was useless even speculating on what might have happened to the victim. 'When was the body discovered exactly?' he asked instead. 'And can I just get you to confirm for me officially that the deceased is in fact Sir Vivian Dalrymple?'

His lips twisted. So many Lords, and Sirs, and learned Fellows. Give him a straight forward crime with normal, everyday working class people any day! Lisle glanced up, saw the look of misery on the Principal's face, and felt instantly guilty.

'Yes, Inspector, it's definitely Sir Vivian. He was a very well liked man. I found him charming. His wife, as I believe I already told you, is in hospital at the moment. I don't know how I'm going to tell her about this.'

Lisle put the notebook away, feeling like a right bastard. None of it showed on his face, however. 'Where is this Tom Jenkins?' he asked instead.

'He's with his wife in the lodge. Shall I go and get him?'

'I think I'll follow you there, if you don't mind. Jim, you stay here with the body. The doc's on his way—I want to know straight away if he has any preliminary guesses as to cause of death for us.'

After all, they must dot all the i's and cross all the t's for the Chief Constable, mustn't they?

'Sir,' Jim nodded, and took up a self-important stance beside the body. Lisle nodded to several of the uniformed constables, standing about the quad at strategic points as he passed them. Their quiet and deferential, 'Sir,' followed the two men as they walked back towards Becket Arch through the moonlit gardens.

Lisle glanced at the rose gardens, the croquet lawn with its hoops and elegance, the pond and with its expensive fish, and remembered, when all was said and done, that the people living here were just that.

People, like anyone else. People, like him.

Tom Jenkins opened the door within a few seconds of their knocking, and nodded at Sin Jun before beckoning them in, turning interested and questioning eyes towards Lisle.

'Principal,' Tom said, and Lisle wondered if calling the Principal 'Sir Roland' had been some sort of social gaffe, then reflected tiredly that he really didn't give a damn.

'Tom, this is Detective Inspector Jarvis. Inspector, this is Tom Jenkins, our porter.'

Lisle looked at the man, guessing him to be somewhere in his mid-fifties. He was solidly built, and the eyes now watching him were steady, if still slightly shadowed, no doubt due to the residue of shock. But, all in all, he made a favourable first impression.

'Did you know the deceased, Mr. Jenkins?' Lisle asked, wasting no time on pleasantries.

'Yes. I did. But not well. Sir Vivian wasn't around college much of late,' Tom confirmed, his voice calm but still just a shade unsteady. 'When I first saw him, I didn't recognise him. Not right off. He was lying face down, see?'

Lisle nodded. Although he had nothing to go on yet—no clues, no doctor's examination, no eyewitnesses, nothing but the fact that there was a dead body where there shouldn't be one—Lisle was beginning to feel that there was far more to this than at first met the eye. Call it instinct—call it experience. Of course, he'd go only on the facts. But he'd be very careful to make sure he *got* all the facts first.

Lisle was not naive. He hadn't climbed as high as he had by not watching his back and knowing the rules. And Lord Roland was a friend of the Chief Constable. The Principal had a potentially embarrassing body on his hands, and had called his old friend for help. The message was clear, to all concerned.

Be quick. Be discreet. Be careful.

But Lisle wondered if it was going to be that simple. Already there was a mystery. If he'd fallen out of the window, how could he fall, face first, right up against a wall? He wasn't much on physics or the laws of velocity or aerodynamics, but surely the body wouldn't have fallen in the position in which it was found?

He gave a mental shrug. No doubt he'd find out soon.

Lisle stepped further into the flat's small living room, then turned in the doorway, subtly blocking the way. 'Thank you, Sir Roland. I take it you have rooms in college where I can reach you, should I need anything further?'

Sin Jun took the obvious dismissal in good part, gave the inspector directions to his rooms in Webster, and assured him he'd be available any time, night or day.

He left, still feeling deeply uneasy. There was a rough edge about Lisle Jarvis that was more than the sum total of his looks, Sin Jun was sure.

Inside, Tom was thinking much the same thing, as he gave the policeman a good long look. The man was built, there was no doubt about it. He obviously worked out, and had that air of being as fit as a butcher's dog that only those with hard-earned stamina were able to generate. His clothes weren't expensive, but he looked good in them. As his old mother would have said—DI Jarvis was a man's man.

His short-cropped hair was a rich shade of nut-brown, and wide hazel eyes looked at Tom with no discernible expression in them at all. He looked tough. He had a pugnacious chin, a nose that had been broken once, perhaps in his younger days, when he'd patrolled the streets and had had to handle some thugs. His forehead was broad and strong.

All in all, the overwhelming impression was one of toughness. But instead of feeling intimidated, Tom felt reassured. It was a reaction that Lisle inspired in most people.

Except in crooks of course. Crooks were never pleased to see Lisle Jarvis heave into view.

'So, Mr Jenkins,' the voice was softer than he'd expected, 'I know this has been a nasty shock for you, but perhaps you can tell me exactly what happened, right from the beginning?'

Without being asked, Lisle sank into one of the two old but comfortable armchairs that flanked a gas fire, and got out his notebook. Tom took the one facing him, and glanced uneasily towards the closed door that led to the main bedroom. It had taken a good deal of persuading to get his wife to go to bed, and he wondered if she was listening at the door.

'Well, Sir, it was like this,' he began, struck by the air of tough competence about the policeman, and for the first time that night began to breathe easier.

Carefully, missing out nothing, Tom took him through his actions that night, whilst Lisle, in rapid and fluent shorthand, took it all down. Only when Tom had finished did he start asking the questions that intrigued him most.

'Did you see Sir Vivian arrive tonight?'

'No, Sir. But then, if people don't come into the lodge, I wouldn't always notice them going by. I have the switchboard to see to, you see, and that puts my back to the window. Then again, Sir Vivian could have come in by either of the side gates. And it was a very busy night, what with the big Prize Dinner and everything. I might not have remembered him, in the crowd, even if I'd seen him.'

Lisle sighed. 'Right. When was the last time, to your knowledge, that Sir Vivian last came in to college?'

But Tom didn't know. Weeks, he thought.

'And on your rounds, you saw or heard nothing out of the ordinary?'

'No, Sir.'

No, Lisle thought, he wouldn't. He would probably learn nothing much until morning—when he got the chance to question the others, and build up a picture of Sir Vivian's last few hours.

He glanced at his watch, saw that it was getting on for the early hours, rose and thanked Tom and let himself out. By now, the doctor would have arrived. He'd have to supervise the removal of the body, do a preliminary check of the victim's college rooms, then ask the Principal if he could make some sort of announcement at breakfast that the police wanted to speak to anyone who'd seen or spoken to Sir Vivian at any time on the day or evening of his death.

So far, he had no clear idea about the character of the dead man. The Principal had said he'd been a well-liked man. But then, he would, wouldn't he?

Half of him hoped for a simple and straight forward 'natural causes' verdict. Another part of him sensed something more sinister was afoot. He sighed and glanced uneasily around the dark and deserted quad.

*   *   *

In her bed in Holywell, Nesta stirred and sighed in her sleep.

The dark stranger was back.

CHAPTER FIVE

Nesta rolled out of bed, sleepy-eyed and yawning. It was a grey sort of day, with a drizzling cold sky guaranteed to depress even the most bright-eyed and bushy-tailed.

She brushed her teeth and changed, shivering, into her faithful pair of denims. She reached automatically for a striped green, blue and gold sweater that did wonders for her geometric cut of deep red hair. The green was the exact same shade of emerald as her eyes.

Nesta couldn't afford to have a huge wardrobe, but what she had looked good on her. Unlike a lot of redheads, she actually liked her colouring, and had learned, over the years, how to dress to suit it.

She made herself a cup of coffee and shivered some more. The one constant thing about cheap rented accommodation, she'd always noticed, was how inefficient their heating was, come the winter time.

She left the cheerless bedsit, shrugging into her see-through plastic raincoat as she went, and walked through the gloom towards a little coffee shop near the centre of town. She didn't mind the rain, and rather liked the cheerful hues of the umbrellas, the bright car headlights, and the general feeling of all-mucking-in-together, that assailed the British public in times of downpour.

She waited patiently in line for the local morning paper at the nearby newsagents, and carried it into the cafe with her. The cheap and cheerful yellow Formica tables and the gum-chewing insouciance of the waitress combined to lift her mood even further. She ordered a coffee, a couple of rounds of toast, and settled back in her window to seat to peruse the news. Wherever she was, Nesta always took a local paper. The national press more often than not carried only news of disaster, death and destruction. Or tales of the rich and glamorous, whose lifestyles failed to move her, or even touch her. She much preferred the day-to-day stories of ordinary, *real* people.

She read and munched and sipped quite happily for half an hour. A local lady had just retired as Dinner lady at a primary school, after 51 years of solid service. Fifty-one years! Nesta couldn't imagine working in the same place for so long. A local boy scout had saved a neighbour's dog from drowning. A charity worker had died at the ripe old age of 92, and the town's grateful residents were busy fund-raising for a memorial in his honour.

Because the newspaper's deadline had long

since passed when news had begun filtering in about a death at St Bede's, a local reporter, roused from his bed, had only just been able to cobble together the bare details. And, because it was too expensive for a small paper to chop and change the front page once the presses had been set, Nesta almost missed the four inch paragraph, tucked away on page 7.

As it was, the dark bold little side headline caught her eye, in between a piece on a village fete, and an advertisement for car tyres.

'OXFORD DON SLAIN IN CAR PARK'

Nesta, who'd just been raising her second mug of coffee to her lips, froze. Slowly, as she read, she put the mug back down on the table, her hands shaking.

She read the piece through twice, not quite believing what she was reading.

'Police confirmed last night, that the body discovered in the car park of St Bede's College, was that of the noted psychologist, Sir Vivian Dalrymple. Sir Vivian was a well-known lecturer and author of many well received works in the field of Experimental psychology.

It is believed that Sir Vivian was attacked by a mugger between the hours of 11.30 and 12.30, after attending a Dinner at the College. Police sources confirmed that the main gates, and the postern gates that led into the car park were, unusually, unlocked at the time of the slaying, and the police are not ruling out the possibility that Sir Vivian was killed by a drug addict, stealing to maintain his habit.

Lord Roland St John James, Principal of St Bede's, has expressed his shock at such a thing happening in the College, and has offered his condolences to Sir Vivian's family.'

And that was it.

Nesta sat and stared at the paper for a long time before stiffly rising to her feet, paying her bill and heading out once more into the cold and damp. It was too far to walk to Park Town, so Nesta returned for her VW Beetle, coaxed it into life, and twenty minutes later, was turning off the Banbury Road and parking more or less opposite Sir Vivian's home.

Her mind, after a sluggish start, had begun functioning again.

As an ex college student herself, she knew about the tragic and insidious drugs culture that plagued University cities. The police obviously suspected Sir Vivian had been the victim of either a junkie (student or otherwise) or an opportunist thief, who'd found the doors to St Bede's unlocked and had wandered in, too see what could be stolen. And Sir Vivian was just in the wrong place at the wrong time.

All of Nesta's previous feelings of wellbeing fizzled out into a depressing sense of anger and despair. It was so pointless! That lovely old man, a victim of some crazed or evil parasite! She supposed that, as a psychologist-in-the-making, she should be more tolerant, but . . . Hell! Being a shrink didn't mean you couldn't believe that some people were just downright *ugly*.

She sighed, trying to control her frustrated anger, and forced herself to calm down. She made a mental note to have a look around St Bede's at some future point, but not just yet. First, she had to get back her father's papers.

She brushed a tear away as she parked, locked the car and stood indecisively on the pavement, high hedges towering over her, dripping cold droplets of water down the back of her neck.

She shuddered, and glanced at his house. She should have been prepared for all the police cars parked outside his residence, of course, but in her shock, she hadn't really been thinking straight.

She hedged around the small gaggle of curious people, who were standing outside the front entrance, and glanced, with the rest, through the closed wrought iron gates.

The garden looked just as she remembered it. Was it only a week or so ago that she'd stood there, watching him dead-head his roses. And now . . . She drew in a ragged breath, feeling ashamed of herself for coming here. And she really should have known better. As if it was likely that she'd really have been allowed to just waltz in and reclaim her things. Even something as important as her father's thesis.

Nesta chewed on her lip uncertainly, and retreated across the road, back to her car with a head full of whirling thoughts. Her papers had to be in the house. Unless Sir Vivian had taken them to his office at St. Bede's, his old college? But why would he do that?

For a long while Nesta stood there, uncertain what to do next. She supposed she could simply ask the policeman on duty when she might see someone in charge, and set about claiming back her property. But on the other hand, she was reluctant to interrupt the police at this important time. More than anything else, she wanted the man responsible for killing Sir Vivian caught and punished. Which meant giving the police plenty of room to do their job. And they wouldn't be interested in her problems, unless they related to their investigation.

Which they obviously didn't.

Nesta was still chewing her bottom lip, a habit of hers when she was anxious, and was moving restlessly from foot to foot, when Lisle Jarvis walked down the path and out through the gates.

The uniformed constable on guard nodded

at him respectfully, but Nesta didn't need this silent salute in order to pick him out as the man in charge. In spite of looking tired enough to drop, there was a raw, rough energy about the man that, even from across the distance of the road, reached out to her and teased at her femininity. All of a sudden, her heartbeat quickened.

'All quiet, Constable?'

She heard the quiet, weary voice, even above the dim drumming of the rain and the murmur of the ghoulish sightseers. The constable nodded, and then, to her utter astonishment, said something and nodded in her direction. Instantly, a pair of brown eyes turned and focused on her.

Nesta had had no idea that her state of worry and agitation had been picked up by the constable, but then, in a sudden flash of comprehension, she realised that her body language must have been fairly screaming 'anxiety'. And, of course, the police were trained observers. No doubt she'd stood out from the rest of the crowd, keeping herself a little apart, and looking more upset than merely just curious.

Nesta took her hands out of her pockets as the tall, tough-looking plainclothes policeman started across the road towards her. For one insane moment, she had the urge to bolt. Why, she couldn't have said.

Perhaps it was a combination of shock and

the fight-or-flight instinct, when faced with a tough predator. Certainly, she had to force herself to stand firm and calm as Lisle Jarvis walked purposefully towards her. His eyes, she noticed, were hazel. Deeply and thickly lashed, wonderful and sharp. They were looking at her with all of a policeman's suspicion.

'Good morning, Miss,' Lisle began.

He was dog tired. He'd been up all night, supervising the removal of the body, and organising his small but experienced team. In just a few short hours he'd got a full guest list of last night's Dinner from Sir Roland, as well as the addresses of all those concerned. He'd set his team into groups of two, who were even now beginning the preliminary interviews of all the potential witnesses. He was waiting on the forensics reports, and had arranged for another forensics team to go over the archery range at St Bede's with a fine tooth comb. Not that he expected much. The room was too public, too well used. The trouble would be not that there was *no* evidence, but that there would be *too much* of it. Unless they could match a fibre from Sir Vivian's body to a fibre in the room, he doubted that he would even be able to prove that the murderer *had* used a weapon from the archery room.

If, indeed, they had.

A little later on he'd be getting the autopsy report. Later on still, he would have to go and see Lady Dalrymple, which was something he was not looking forward to one little bit.

He'd been about to go home to get a few hours much needed rest, but had decided to take a quick look at Sir Vivian's home first.

It was already full of policemen, going about their business, and, as he'd half-expected, coming up with nothing useful. So when he'd trudged tiredly back to his car, and the constable on duty had pointed out to him a pretty, redheaded spectator who seemed to have a lot on her mind, he'd been both disgusted and hopeful. So far, even though it was such early days, they had nothing concrete to go on. Not even a motive.

But a pretty redhead always had potential. Could she be the murder victim's mistress, perhaps?

Now, drawing up in front of her, Lisle could see that this redhead had an awful lot of potential indeed.

Her hair, cut in the shape of a bell, and coming to sharp points either side of her well-shaped mouth, was sprinkled with raindrops. Her figure, even beneath the see-through plastic raincoat, looked curvaceous and full. Her eyes were the colour of Irish fields.

Lisle dragged in a quick breath, taken by surprise by the tug of sexual pleasure and interest that suddenly started stirring, deep in his abdomen.

Since his divorce, he'd been living a celibate lifestyle, and hadn't even noticed it much. Suddenly he was very much aware of a woman's power. She'd nudged awake the dragon that had been sleeping within, and he wasn't best pleased.

'Can you tell me what you're doing here?' he asked, as usual, getting straight to the point. He was too damn tired to start making polite conversation.

Nesta blinked, opened her mouth, and then shut it again. What, after all, could she say? Explaining about her father's thesis would involve a long, complicated, and totally irrelevant story, and she could already see this man was practically dead on his feet. As a psychologist she could see the symptoms of fatigue in his hollow eyes and gruff voice, and inaccessible approach.

So she smiled and shrugged one shoulder. 'Nothing really. I just saw the crowd and wondered what was happening.'

But that sounded even worse. It made her sound like nothing more than a ghoulish sightseer. She didn't know why, but she didn't want to belittle herself in front of this man. She felt herself flush in shame and, unable to meet the disappointed look in his eyes, glanced down at her wet feet. Her shoes, she noticed belatedly, had a hole in them.

Lisle's eyes narrowed.

Lying. She was lying to him. But perhaps he was just so tired he was getting suspicious of everyone?

114

'I see,' he said flatly, and saw her pretty head rear up. She was still flushing.

'I don't normally . . . I mean, I'm not one of these people who like to stop at accidents and . . .' her voice trailed off miserably. 'I was just out for a walk . . .'

Oh, shut up, Nesta, she told herself grimly. You're making a complete fool of yourself.

Lisle smiled. He couldn't help it. She looked so woebegone.

'So you didn't know the man who lived there?' he asked, nodding back at the house.

Again Nesta opened her mouth, and again she closed it. She realised, a bit late in the day, that she shouldn't have come here. She should have gone back to her bedsit and done some solid thinking, and then worked out a campaign of action. Now she was caught in the cleft of a dilemma, and had nobody to blame but herself. She didn't want to be in the position of lying to the police, but on the other hand, she didn't feel able to come out with the whole truth just yet.

She shook her head, more at her own stupidity and rashness than anything else, but Lisle took it for a negative answer.

'I see. Then in that case, I suggest you go home, and get out of this awful weather.'

For one moment, Lisle wanted to ask her where she lived. He told himself it was merely a precaution. If, after all, it turned out that she *was* involved, he needed to know where to contact her. But a little voice was jeering away in the back of his head. Precaution hell! He just wanted to see her again.

'Oh, er . . . right,' Nesta said, backing away reluctantly. She couldn't, for some reason, seem to tear her eyes away from his.

Really, he was not her type. He was too old for her for a start—surely by more than a decade or maybe even a dozen years. And he was too rugged and tough. Too in charge and sure of himself. Whilst it made her feel challenged and protected and excited, all at the same time, she didn't see herself playing a submissive role in any relationship with a man.

She fumbled at the door of her VW Beetle, fumbled for her keys, got the car open and sat inside. What on earth was she thinking of? She'd met the man two minutes, and her mind was already thinking along the terms of a relationship?

She turned on the ignition, and put on her seat belt. And still he was looking at her—she could feel his gaze through the glass of the windscreen.

Lisle watched her drive away, holding up his hand as she gave him a timid wave through the steaming-up window.

He memorised her car number plate, just in case. And, less than a minute later, was glad that he did.

He was just climbing back into his own car, and had wearily told Jim that it was time they went home and got some sleep, when one of the constables, engaged on the door-to-door questioning of the victim's neighbours, beckoned to him sharply. He came running down from the house next door to Sir Vivian's, on the right hand side.

Lisle sighed but waited patiently, winding down the window.

'Sir, I thought you should hear this straight away,' the constable, who looked about 15 to Lisle's jaundiced eye, leaned in through the window, red of cheek and sparkling eyed, and earnestly began reading from his notebook.

'Mrs Sayers, who lives next door, remembers Sir Vivian receiving a visitor last Tuesday or Wednesday afternoon, she's not sure. She says a young woman called in, and stood talking to Sir Vivian for a few moments, out in the garden. They then went inside, and stayed inside for over an hour.' The constable broke off with a grin. 'Apparently, Mrs Sayers was much upset, because Sir Vivian's wife is in the hospital, and since retiring as a Tutor, Sir Vivian hasn't been teaching any undergraduates. Or taken on any private tuition, for that matter.'

Lisle smiled wearily. 'So a young lady, staying for over an hour when the lady of the house was away, ruffled Mrs Sayers' feathers?'

'Yes, Sir. So far, it's the only lead we've been able to come up with.'

Lisle rubbed his eyes. They felt like grit. It

wasn't much, but it was a starting point. 'Does she know who the lady was?'

'No, Sir. But she gave me a good description.'

'I bet she did,' Lisle laughed humourlessly. 'Come on then, let's have it.'

'Yes, Sir. She was in her early twenties, medium height, curvaceous in build, with a distinctive red hair cut, shaped like a bell, and curving into her cheeks into a point either side of her mouth.'

*   *   *

The pathologist looked across his office at Lisle standing in the open doorway and smiled knowingly. 'That's bad timing, Lisle, I've just finished the autopsy on your man Dalrymple,' he said cheerfully.

A middle-aged man with thinning hair and a wide smile, the medical man had known and worked with Lisle for many years now. And certainly long enough to know now that he'd reached the lofty heights of Inspector, he always delegated the chore of actually attending an autopsy to someone else.

Although he'd never yet actually passed out during the procedure, it was no secret that it was one aspect of police work that he'd always hated, and had been glad to avoid.

'I see no point when I know you'll always be able to tell me what I want to know, Jack, without having to watch the gory details myself,' Lisle said with a weary grin. 'And right now I'm hoping you'll tell me that the old man died of natural causes, like a nice simple heart attack.'

Dr Jack Underwood laughed. 'Not unless you call an arrow through the chest a heart attack,' he said, then laughed again. 'Although, in a way, I suppose you could say it was exactly that. His heart had a very neat hole in it, so you could say it got attacked all right.'

Lisle blinked. 'Are you serious?'

'Absolutely.'

'He was killed with a bow and arrow? Like cock robin, for pete's sake?' Lisle heard his voice rise in disbelief.

'Well, not exactly a bow and arrow like you're probably thinking. Not Robin Hood, longbow stuff and all that. It was more of a crossbow bolt that did for him, probably from a small, modern, compact but powerful bow.'

Jack Underwood reached for a small plastic evidence bag and tossed it across to him. Lisle neatly caught it, and found himself looking at a thin, barbed piece of what looked like steel. It was barely four inches long. 'A crossbow bolt, I take it?' he said flatly.

'Yes. I removed it from the body of Sir Vivian not an hour ago. It was without doubt the cause of death,' he said wryly. 'And before you ask, I put time of death at any time between ten p.m. and midnight.'

Lisle smiled grimly. 'Let me guess. He was last seen talking to someone alive and well at ten, and the porter found him at not long after midnight?'

Jack Underwood laughed. 'That's it. You know it's always notoriously difficult to accurately gauge the time of death on the physical evidence alone. Body temperatures, ambient temperatures, the quirks and vagaries of rigor—they can all trip you up. You're far better off having eyewitness accounts to place time of death any day.'

Lisle sighed glumly. 'Any defence wounds?'

'None.'

'Anything else you can tell me?'

'The arrow went in from behind, I'd say. Death would have been pretty instantaneous. That's why there wasn't much blood at the scene. And, of course,' he pointed at the small, lethal piece of metal in Lisle's hands, 'the whole thing was buried in the body, so there was no feather-lined arrow sticking out of his back to make you suspicious at first sight. It wasn't until I got him undressed and on the table that the wound became obvious. A very neat job.'

'And the arrow . . .'

'Bolt,' the pathologist corrected pedantically.

'Fine, bolt, whatever—it went straight through the heart? A good shot, do you think, or just lucky?'

Jack Underwood laughed. 'Do I look like an archery expert to you, Lisle? I can tell you which rib the bolt nicked, and exactly where, if it helps you any.'

Lisle sighed heavily. 'Hardly.'

*   *   *

Back at the incident room, Lisle sat at his desk and read the pathologist's report in detail. Then he reached for the phone and dialled his sergeant's mobile.

'What have you got?'

'Still going through the party guests' witness statements, Sir. Sir Vivian did attend the party, but not the actual Dinner, for some reason. He was seen both before and after the meal, though. So far we've got him leaving the party somewhere around ten forty-five. He was staying the night in his room, Sir, rather than return home at that late hour.'

Lisle grunted. 'That accounts for his body being found where it was then. He was probably on his way to his bed, when someone shot him.'

'Sir?'

Briefly, Lisle filled him in on Dr Underwood's findings. 'All right, carry on with what you're doing. Meet me back here when you've finished. If you want me, I'll be at the college.'

121

'Sir.'

*　　　*　　　*

In his own office, Sin Jun paled slightly when Lisle told him the news, about fifteen minutes later. 'But that's appalling,' Sin Jun said. 'Who'd want to do something like that to that dear old man?'

Lisle nodded. 'That's what I've come to ask you, Sir. Did Sir Vivian have any enemies?'

'What? No, good grief, no. He was liked by everyone. Yes, I know, Inspector, that sounds like an old chestnut, but in Vivian's case it was true. Sometimes academics can be bitchy, I'll give you that,' Sin Jun went on, with a small smile. 'The amount of cat fights that I've had to break up you wouldn't believe. Glad that I made my fortune in the business world, I can tell you. But Vivian wasn't like that. He didn't do petty bickering or back-stabbing.'

Lisle sighed. 'Money troubles?'

Sin Jun blinked. 'I seriously doubt it.'

'Womaniser?'

Sin Jun barked a laugh, and Lisle sighed, then noticed a stack of that year's newly produced College Prospectuses on the desk. He reached for one, and leafed through it absently. It was a glossy, high-end piece of literature, with photographs of the picturesque college grounds and members of staff, with blurb designed to attract the next batch of

122

students and their grant money.

Then Lisle turned a page, and froze. It was a section dedicated to sport—as well as the famous Boat Race, Oxford was known for inspiring sporting greats from the field of athletics to boxing.

And, in St Bede's case, archery.

'You have archery facilities here,' Lisle said flatly.

'What? Oh yes, we've had one or two successes over the years. One of our Fellows, Callum Fielding, is almost good enough to compete at National level. And in the past we've had . . . .' Sin Jun's voice suddenly trailed off, and he shot an appalled glance at the policeman.

'Oh surely you don't think . . .'

'I'd like you to show me your sports hall, Sir,' Lisle said flatly.

*   *   *

Ten minutes later, he reached for his mobile and called out a SOCO team. St Bede's boasted a fully-equipped sports hall, complete with archery targets, crossbows of all sorts of descriptions, as well as bows and arrows that Robin Hood himself would very much have appreciated. And every one of them would need to be checked.

'I take it this hall was closed and locked last night?' Lisle asked, folding away the phone and glancing around.

'I imagine so, Inspector,' Sin Jun said miserably. 'I'll check with the porter.'

'But a lot of people will have keys?'

'Yes.'

'But only those from this college,' Lisle pressed. 'Most of the party guests were from other colleges within the university I take it. There'd be no reason for them to have keys?'

'Er, no,' Sin Jun agreed reluctantly.

Lisle nodded. Perhaps this was a lucky break after all. If the bolt recovered from Sir Vivian's body could be matched to one of those from the St Bede's archery club, he might just have shortened his suspect list considerably.

Because there was no way now that this could be a casual, random killing. Nobody wandered around at night with a bow and arrow looking to mug someone. This had to be premeditated.

'I think you were saying that one of your Fellows was a good shot, Sir. Dr Fielding, was it? What can you tell me about him?'

Sin Jun shot him an appalled look. 'Now look here, Inspector, Sir Vivian was one of Callum's tutors when he was an undergraduate here. They got on like a house on fire. Callum respected Sir Vivian enormously, and for his part, Vivian regarded Callum as one of his star pupils. Not only did he go on to produce a blindingly good D.Phil thesis of his own and become a member of this college, but he's just

124

been awarded the Kendall Prize as well.'

'This would be at the Prize Dinner that was just held here?' Lisle asked sharply. 'Worth a lot is it? This prize?'

'It fully funds a Fellow's research for five years, Inspector. Believe me, that's like the holy grail to an academic!' Sin Jun said with pride.

'And Dr Fielding won it,' Lisle said sharply 'Was Sir Vivian in the running to win it too?'

'What? Good grief, I have no idea. I'm not sure who was on the short list. You'd have to ask the Kendall family that. But Vivian is all but retired now, and besides, he had won it before anyway.'

'So it might have caused bad feeling, if he'd been counting on winning it again?' Lisle pressed.

Sin Jun shook his head helplessly. 'Inspector, I can assure you, you're barking up the wrong tree.'

'Nevertheless, Sir Vivian was murdered in your college, with a crossbow bolt. And I'm sure I don't need to tell you, Sir, to keep that information to yourself. At the moment, the press is under the impression that this was a random, common-or-garden mugging. I don't have to tell you what will happen if the real cause of death is leaked to them.'

Sin Jun paled visibly. 'Nobody will hear it from me, Inspector, I assure you.'

Lisle nodded. Good. The longer they could keep it under wraps, the more complacent and safe the killer would feel. Which was just how Lisle wanted it.

For now.

CHAPTER SIX

Lisle parked the car in front of a slightly inauspicious-looking building, and climbed out. He hadn't brought Jim with him, telling his sergeant instead to report in later. There was no reason why they should both lose out on their sleep.

He wondered, as he locked the car and went in search of the building's landlady, if he was doing the right thing. Normal procedure called for two police personnel to be present at any interview. But in reality, budget cuts being what they were, they were so short-staffed that single-personnel interviews were actually the norm. Jim was dead on his feet and . . .

Lisle smiled to himself grimly. If he was going to be totally honest, he'd simply wanted to talk to the redhead alone.

Strictly in the interests of his investigation, of course. The fact that she'd been on his mind all morning, the memory of her green eyes intruding into his consciousness about every five minutes or so, had absolutely nothing to do with it.

The landlady, a fifty three year old bleached blonde, with expert make-up and a warm heart, was aghast to be called on, in the middle of the day, by a policeman. Appalled that one of her 'people' should need to be interviewed by the police. Totally innocent of any knowledge of wrong doing, and, of course, she personally really *admired* the police, and thought they did a good job. And told him so. At length. All the time, her pale blue eyes running over the impressive length and look of him.

As Lisle followed her upstairs, parrying her curious questions and none-too-subtle hints for information, he began to feel more and more weary. He'd got past that dog-tired state, where he could have slept for twelve solid hours had he gone home, like he'd meant to. He was now in that restless-but-listless stage, where he felt wide awake, but like something the cat had dragged in.

As soon as he'd heard the description of Sir Vivian's mysterious female caller, he'd spent the last few hours tracking her down. And the thought of seeing her again was not a displeasing one.

For a woman he'd only talked to for a few minutes, she'd certainly made her presence felt.

The landlady finally paused for breath, and hesitated outside a slightly warped door before tapping timidly. A moment later, Nesta Aldernay opened it and looked in blank surprise at her landlady, who was never usually a lunch time caller. Then her green eyes slid past her to the tall, menacing figure standing behind her.

She became suddenly still. Then she smiled. 'Hello again,' she said quietly. She knew her landlady's eyes were avidly watching her every expression, her big ears straining for the slightest hint of scandal or intrigue, and she was damned if she was going to give the old girl any more ammunition.

Lisle understood her predicament at once. He smiled back. 'Miss Aldernay,' he said crisply, but pleasantly. 'There are just one or two questions that need clearing up.'

'Oh, of course,' Nesta said, her heart suddenly thumping against her ribs. How did he know her name? She hadn't told him this morning, of that she was certain. But then, he was a policeman. Her name must be on many databases available to the police.

She opened the door a little wider. 'Please, do come in. Would you like some tea?' Then, turning to her landlady, she smiled at her sweetly, and gently shut the door in her face.

Alone in the room, the two of them stood in silence, warily looking at one another as they patiently waited until they could hear the heavy tread of the landlady going back down the stairs.

Nesta swallowed a strange lump in her throat, wondering why her feet were so reluctant to move. She felt, ridiculously, rooted to the spot. Then she firmly took herself in hand, and forced herself to start towards the small sink and the waiting kettle. 'Sugar? Milk?'

'Please. One sugar.'

He watched her cross the room, rather like a cat watches an unfamiliar mouse. Curious. Wary. Purring just a little . . .

Nesta had changed her clothes the moment she'd returned. In spite of the supposedly waterproof mac, they'd felt clammy and cold. She was now wearing a long, mid-calf length tartan skirt in a vivid blue, green and yellow pattern, and had pulled on her one really good piece of clothing, a mint green cashmere polo-necked jumper. It had been warm and comforting, snuggling into its woollen folds.

The contrast of the colour however, with her bell of red hair, and her sparkling emerald eyes was breathtaking, even to a man who wasn't already punch-drunk on lack of sleep.

Lisle reluctantly dragged his eyes from the wonderful sight of her, and looked around the room, his mobile lips twisting into a grimace of sympathy.

The wallpaper was a little too dark. The windows a little too grimy. The carpet a little too worn. The lampshade looked as it if belonged in the 1940's. A typical cheap bedsit in fact. Not that that meant anything. Now, if she'd been putting up at the swish Randolph hotel . . . Lisle's policeman instincts would have been twitching, even more than they were now.

But, he thought with a pang of depression, a woman like this belonged in a four-star room.

Too bone-weary to sit, he prowled the room, checking out the atrocious artwork, her old-fashioned alarm clock, his eyes taking note of her mac, drip-drying over a chair and the few toiletries she had scattered beside the washstand cabinet.

Nesta made the tea, very well aware of his roving eyes. They would, she was sure, miss nothing. He had the eyes of a hawk. Far-seeing. Sharp. Trained to predator-perfection.

It made her shiver in the most odd way . . .

She made the tea and turned, once again having to force herself to walk across the room towards him and smile naturally. It wasn't easy. The man brought an aura of menace into the room that was, perversely, not so much frightening, as exciting. He had the same aura about him as the film idols of her grandmother's day. Bogart. Lancaster. Gable. A man's man, who should have seemed out of place in the second decade of the brand new millennium, but somehow didn't. He was the kind of man who had the power to force his environment to suit *him*. Not, as with all of the other men of her acquaintance, the other way around.

No doubt about it, the man oozed power. Sex appeal. Charisma.

She became aware of his hazel eyes narrowing on her face, and she blushed furiously, aware that she'd been caught out staring.

Lisle, at the sight of that blush, instantly felt his body come abruptly awake. His blood, instead of running around apathetically in his veins, suddenly began to pound. He could feel his nerve-ends tingle, his body harden. He knew that look. What man didn't? The look of a woman who found him attractive. The look of a woman who'd been speculating.

He took a deep breath. It had been so long since he'd even thought about sex in any serious way. Since his divorce had become absolute, things had just slid into . . . well . . . limbo. Women were often put off by his occupation. And the antisocial hours he worked had made dating difficult. Eventually, he'd ceased to even bother. Now though . . .

He ran a harassed hand through his hair, unaware that the gesture set Nesta's own body tingling. His crisp brown hair crackled with electricity, and the sight of fingers running through it made her own fingertips itch to run through the dark locks.

'May I sit down?' he finally said, taking a sip of the tea, and discovering that she'd made it just how he liked it.

'Oh, of course,' Nesta said, flustered. 'I'm afraid the chairs aren't very comfortable.'

Lisle smiled and shrugged, sinking down into a very uncomfortable chair with a heart-felt sigh. This interview was definitely not going according to police manual instructions.

'I should have introduced myself,' he apologised, setting his mug by his feet and reaching into his jacket for his ID. He held out the identification card to her, and Nesta reluctantly took it.

Detective Inspector Lisle Jarvis.

Two things struck her at once. Firstly, how well the name suited him. And secondly, how serious things had suddenly become. He was not just a gorgeous man any longer, a creature who'd brought a dash and masculinity into her rather feeble little room. He now represented the law. And all that it implied.

In spite of herself, Nesta felt instantly worried. Even though she understood the psychology of the moment, it didn't help her much. She told herself that many people felt guilty and nervous in the presence of police authority, even though, like herself, they'd done absolutely nothing wrong. But none of that could prevent her from feeling, suddenly, acutely vulnerable. Which made her, naturally, acutely angry. Being angry was much easier on the nerves than being afraid.

She moved purposefully to the equally uncomfortable chair opposite him, and sat down, calmly crossing her legs. Wordlessly, she handed his wallet back to him. 'Inspector Jarvis. What can I do for you?' she asked bravely.

She might just as well take the bull by the horns.

Lisle smiled grimly, mentally shaking his head. So, she wanted to take the initiative did she? Put him in his place? Hah! Who did the lady think she was dealing with? A rank amateur? Even dog-tired, he could play her at any game she chose to play, and win. Hands down.

'You can start off by telling me why you told me a pack of lies this morning,' he said savagely.

Nesta blinked, totally stunned. Whatever she'd been expecting, it hadn't been this. Her whole body jerked, both under the lash of the power in his voice, and the instant reaction to danger.

'I beg your pardon?' she said coldly.

Lisle looked at her stormy eyes. They really were the exact colour of emeralds. They sparkled like jewels too. He shook his head, and made a great show of bringing out his notebook.

'You are Nesta Janice Aldernay, of 31 Brook Close, Durham?'

Nesta gaped at him. 'How . . . ?'

'Your car number plate,' Lisle explained briefly. He'd tracked her to this residence by the simple expedient of getting a much put-upon WPC to check up on all the hotel and hostel registers that landlords, by law, were required to keep. It hadn't taken as long as he'd thought.

Nesta blinked again. 'But why did you take down my car number plate? And,' her eyes sharpened accusingly, 'I didn't see you write it down anywhere.'

Lisle sighed. 'I have a very good memory, Miss Aldernay. As, so it happens, does Sir Vivian Dalrymple's next-door neighbour.'

Nesta, wide-eyed over the thought of his almost photographic memory, suddenly felt herself go a little cold. And a little pale. She cursed her fair skin, which she knew from experience, regularly gave the game away. It was almost impossible to stop her emotions and reactions from showing on her face.

'Neighbour?' she echoed stupidly, biting her lower lip and desperately trying to guess ahead. Somehow, without quite knowing how, she seemed to have wandered into a minefield.

Seeing his hazel eyes flicker in interest, she leaned back in her chair and let her brow furrow in puzzlement. 'Who did you say this neighbour was?'

Even as she said it, she wondered what the hell she was doing. And, quick as a flash, the ironical answer came back. She was letting him get under her skin—*that's* what she was doing. She felt a rush of sudden shame, as

134

she realised that this was far, far too serious a matter to be playing games. Of course, she must just admit . . .

'Miss Aldernay, don't play games with me,' Lisle said, his voice as soft as velvet, as deadly as dynamite. 'I'm tired, I'm cranky, and I'm in no mood to be toyed with.' His voice rose to a sharp edge, then subsided again.

Nesta felt her nipples suddenly begin to ache. Sweetly. Unsettled, she sat up very straight on the chair. She took a breath.

'I'm not sure . . .' she began, ready to tell him all about her father's research, but not sure she should even waste his time with it.

Lisle, however, glanced down at his notebook, and ruthlessly cut her off. Although, in his line of work, he was used to being lied to, there was something about being lied to by *this particular woman* that was oddly painful to him. He just didn't want to hear it.

'According to our witness,' he began grimly, 'a young woman, between the age of 20 and 25, called on Sir Vivian on Wednesday last. This woman was about five feet five in height, with a bell-shaped cut of red hair that came to a point either side of her lips.'

Lisle looked up suddenly, his eyes softening on the wings of her hair. They seemed to point, like arrows, to her mouth, which was slightly open, and breathing in air rapidly. Her lips were perfectly formed, lipstick-free, and had a deep, appealing, cupid's bow.

He dragged his eyes from them with something of an effort, and looked into her eyes. And found that they were no longer flashing in furious emerald temper, but darkening in despair. He felt his heart sink. So she *was* guilty of something. Please, let it only be prevarication. Nothing worse. Please.

But he was in no mood to be merciful. 'Does that description remind you of anyone, Miss Aldernay?' he jibed.

The voice was so soft, so sure, so damned wonderful, that Nesta once again felt herself getting angry.

'There must be a fair few redheads in this city, Mr Jarvis,' she pointed out grimly.

'*Inspector* Jarvis,' Lisle corrected ruthlessly. 'And I dare say there are. But how many of them showed up outside Sir Vivian's home this morning, looking worried and anxious?'

Nesta watched him suddenly get to his feet and begin to pace restlessly. Like a caged tiger, all frustrated power and animal angst. Instinctively, she opened her mouth to tell him everything. Let him waste his time, what did it matter to her? But before she could do so, Lisle, alerted by the title of a book by her bed, suddenly lifted it up and read the title.

'The Psychology of Sin' by Dr Callum Fielding.

He spun around, catching her just as she was about to speak.

'You study psychology?' he snapped. It

sounded so much like an accusation that it caught her totally unawares.

'No. I mean, yes. I mean . . .' she flustered, 'I've just finished a B.A. course in the subject at Durham.'

Lisle suddenly felt like laughing. And cursing roundly. Because, suddenly, the mystery was no mystery at all. And he should be glad, but he wasn't. He was disappointed.

'Oh, I get it,' he nodded, rubbing his eyes tiredly. The sensible part of him knew that he was acting like an idiot because he was just too tired to think straight. But another part of him simply failed to care.

Nesta, not liking the sneer on his handsome face, or the tone of his voice one little bit, got rapidly to her own feet, her hands curling and uncurling into fists by her side.

'And what exactly is it that you get, *Inspector* Jarvis?' she asked coldly, her chin coming up in a challenge, her body tensing.

Lisle looked at her, thinking what a waste it was. All that fire and beauty, thrown away on an old man.

No, a little demon voice popped up in the back of his mind. Not just any old man. A titled old man. A powerful old man. A man with a great academic reputation. The boy who'd grown up on the wrong side of the tracks suddenly raised his ugly head.

As if he would ever be good enough for a woman like this. Well-educated. Beautiful.

137

Classy.

'You thought he could get you in, did you?' he asked grimly. 'Is that what he promised you? To get you a post-graduate course in this mighty, wonderful University of ours?' he goaded. 'And just what did you have to do to fulfil your part of the bargain? And was it just the once? Or have you been seeing each other for a while?'

Nesta stared at him, trying to make sense of the bitter, mocking words. He was obviously grinding some personal axe. His ugly tone made her wince at first, and then, in a sudden wave of understanding, his equally ugly meaning had her exploding in indignation.

Her eyes widened, flaring into green lasers as he walked towards her and tossed the book he was carrying onto his now empty chair seat.

'If you'd just told me this morning that you were Sir Vivian's mistress we could . . .'

Nesta hissed. There was no other word for the small expulsion of air that escaped her throat. Of all the condescending, self-righteous, mean-spirited . . . She felt her hand come back, and had just about a split second to wonder what the hell she thought she was doing. Then she was watching her hand swing out in front of her, heading for his face like a guided missile.

If he hadn't been so tired, she would never have been able to land the slap on him. As it was, he saw the movement, felt a brief-lived desire to laugh, and then felt the shocking, stinging slap numb the left side of his face. It was, he thought blankly, a rather good backhander.

The noise of the blow echoed through the room with all the panache of a gunshot.

Nesta's green eyes widened even further.

Had she really just hit him?

She saw the white imprint of a hand slowly appear in stark relief in his reddened face, and realised that, yes, she had indeed just hit him.

She, the psychology major, had just lost control.

Lisle blinked, still fighting off a vague desire to laugh. It had been so long since he'd been slapped in the face by a beautiful woman. Who'd have thought he still had it in him?

'You do realise,' he heard himself say, clearly and mockingly, 'that I could arrest you for assaulting a police officer?'

Nesta boiled at that weary, mocking tone. So he didn't take her seriously? Her heightened senses hummed, demanding that something else happen.

Something even better. Even more dramatic.

'Really?' she snarled. And thrust herself against him.

Taken by surprise, Lisle took a staggering step backwards. He felt her hands cup his face, and then her eyes were so close to his, the green fire of them wiped out everything else.

He felt her sweet breath against his tired skin and then . . .

Her lips met his with as much passion as sweetness, forcing his mouth open, her tongue darting into his mouth to assail and tantalise. He could feel the super-softness of the cashmere sweater pressing against the cool cotton of his shirt. And, beneath the wool, the two hard discs of her nipples, grinding against his lower ribs, turning his knees to water.

He could smell her perfume, a delicate, light, floral scent that invaded his nostrils, settling around him, confining him, trapping him, like a fly in a gossamer web.

Her fingers dug in to the vulnerable flesh of his cheeks, but he didn't care. Her touch awoke with a vengeance something that had been long dormant inside him. Something male. Something animal. Something tender, and precious, and worrying and . . . .

Nesta broke the contact and stood back, trembling.

'Can I get arrested for that too?' she asked, her angry defiant challenge coming out more like a soul-shaken croak.

Lisle smiled grimly. 'I'm not sure,' he said shakily. 'But it felt too good to be legal.'

And with that, he decided that it was probably a good time to beat a tactical retreat. He had other things to do and people to see. And to continue questioning Nesta Aldernay whilst they were both in such an agitated state was probably *not* a good idea!

*   *   *

Callum walked into the lobby of the city's most famous hotel and glanced around curiously. Like most Fellows who lived in their college, he only ever came to the Randolph to dine. Now he approached the desk and smiled briefly.

'Is Miss Kendall in, please?'

The desk clerk smiled tightly. Another one for the supermodel. The press and fans never gave any of them any peace. 'I'm afraid Miss Kendall is not seeing anyone, Sir,' he repeated the words by rote. A young man in his late twenties, he'd been on duty for the last four hours, and felt as if he'd said it a thousand times.

Callum, who knew all about body language and had an acute ear for human emotion, read his irritation easily. 'Popular is she?' he asked sardonically. No doubt a woman who looked like she did was bound to be popular. She probably had to fight men off with a cricket bat. 'Would you please just tell her that Dr Callum Fielding, the winner of the Kendall Prize, is downstairs and would just like a quick word?' he asked, and the desk clerk smiled brightly.

'Of course, Dr Fielding,' he said, reaching for the telephone and giving himself a mental

141

head-slap. Now that he thought about it, it was obvious the blond giant wasn't the usual run of the mill Marcheta fan!

He turned aside slightly and quietly repeated Callum's request, then hung up and smiled. 'Miss Kendall will be right down, Sir. If you'd like to take a seat?'

Callum ignored the proffered seat and was standing staring out of the window and across at the Ashmolean Museum when Markie came down. Her eyes instantly found the tall figure, of course. With the autumn sunlight streaming in through the window, giving his fair hair a silver halo, he was a magnet for every eye in the room.

'Dr Fielding, how nice,' Markie said. She was, in fact, dying to know what he wanted. All night long she'd been tossing and turning restlessly, and it was mainly the memories of this man which had kept her awake.

She was wearing a pair of deep cream slacks, with fairly high-heeled, calf-high brown leather boots. With it she was wearing a peach coloured top with a metallic sheen, and a matching cream jacket. Her long black hair fell free and cascaded down past her shoulders and down her back in a mass of gentle ebony waves. Her make-up was light, and she was wearing long dangling gold earrings. She looked stunning.

'I was just going out for a walk in the park, while the sun was shining. Care to join me?'

142

she asked brightly.

Callum smiled and politely held the door open for her. They didn't say much as they walked past the crowds at the Martyr's Memorial on St Giles, conversation being difficult. Then they had to dodge the tourists on the pavement as they passed the red-and-white brick monstrosity that was Keble College, but once they were inside the parks on Park Road, and the sound of traffic faded, Callum glanced across at her and decided to waste no more time.

'I rather think we got off on the wrong foot, Miss Kendall,' Callum began somewhat awkwardly. With her high-heeled boots, she was only a few inches or so shorter than himself, and he found he was looking right into her lovely blue eyes.

He felt his loins begin to harden, and he quickly glanced away again, telling himself not to be so juvenile. He was hardly a sex-starved teenager anymore with hormones running amok!

'I may have given you the impression at the Dinner that . . . Er . . .'

'You wanted to be rid of me?' Markie asked bluntly, delighted to see a dull flush creep across the fine angular lines of his face. Not many men knew how to blush in this day and age, Markie thought with a tender pang that caught her by surprise.

'It's all right you know,' she said quickly.

143

'I could see that you wanted to be alone with your friend. He'd had a little bit too much to drink, I think. I hope he's all right now?'

Callum paled. 'I take it you haven't seen the papers?'

'No. Why?' Markie asked sharply.

'Sir Vivian died right after the party. The newspapers are speculating that he was mugged, but as far as I know, the police haven't issued any official statements yet.'

'Oh no! That's awful. Was he feeling ill, do you think? Perhaps he wasn't tipsy after all.' And now Markie felt acutely guilty. All the time she'd been scoring points off Callum Fielding because she'd felt slighted, and had her ego bruised, that poor old man had been feeling ill. Damn it, she shouldn't have left him on the bench alone like that.

She said as much.

'I know how you feel,' Callum agreed bleakly. 'Ever since I heard the news, I've been thinking the same thing. But what worries me most is what Vivian said just before you joined us.'

'Interrupted you so rudely you mean,' Markie said dryly, then waved a hand vaguely in the air as he made to demur. 'No, it's OK, that's what it amounted to really. But you seemed to be talking so intently to Dr Ngabe that I was curious. So, what did Sir Vivian say?' she insisted.

'He told us that somebody at the party

didn't deserve to be in Oxford,' Callum repeated boldly. 'He intimated that somebody had somehow cheated, which usually means either on their exams, or via plagiarism. It's one of the worst things that most academics could be accused of, and Sir Vivian wasn't the sort of man to make such an accusation lightly. He loved Oxford with every atom of his being, and something like this, a scandal of this type, would have hurt him very badly.'

Markie stopped walking, and put a hand on his arm. She understood at once the importance of what he was saying. 'Do you think it was playing on his mind? Could the stress have been too much? You fear he had a heart attack, don't you?'

Callum sighed and shrugged. 'I don't know. I didn't see him sit down to Dinner, and afterwards I wanted to find him and ask him to explain further. But then I won the award, and everyone wanted to congratulate me, and I never saw him again.' His voice cracked just a little on the final words, and he scowled at his weakness.

'I'm sorry,' he said gruffly. 'Sir Vivian was one of my tutors. More than that, I regarded him as my mentor.'

Markie felt his distress and took a step towards him, then groaned aloud as three men with cameras came running up to them.

'Marcheta, this way!'

'Give us a smile, Marcheta, you look

gorgeous.'

The youngest one shoved his way between them, and Callum took a few steps backward, looking non-plussed. His body tensed for a moment, as he was clearly wondering if she was being attacked, then, as she went into 'posing mode' he shot her an astonished look.

'All right, boys, just a few shots, then you must go and promise not to be a pest. I'm talking with the winner of the Kendall Prize, and we have business to discuss.'

She gave them a few more minutes, then with varying degrees of good-natured reluctance, they left them.

'Sorry about that, but I've found it's easier in the long run just to give them what they want, then they stop pestering you,' Markie said. Then grinned at him widely. 'You really do have no idea who I am, do you?'

Callum, his face tight, smiled grimly. 'Clearly not. I'm sorry, I don't watch much television, so please don't take it the wrong way if I've never seen any of your films. Or, er, music videos or whatever,' he added vaguely. Perfect. He'd come to apologise for his boorish behaviour, now he was insulting her again. What was it about this woman that made him feel so tongue-tied?

Markie laughed. 'I'm just a model, Dr Fielding. I don't have any acting talent I'm afraid, and I couldn't carry a tune in a bucket.'

Callum blinked and found his mouth was

hanging open, and closed his jaw with a snap. This bewildering woman was like nobody he'd ever met before. One moment she was a vamp, and the latest love interest of the College Casanova. Then she was the all-important Kendall family representative who was awarding him the Kendall Prize, no less. Then she was a supermodel, surrounded by adoring paparazzi. And now she was a down-to-earth girl-next-door who could laugh at herself and knew how to call a spade a spade.

Which one was she?

She smiled across at him, the breeze blowing a strand of hair across her eyes. Raising a hand to brush it away, Markie moved a step closer to him. 'I'm really sorry about your friend,' she said softly. For all of his height and the solid build of him, there was something touchingly vulnerable about this man.

It made her want to comfort him, and at the same time, throw herself into his arms and demand he take her somewhere private, where she could . . . .

'Dr Fielding?'

Callum turned abruptly, his eyes piercing the man who'd come up beside him. He didn't know what Markie Kendall had been about to say next, but he knew that he'd very much wanted to hear it, and to have some stranger barge in was enough to make his eyes darken ominously.

Lisle Jarvis stood stock still and tensed.

147

'You are Dr Callum Fielding?' he asked bluntly. He'd been told by the St Bede's porter that Dr Fielding had been asking after a Miss Kendall, who was registered at the Randolph. And at the hotel, the desk clerk, after some persuasion, had told him that he'd overheard Miss Kendall and her visitor say they were going to walk in the park. Now, having had to spend a good half an hour tracking down his quarry, Lisle was in no mood to be given the run around.

The porter at St Bede's had given a very accurate description of Dr Fielding. Very tall, very well built, and very fair. He'd failed to mention that Dr Fielding also had eyes that could stop a charging bull in its paces.

He wondered what had made the man look such daggers at him. And wondered, even more, if Dr Fielding usually had such a temper.

'Yes, I'm Callum Fielding,' Callum said calmly. The moment of anger had quickly passed, and he was already telling himself that he should be glad of the interruption. He'd probably been just about to make a monumental fool of himself with Markie Kendall anyway.

Although he'd had his fair share of female company since hitting his late teens, he was hardly anyone's idea of a ladies man. He'd spent all of his adult life at Oxford, both living in college, and remaining unmarried.

If anyone had asked him, he would have said that he would probably just fall into perpetual bachelorhood and become one of those old men that never seemed to leave the city.

A woman like Markie Kendall was way out of his league.

'I'm DI Jarvis sir,' Lisle said, showing the academic his ID and relaxing slightly as he sensed the tension in the big man subsiding. 'I have a few questions for you about the murder of Sir Vivian Dalrymple.'

Callum felt a cold hard knot clench his insides. He went pale. For a moment, he felt and heard a roaring in his ears, and the world seemed to recede then suddenly flow back. He blinked.

Lisle watched these signs of shock with interest.

'Murder?' Callum repeated bleakly. 'Someone murdered him?'

Beside him, he heard Markie gasp.

'Yes, Sir. I need to talk to you about the Dinner you attended. I need to know when you last saw Sir Vivian alive, and what you talked about. I think it would be easier if you would follow me back to St Aldates Police Station, Sir. We'll be more comfortable in an interview room, I think,' he added firmly.

'Just a minute, are you arresting him?' Markie demanded, and Lisle looked at her curiously. He recognised her at once, of course, but until then he hadn't made the connection. So Miss Kendall was also 'Marcheta' was she?

He also instantly picked up on the aggression in her voice, and smiled bleakly. She was expensively dressed and looked just the sort to know all about her rights, and have hot-and-cold running solicitors on tap.

'No, Miss Kendall, is it? I'm not arresting Dr Fielding. But I am questioning all of Sir Vivian's associates and the people who attended the Dinner the night Sir Vivian's body was found.'

'In that case, you'll be wanting to talk to me then as well,' Markie said. And smiling brightly, she moved closer to Callum and looped her hand firmly under his elbow. 'We'll come in together. We both talked to Sir Vivian at the same time, so you can get both our stories at once.'

Her bright hard eyes met Lisle's with a challenging stare, and Lisle nodded slightly in acknowledgement.

He glanced at the tall, silent blond man, who seemed to be thinking furiously, and wondered if he realised that he had an unlikely champion in the supermodel.

CHAPTER SEVEN

Markie Kendall had never been inside a

police station before and she rather thought it might be the first time for Dr Callum Fielding as well. Lisle wanted to separate them for interview, but the supermodel was having none of it, and threatened him with a barrage of her father's solicitors if he wanted to make an issue of it.

So Lisle smiled wryly and showed them both into interview room three. At this point, he didn't want to antagonise possibly vital witnesses. Or unnecessarily alert his best suspect to date. He wondered if the psychology Don had realised yet that he'd been earmarked for that role.

He didn't look particularly worried, if he did.

As he took his seat, Callum was far more interested in his female companion than in what the police might be thinking, and he looked at Markie with a mixture of irony, sexual awareness and annoyance. Was she always this bossy and aggressive? And why did it attract him so? If he'd been asked, he'd have said that he liked his women more contemplative and thoughtful. She was definitely not his type, so why did she keep getting under his skin?

'So, what can you tell me about the night Sir Vivian died?' Lisle began, once the tape was rolling, and they'd made themselves as comfortable as they could in the moulded plastic chairs. 'Miss Kendall, we'll start with

151

you shall we?'

Markie nodded, and began by telling them why she was in Oxford, and everything she could remember about the night of the party. Since her meeting with the victim had been relatively short, this didn't take long.

After getting a few things clarified, Lisle turned to his real target. 'Dr Fielding. I understand you knew the victim well?' he began easily.

'Yes. He was one of my tutors when I did my postgraduate course, and he was my mentor at St Bede's.'

'So you were close?'

'Yes.'

'Did you expect to be left anything in his Will?' Lisle asked bluntly, and Markie stiffened in her chair. She knew she was here under sufferance, and that if she made a nuisance of herself, this Inspector Jarvis was more than capable of sending her out of the room, so she forced herself to be calm. Even so, she had to bite her lip to keep from asking exactly what the Inspector was implying, and her hands clenched into fists under the table.

Callum regarded the policeman across the table warily. 'I wasn't expecting anything,' he said calmly. 'Sir Vivian and his wife have children and grandchildren. I would imagine all his property and assets will be divided between them.'

Lisle nodded impassively.

'Would you consider yourself a wealthy man?'

'Relatively, yes,' Callum said easily. 'Let me make this easier for you, Inspector. I have nothing to gain from the death of Sir Vivian.'

'And this prize, the Kendall Prize, it's worth a lot of money. Was Sir Vivian a serious threat to your chances of winning it? I understand that it means a lot to have your research funded for five years?' he carried on remorselessly.

'Yes it does, and I can tell you that Sir Vivian wasn't even Short listed this time,' Markie couldn't resist interrupting this time. 'As a Kendall, I was one of the few who knew who'd made the Short list. So you see, Sir Vivian posed no threat at all to Dr Fielding.'

Lisle smiled wryly. She was like a tigress defending her cub. Which was interesting. He glanced at the academic to see how the big man was taking it, but Callum's face was totally inscrutable. Lisle knew he wouldn't like to have to play poker with this man.

'Have you've known Dr Fielding long?' he asked the beautiful woman mildly, and Markie felt herself go hot then cold at the knowing look in the policeman's eye. Damn! Was it so obvious that she was smitten by the blond giant? She hoped not. 'Marcheta' never did the chasing. She was always the one who was chased.

Well. Until now, maybe.

153

'We met for the first time at the night of the party. This is only the second time we've had a chance to speak,' Markie corrected the Inspector stiffly.

Callum Fielding smiled at the surprised look on the policeman's face. 'Were you thinking we were part of some kind of conspiracy, Inspector?' he asked dryly. 'In which case, please let me assure you that we're not. And, as you can tell, we are far from close. In fact, the only reason I approached Miss Kendall today was in order to apologise to her.'

'Oh? For what?'

Callum shifted uncomfortably in his seat. 'We didn't exactly get off on the right foot at the party,' he said, hoping he could leave it there.

He couldn't, of course, and Callum had to explain why he'd been concerned that Markie Kendall might have found his attitude towards her a little cold and aloof. And Lisle's eyes sharpened when the psychology Don repeated the murder victim's words on the night he died.

'Let me get this clear,' Lisle said, tensely leaning forward in his chair when he'd finished. 'Professor Dalrymple intimated to you that he'd discovered a cheat and a fraud amongst the academic body within the university?'

'That's what I took him to mean, yes,' Callum agreed cautiously. 'But you must

154

understand that he'd had a little too much to drink and that there wasn't time for him to actually elaborate. You can ask Dr Ngabe, she was there with us at the time.'

Lisle nodded. He would most definitely be doing that. Because, for the first time, he'd finally got the whiff of a proper motive—if what Fielding had to say was true.

And after all his years on the force, Lisle never took anybody's uncorroborated word for anything.

'Would you say that an academic would be willing to kill to safeguard his or her professional reputation, Dr Fielding?' he asked bluntly. 'I mean, you are a psychologist, yes?'

Callum sighed. 'I'm not a practising psychiatrist, Inspector, and I don't have patients or give out therapy. I'm purely a research man. But I think I can safely say that most rational, mentally well-balanced people wouldn't react with such extreme violence,' he said carefully. 'Of course, the stress of exposure would be enormous. In Oxford, your perceived intelligence and reputation are paramount. And if the person threatened was drunk, or panicked—I suppose the situation could have escalated out of control.'

Lisle nodded. A very careful answer, that. 'And how is your mental well-being, Dr Fielding?' he asked casually.

'That's enough!' Markie shot to her feet.

Now the man was implying that Callum, of all people, was out of control. Which, she thought a shade hysterically, was almost funny. A more buttoned down, aloof, and aggravatingly controlled person, Markie had never met. It made her want to rip off his mask and see the naked face of the man underneath.

And rip off his clothes whilst she was at it.

'We've told you all we know, and unless you intend to make an arrest, we're leaving,' she threatened. She shot Callum a frustrated look. Couldn't he see what the policeman was getting at? Why didn't he fight back?

Callum read her glance in an instant, and although his eyes flashed, his body language remained calm. In fact, he smiled across at the policeman wryly. 'It's fine, Inspector. My mental health is just fine, thank you. And I didn't kill Vivian, and I'll do anything I can to help you in your efforts to find out who did. All you have to do is ask. Is there anything else you want to know?' he continued, ignoring the beautiful woman who was standing beside him, fulminating.

'Not at the moment, Sir, thank you,' Lisle said, turning off the tape and showing them to the door. Once they'd left, he sat for a moment, thinking.

He had to smile. Dr Callum Fielding had a wildcat on his hands there, whether the man liked it or not. And, unless Lisle missed his guess, the St Bede's Fellow probably hadn't made up his mind if he was happy about that or not.

But the interview had raised some distinct possibilities.

Thoughtfully, he reached for the phone and rang St Bede's to find out the likely whereabouts of Dr Ngabe.

*　　　*　　　*

Outside the police station, Markie stormed up the road towards Christ Church College.

'You do realise that man thinks you're a suspect, don't you?' she fumed to Callum, who was silent as he walked alongside her. 'It's ridiculous. You're a well-respected academic!'

Callum smiled dryly. Several tourists moved off the pavement to give the big blond man room, and he smiled a vague thank-you at them as Markie power-walked her way through them obliviously. 'I've a good mind to hire the most high-powered and obstructive solicitor I know, just to get on Inspector Jarvis's nerves.'

'I'd rather you didn't,' Callum said mildly. Inwardly he was both amused by her passionate defence of him, and just a little alarmed. And excited too. Was he reading the signals wrong? Or was she actually being proprietorial towards him. And if she was . . . He felt a hot flash of sexual desire hit him, which in turn set off a warning in his head.

'Why not?' she stopped by the famous Carfax clock with its moving figures, and looked at him challengingly.

'Because that's the person responsible for finding my friend's killer,' Callum said reasonably. 'And I don't want him distracted. And I wouldn't have thought you would want that either. When the press get a hold of this, the name of the Kendall Prize is going to be associated with a murder, you do realise that?'

Markie stared at him aghast. 'Oh no! That's terrible!' The first time her father asked her to be the family figurehead, and this had to happen!

'We've got to find out who really did it,' she said, making Callum gape at her, dumbfounded.

'Now hold on a minute,' he said sharply. 'Just who do you think we are? Sherlock Holmes and Dr Watson?'

Markie Kendall sighed. 'Only if I get to be Sherlock,' she said, feeling subdued. He was right. It had been a foolish thing to say.

Callum shook his head.

'But we can help somehow, can't we?' she persisted, her voice hopeful but small. 'I mean, he was your friend. And this is your city,' she said, waving a hand around at the spectacular scenery. 'You're an academic, you'll be able to find things out that the police probably won't. If Sir Vivian suspected someone of being a cheat, people will speak more freely to you than they will to that Inspector Jarvis!'

Callum smiled grimly. 'Perhaps,' he agreed warily. And she was right, in a way. As soon as it became clear what the Inspector was implying by way of motive for Vivian's murder, the whole academic community would curl up on itself like a prickly hedgehog repelling intruders.

'So, where do we start?' Markie asked, her eyes glowing.

'We?' Callum said sharply. 'What's this "we" business?'

'It's my family Prize. It's up to me to defend the family name. Besides, whilst you might be the high-and-mighty brainbox of this outfit,' she grinned at him cheekily, 'there might come a time in our investigations when you need a woman's touch.'

'We're not investigating,' he said warningly. 'We're just going to ask around, see if we can get a few hints, a lead or two, and then hand them over to Inspector Jarvis. Before he arrests me,' he added under his breath, but Markie heard him.

'See! We need to stick together. And if they do cart you off to jail, I'll bake you a cake with a file in it.' And then she thought about her lack of prowess in the kitchen, and added, scrupulously honestly, 'or rather, I'll hire a baker to bake one for you and I'll put the file in.'

Callum Fielding burst into spontaneous laughter.

And it was, he realised with a sudden pang in his heart, the first time he'd done so in a long, long time.

*   *   *

Rosemary Naismith watched her lover packing, and tensed when he took down the specially shaped, nylon case that would house his bows.

But Jerry simply picked up his selection of crossbows and carefully stowed them away without a qualm. Slowly, she began to relax. He hadn't suspected a thing. She'd been very careful to make sure they didn't look disturbed from the last time he'd practised with them.

'Right then, I'd better be off. The plane leaves at six,' he said with forced brightness.

Rosemary smiled briefly. 'You'll call from the States when you arrive?'

Jerry didn't quite meet her eyes when he smiled back. 'Sure,' he said.

He was lying, they both knew that.

Their affair had been brief but passionate, but it had run its course, and they both knew it. But for form's sake, and because it was easier, they were both willing to pretend that this wasn't the final break up.

After he'd gone, Rosemary let herself out of the house that Jerry had shared with three other students, and walked back towards

Truman Hall. She felt restless and nervous. The newspaper reports about Sir Vivian Dalrymple's death were surprising, inaccurate. They still thought he was the victim of a random mugging, although they must know that wasn't the case by now. She could see why the police were keeping the details from them though, of course, but surely the story would break soon?

But she was confident there was nothing that would lead back to her. How could there be?

Nevertheless, she felt keyed up and unable to settle down. What she needed was a distraction.

With a sudden glint in her eye, she changed direction and headed towards St Bede's College instead.

*   *   *

Markie watched Callum unlock his door with a decided feeling of anticipation. They had decided to go back to his place to set out a plan of campaign, and she was surprised to find him leading her to St Bede's.

'You actually live in the college itself then?' she asked him, rather redundantly, as he opened the door and allowed her to precede him.

'Yes. I find it convenient,' he said, not liking the implied criticism. And it was a very easy

161

way to go on. The College scouts kept the rooms clean and he took all his meals in the dining hall. His rooms consisted of a sitting room, where he taught his students, and a large bedroom with en-suite bathroom. Both had big bay windows that looked out over the gardens, and famous weeping willow trees. It was a peaceful, quiet and well-ordered way to live, and it had suited him for many years.

So why did it suddenly feel so inadequate, once Markie Kendall stepped over the threshold? He watched her walk around, examining things like a wary cat just released into a new environment. He too, looked around, seeing the place where he lived through new eyes.

It was a very masculine room, filled with books, of course, that lined three of the four walls. A fireplace lay unused at the moment, although he sometimes had a real fire in the depths of winter. Big heavy furniture, comfortable for his large frame, dominated the room. Wooden floors—centuries old and original oak, played host to a large oriental carpet. He supposed that, according to the latest fashions in modern living, his home must strike her as an anachronism.

Markie watched him as he went to a small sink set in one corner, where he could make tea and coffee and toast, and put the kettle on.

'Tea?' he asked.

'I prefer coffee if you have it.'

'I do. Milk, sugar?'

'Milk, no sugar.'

Callum nodded, feeling a rare sense of intimacy as he made her, for the first time, a hot drink. It felt like a landmark of some kind, and again he felt a warning siren sound in his head.

This woman was getting way too close to him, way too fast. It made him feel both hunted and deliciously excited at the same time. His relationships in the past had always followed the same tried and true pattern. He would meet someone, usually a visiting academic, and a mutual cautious sounding-out period would begin. Were they both single or at least unattached? Were they compatible. Were they both sure they were seeking the same thing? In Callum's case that always fell a fair distance from a one-night stand, but well short of a long-term relationship.

His affairs tended to last between three and six months, and usually ended when the lady concerned went on to pastures new. He never promised anything, and never took anything for granted. He enjoyed being friends as well as lovers, and none of his partings had been anything but mutually amicable, with just enough regret on both sides to be healthy, but never enough to make either one heart sore.

He'd always felt that that was both sensible and to be desired.

Somehow he couldn't see that pattern

163

repeating itself with a woman like this. She was a supermodel, for pete's sake. Men adored and wanted her. She could have her pick of men.

And yet, he was fairly sure, she was interested in him.

And, OK, he'd learned from the college gossip mill that she was in Oxford only for a few months, whilst she was sorting out some sort of perfume launch. So in theory, she met at least some of his criteria.

But it was pointless even speculating about it. There was no way he was going to allow anything to happen as far as this woman was concerned. He hardly needed to have all his degrees in psychology to know that she spelt trouble with a capital T.

He made her coffee and took it over to her. She was sitting in a chair opposite the window, and the light fell over her, highlighting her fabulous high cheekbones and the glory that was her hair. He felt his breath catch, and took a long, slow inhalation of breath.

She reached up and took the mug from him, smiling a thanks and watching him as he took his own mug of tea and stood looking out of the window with his broad back to her. He was so damned tall—and fit! More than ever, Markie was determined to see him naked. The thought of it thrilled her in a way she'd never felt before.

'I'll have to talk to June,' Callum said softly. 'Sir Vivian's wife,' he added, when she gave him a questioning look. 'If he confided to anyone about what was bothering him, then it would be her. But she's in the hospital, so I'll have to be delicate.'

Markie sipped her coffee, but her eyes couldn't help but stray to his large, capable hands. She could almost feel them being 'delicate' on her skin, and she caught her breath on a wave of sudden, giddying desire.

'Perhaps she'll give me permission to go through his papers,' he carried on, seemingly oblivious to her thoughts. 'And I don't think Sin Jun would have any objections to me searching Vivian's rooms at college. Not that he was there much, but he might have left something of interest behind. Because Sir Vivian was an academic through and through, and he would have left research, and well-documented notes behind. I just can't see him making such an allegation without having solid proof as back-up. Are you listening to me?' he asked sharply.

Markie, who'd been wondering what his bedroom looked like, and if he had one of those old-fashioned but really roomy four-poster beds in there, abruptly blushed at his sudden question and sat up straight guiltily. Instantly sloshing hot coffee onto her top.

'Oh damn!' she said, standing up.

'The bathroom's through there,' he said, his lips twitching in a suppressed smile, and indicating the door further across the room.

'Help yourself to a towel.'

'Thanks.'

But Markie had no sooner gone through into the bedroom, than he heard a knock at the outer door. He frowned, knowing that he wasn't expecting a student for a tutorial for another hour at least. He answered the door and sighed when Rosemary Naismith sailed past him before he could even attempt to stop her.

She was wearing a long brown, orange and black dress that clung to all her curves, and she shrugged off a beige mackintosh as she passed him, slinging it across the back of one of the chairs.

'Well, congratulations on the Prize,' she said dryly. 'I didn't get the chance to say it at the party. You were too busy being feted by everyone else,' she added waspishly.

Callum took a long, slow breath. 'Rosemary,' he said flatly.

Rosemary laughed, a brittle tense sound that made his eyes sharpen on her. He noticed that she'd lost weight recently, and was suddenly looking her age. Was she ill?

'Would you like something to drink?' he asked, and as expected, she immediately requested a Scotch. She'd always preferred alcohol whenever she could get it, he remembered, as he poured her a small quantity into a tumbler. As he did so, he cast a quick, anxious look at the open bedroom door.

He thought he could detect, just faintly, the sound of running water. But he wouldn't have long before Markie came back.

'Look, Rosemary, I'm busy right now,' he began, but to his dismay, when he turned with the drink in his hand, she was right behind him. She took the glass from his hand and swallowed the drink in one go.

'Relax will you?' she purred. 'Anyone would think you were frightened that I was going to ravish you.' Her voice dropped to a husky purr. 'Unless of course, that's what you're hoping for? Because you know I'd be only too happy to oblige,' her voice carried clearly across the space to the woman who was just emerging from the bathroom.

Markie Kendall froze.

'Rosemary,' she heard Callum say, and his voice seemed to have a warning edge. Then she strode forward, and stopped in the doorway, surveying the scene.

A blonde woman had wrapped herself around the stiff and immobile figure of Callum Fielding, and she was kissing him as if her life depended on it.

Markie felt a fierce flash of jealousy and possessiveness, and forced it down. After all, what had she expected? Callum was a gorgeous, unmarried man. There was bound to be a woman in his life.

As she watched, his large hands came up and forced his companion away. Then she saw

167

his eyes fall on her, and his jaw clenched.

'Sorry, didn't mean to play gooseberry,' she called gaily, and heard the other woman gasp as she turned to look at her. But already Markie was making her way to the door, barely giving her a glance.

'I'll probably see you around some time, Dr Fielding,' Markie tossed casually across her shoulder as she forced herself to walk nonchalantly to the door and let herself out.

Once outside, she scowled ferociously at an innocent passing student, and stomped off towards her hotel.

In his room, Callum stared at the closed door, then shot Rosemary Naismith a curious glance as she laughed grimly.

'Sorry about that,' Rosemary lied. 'I had no idea you had some floozy waiting for you in the bedroom.' She grabbed her coat and sauntered to the door.

'When you've finished with her, why don't you give me a call, Callum?' She laughed again, but it was strained and tight, and again Callum wondered at the stress in her body language.

'Rosemary, are you all right?' he asked softly.

Rosemary, sensing the pity in his voice, turned on him furiously. 'Oh go to hell, Callum,' she hissed. 'You're a joke, do you know that?'

And her taunting words seemed to echo

around the room long after she left, leaving him feeling very uneasy.

Was he a joke? He was not yet thirty-five, but what did he really have to show for his time on the planet? Suddenly, he knew he was at a crossroads, and knew that there was only one person to blame for this sudden upheaval in his once orderly and comfortable life.

Markie Kendall. Or shouldn't he really be calling her Marcheta the supermodel? A woman used to the glitz and glamour of a world far removed from his dreaming spires. Now that really had to be a joke, didn't it? A woman like that, and him? They were chalk and cheese. Oil and water. He was insane to even contemplate it.

'Damn that woman,' Callum Fielding said with feeling.

CHAPTER EIGHT

Lisle glanced out of the window of the incident room, watching a group of amicably arguing undergraduates sprint across the Wallace quad, towards the main gates.

Lord St John James had acted swiftly to his request for a room in college, where he and his team could work in peace, and had allocated them a large lecture-cum-theatre room in Webster. The stage that ran the length of one

169

entire wall was empty now, and the police computers, bulletin boards, desks and other paraphernalia looked oddly out of place in the high-ceilinged, elegant room.

He sighed and got back to the report he was reading. It was not only dry stuff, it was getting him no farther forward. Although it was only the third day, and after a few good nights of reasonable sleep, he was feeling much more alert and fresh, he was getting that sinking feeling in his stomach that told him that a case was going nowhere, and not particularly fast at that.

He had yet to interview the widow, a task he was definitely not looking forward to, and all the preliminary reports to get through, where he might just come across the odd nugget or two if he was lucky.

An image of flashing green eyes swam across his vision and he blinked them away quickly. Had he really kissed one of his prime suspects! Hell, if his superiors ever found out . . .

He made a grim sound low down in his throat and tried to concentrate, and forget about her. He'd left Nesta Aldernay's bedsit, shaken and utterly stirred, but that was all over now. Unless something else came up, there was no reason to ever see her again.

Which was just as well, considering. He was getting too damned old, and had always been too damn mean, to get bowled over by love's sweet dream. Red hair and green eyes or not!

The report he was reading was by one of the men who had sealed off Sir Vivian's room in his old college. Although no longer strictly active, the old Don's status had ensured that his office remained his domain, and probably would have remained his for life, if he understood the way Oxford Colleges functioned.

The neat and conscientious handwriting listed lots of academic papers, the beginnings of a new book, diaries (nothing juicy) and the usual run-of-the-mill finds. Nevertheless, Lisle knew he'd have to look the office over for himself, in more minute detail. He could afford to miss nothing.

The antiquated telephone on his desk, ferreted out by a disgruntled Bursar, trilled like a canary with a bad cough. He reached for it quickly, glad of the distraction, and listened to a report on the last of the party-goers to be questioned. As with most of them, they'd seen or heard nothing out of the ordinary that night.

Lisle thanked the detective constable for the report and hung up, and then began to pace. Every few minutes he'd glance at his watch. Two constables, who were collating data, watched their chief anxiously. Nobody wanted to get on the wrong side of DI Jarvis.

Again the phone rang, and again it was bad news. The forensics people assigned to St

Bede's archery room had been through every bow and arrow in the place. The bolt found on the victim did not match any bolt used by the students or staff of the college. Nor could it be forensically linked to any of the various bows and crossbows in the St Bede's arsenal.

He again thanked the messenger of bad news, sighed, and walked to his car. No point in putting it off any longer. He headed up the Woodstock road, turning off up Bevington Road to get onto the Banbury Road, telling himself it was always best to get unpleasant duties over with quickly. He turned onto the Marsden Ferry Road towards the suburb of Headington, trying not to think ahead too much.

Long before he got there, the big white building on top of the hill was clearly visible— the John Radcliffe Hospital. The big white elephant, as his mother had always called it. One of the finest teaching hospitals in the world, it was closely allied to the Medical school within the Oxford University system itself. No wonder Oxford had to turn away more potential students in Medicine than almost any other subject.

He had the usual trouble finding a parking space, and the even more usual trouble of trying to find one patient in such a mammoth place. But eventually, on the sixth floor, he quietly approached a four-bed women's ward and whispered a word or two to the sister on duty there. After showing her his badge, he was quietly ushered to the bedside of Sir Vivian Dalrymple's widow.

June Dalrymple looked very ill indeed. He hadn't asked the sister for any medical details, but one look at the sunken cheeks and the hollow-eyed glance that turned his way, and Lisle felt his heart lurch. Her white hair hung in limp wisps against her cheeks. Her hands on the blanket, both hooked up to IVs, looked gnarled and painfully thin. But the smile she gave him radiated out of the wreck of her face like a sunburst.

'Visitors?' she asked. Her voice lacked the power it must once have had, but it was still defiantly full of life. 'How nice.'

'My name is Detective Inspector Jarvis, Lady Dalrymple.'

'Oh, yes. The police.' The smile faltered, but only briefly. 'I've been expecting you. My sister-in-law called in yesterday to tell me the news about my poor Vivian.'

Lisle couldn't help but show his relief. June Dalrymple smiled again. 'Please, take a seat, Inspector. And ask me anything you like. I'm over the worst of the shock now. Or at least, I think I am, which is more or less the same thing, isn't it?'

Lisle took one of the garish orange plastic chairs from a sleeping woman's bedside, and sat down beside the old lady. As he did so, he began to breathe more easily.

Lady Dalrymple was obviously of the old school. Her generation had been raised to keep a stiff upper lip at all times, remain polite, even in the direst of circumstances, and always, always, to respect authority. And no matter what modern thinking espoused on the repression of emotion prevalent in her generation, right at that moment, Lisle could have kissed her.

Like all big and tough men, weeping women totally flummoxed him.

'Thank you, Lady Dalrymple. I really am very sorry about your husband,' he said sincerely.

For a moment, the old lady looked at the policeman. Liking what she saw. Liking what she heard. A *genuine* man. One that she instinctively trusted.

'Can you tell me how he died, Inspector?' she asked quietly. 'Maud just said that he'd been . . . murdered.'

Lisle met the frank, unwavering gaze, still feeling a little unnerved at her obvious fragility. But there was a no-nonsense look in those dark, ravaged-by-pain pupils that aroused his sense of honour.

He nodded once, briskly. 'He was shot with a bow, Lady Dalrymple. The arrow passed clean through his heart, stopping it instantly. He wouldn't have felt much pain. I doubt he would even have known what was happening to him.'

For a long few seconds they were both silent. At last, June Dalrymple sighed heavily. 'He would have been most put out by that, you know. He always said death was the last great adventure. He'll have been miffed to have missed it, so to speak.'

Lisle blinked in surprise but then smiled. For a second, in perfect accord, the two people—the old dying woman, and the young, vibrant, powerful man, sat in quiet and gentle understanding.

Then Lisle got out his notebook. 'Do you know of anyone who might have wanted to kill your husband, Lady Dalrymple? A disgruntled ex-student, someone he might have crossed, a colleague he upset. Anything of that nature?'

'No, Inspector. You're barking up the wrong tree there, I'm afraid. Whoever did this, if it was not a random act of violence, did it for a specific reason. My husband was not the kind of man who made enemies. He understood human nature too well for that.'

It was a simple statement, and right to the point. And had she been any other woman, any other wife, he would have taken it with a good pinch of salt. He'd been a policeman too long, and knew that usually the spouse was the last one to know anything. But this couple, he realised instinctively, were not of the usual mould.

He found himself believing her. So, Sir Vivian was not a man who was likely to just easily get himself murdered.

'I see,' he said softly. Her words only confirmed his own thinking on the matter. 'Your husband was attending a prize-giving Dinner at St Bede's the night he was killed.'

'The Kendall, yes I know,' June said quickly, with a smile. 'A very prestigious award, Inspector. And one that carried a considerable amount of money with it.'

'Did your husband expect to get it?'

June laughed. 'Good grief, no. He expected either Dr Ngabe or dear Callum to win it.'

'Dr Fielding did indeed do so,' Lisle said simply.

'Did he? Oh good. I am glad.' Briefly, the old lady's face lit up. Pain seemed to recede for a moment or two.

'You like Dr Fielding I take it?' Lisle said, making it a statement. 'Did your husband get on well with him also?'

'Like a house on fire, Inspector,' June said with a small laugh. 'My husband tutored him, you see, and he always said that Callum was one of those pupils that you pray for—one that can surpass the master, as it were. And he went on to do so well. Yet he still always came to Vivian for advice and help whenever he needed it. Which wasn't so often of course nowadays.'

Lisle nodded. It confirmed what Callum had already told him—that he liked and respected the man. Still, a lot of his team had now

176

reported in that, during the pre-Dinner party, Sir Vivian had become progressively more and more drunk, and had more or less accused someone present of being a cheat and fraud.

Which meant that someone had a motive. He took a deep breath. 'Lady Dalrymple . . .' something in his tone made the old lady look at him sharply. 'Did your husband say anything to you about suspecting somebody of cheating? That is, of either plagiarism or something along those lines?'

Lisle understood only too well what a charge of cheating would mean to an Oxford Fellow.

'No. Never,' she said simply. 'Why?'

Gently he explained to her the picture they were building up of her husband's behaviour on that night, and the things he'd been saying. When he'd finished, the old lady was shaking her head in astonishment.

'That's not like Vivian at all. Not at all,' she said fretfully. 'Either the drinking, or the speaking out of turn. It just wasn't *like* him. He must have been really upset . . . *really upset*, Inspector, to do something like that.'

Lisle believed her. And, instinctively, he believed that that was the reason Sir Vivian had been killed. Someone at that party had been doing something he or she shouldn't. And Sir Vivian hadn't liked it. And had hinted broadly that he knew about it. And someone, who owned a very powerful bow and knew how to use it, had slipped out, retrieved that bow and lay in wait for him in the car park, and killed him.

But who? Common sense told him that the short-listed candidates had to be high on the list. Otherwise, why would a man of Sir Vivian's obvious restraint have been quite so verbal and upset at that particular social event?

Callum Fielding had actually won the Prize. And he'd always been Sir Vivian's golden boy. It would really upset the old man all right to discover that his prayed-for pupil had feet of clay. And, of all of them, he was the only one known to be a keen archer, and have a key to the archery room. Except that the weapon hadn't been one of those. Would he buy an expensive bow, when he had all the bows and arrows he needed right on tap? He even lived in the same House as the archery room.

Perhaps. Human nature always wanted the best. To own something bigger and better than everyone else.

He made a mental note to get a search warrant to check the Fellow's room. Not that he was optimistic of finding anything. If the Don had killed his mentor, he was way too smart to have the murder weapon lying about in his rooms.

'Do you know if Dr Fielding and your husband had had an argument recently?' Lisle asked curiously.

June Dalrymple flushed. It was just a pale wash of pink, but it came and went angrily, indicating more clearly than words what she thought of that question.

In obvious pain, she turned a little on the bed, the better to look at him. 'Young man,' she said, a shade breathlessly, 'if you're looking at Callum as a possible killer, you are most definitely wasting police time.'

Lisle smiled. 'I see. Well, thank you for seeing me, Lady Dalrymple. And if you can think of anything else . . .' he rose and put the chair back, wanting to leave but knowing that he couldn't. He had one more question he really didn't want to ask—for a number of reasons—but ask it he must.

'Lady Dalrymple, I'm sorry to have to ask this, but did you suspect your husband of having an affair?'

June Dalrymple looked at him blankly for a moment, and then, unbelievably, began to laugh. It hurt her to do it, and she began to cough, but she couldn't stop. 'Oh, Inspector . . .'

Lisle, feeling suddenly very foolish and thoroughly ashamed of himself, backed out of the room as the sister hurried in to try and calm her patient.

Lisle still felt all kinds of a fool as he drove back towards the city and St Bede's, where the porter gave him directions to Sir Vivian's office. And as he climbed the spiral stone staircase, he was still shaking his head.

Somehow, if June Dalrmple didn't believe her husband was a philanderer, he couldn't believe it either. So exactly *what* business did Nesta Aldernay have with the dead man? Which reminded him—he'd been so shaken by the sexual explosion that had happened between them, that he'd forgotten to ask her exactly where she'd been the night Sir Vivian was killed.

Hell! He really was walking on quicksand.

The yellow police tape hung down at the side of the door, but he wasn't surprised. The damn stuff was always unpeeling.

But the instant he opened the door to the rather dark and cramped office, he sensed that he wasn't alone. Belatedly, he realised that his steps, echoing off the stone staircase as they had been, would have alerted anyone inside to his presence. It was not that he could see anyone, or any signs of recent human activity. He just knew he wasn't alone. The hairs stood up on the back of his neck.

Although it was only early afternoon, the windows were so small, and the day so cloudy, he flicked on the light switch.

His eyes scanned the room. A cupboard. No doubt full of stationery and files. A big desk and with a big kneehole . . . His eyes narrowed. That kneehole should not be as shadowed as it was.

'All right,' he said grimly, his voice deep

180

and growling and dangerous. 'Come on out of there. Police. Come on out damn you!'

And a second later there was a reluctant scuffle of movement. Then, rising from behind the desk, a familiar gleam of dark red hair.

Nesta Aldernay's green eyes shone at him, like a cat's, above the line of the desk top.

'You,' Lisle barked.

He might have known.

*　　　*　　　*

Callum walked reluctantly into the foyer of the Randolph hotel, and once again asked for Miss Kendall. The clerk, recognising him this time, smiled brightly and quickly reached for the phone. Callum tensed, feeling the potential for embarrassment wash over him if she refused to see him.

But the clerk told him that Miss Kendall would be right down, and with a sigh of relief Callum moved back to the open doorway and glanced down Broad Street.

His working day was over, and the last of his students had been seen. Evening approached, and when he felt her presence beside him, he turned and smiled briefly.

'Miss Kendall.'

She was wearing a midi-length black silk dress, with a silver and black shawl thrown about her shoulders. Her jewellery was chunky silver, and she looked as stunning as ever.

181

He was about to apologise for the scene with Rosemary, then stopped himself. Although she'd almost certainly misinterpreted what had really happened earlier on, he thought that perhaps it would be better to let the misunderstanding continue. If she thought he was involved with someone else it could give him some much-needed protection from his growing attraction from her. After all, she'd be far less likely to continue to be interested in him if she thought he was taken, so to speak, and with a little luck her own indifference might help him stem the tide of his own growing attraction towards her.

Unless, of course, she was the kind of woman who didn't care if she poached on someone else's territory.

'You can't keep calling me that,' Markie said with a wry smile. 'Markie, please.'

'Markie then,' Callum repeated a shade reluctantly. 'I've had an idea about where Vivian might have left his notes. According to Sin Jun, the police found no interesting or suspicious documents in his rooms at College, and if they found anything at his home, they're hardly likely to share the knowledge with us.'

'I can't see that Inspector Jarvis exactly being forthcoming, no,' Markie agreed sardonically.

'But Vivian kept a country cottage in Cornwall. And he always liked peace and quiet if he was writing an especially difficult paper.

So he just might have taken his research about our cheater down there.'

Markie's face lit up. 'Then we must go.'

Callum took both a mental, and a literal, step backwards. 'Now just a minute, I only told you to keep you in the loop. I was thinking of driving down there this evening and spending the night. That'll give me plenty of time to search the place. A long time ago, Vivian gave me a key, and said I could use it whenever I needed to. In fact, I spent a few weeks down there just last Spring. But . . .'

'You can't keep me out of this,' Markie warned fiercely. 'Give me five minutes to pack.' She turned and headed towards the staircase, then shot a sharp look back over her shoulder, her eyes sparking jewelled fire. 'And don't even think about giving me the slip, otherwise I'll get the address from either Sin Jun or Lady Dalrymple and just arrive on the doorstep anyway.'

Callum opened his mouth, realised at once the futility of arguing with her, and closed it again.

Markie smiled sweetly. 'I'll only be ten minutes.'

Callum smiled wryly. And pigs might fly. He might be a crusty and confirmed bachelor, but even he knew that women and packing and a ten-minute time-frame should never be used in one sentence.

                    *   *   *

They made good time travelling southwest, but just before they hit the Devon/Cornwall border, Callum's bottle-green Jaguar XJS began to loose power. The engine made a very un-Jaguar-like growl, and he was relieved to see signs to a market town just a mile ahead.

He nursed the car carefully to the nearest garage, which was thankfully open until midnight, and got out to talk to a mechanic. Markie used the time whilst a gaggle of men stood about looking under the hood of the impressive car, to visit the facilities. A quick touch-up of her lipstick and mascara and a quick squirt of perfume was all she needed.

Back outside, it was obvious from the look of disgust on Callum's face that the news wasn't good.

'It won't be ready until mid-morning tomorrow at the earliest,' he said grimly. 'The old girl's never let me down before,' he added, giving the car bonnet a brief tap.

'Well, we'll just have to find a hotel,' Markie said fatalistically. 'Perhaps he can recommend one,' she added, nodding towards the chief mechanic who was talking on his mobile, and obviously ordering some part for the car from a 24 hour service.

'*The Three Pigeons* is a nice place,' he informed them helpfully when asked, and gave them directions. It wasn't hard to reach, and turned out to be a lovely old 17th Century coaching inn facing a flower-bedecked market square.

Inside, it was all old wood, opulence and atmosphere. 'What a lovely place,' Markie said, glancing around. 'I bet it's popular with the tourists,' she predicted.

And alas, so it was. The receptionist, a pretty brunette who was obviously well-impressed with Callum, had to admit that they only had one room left—a double.

'We'll take it,' Markie said at once, before Callum could say a word. The brunette sighed and offered the register for their signature. Callum debated going off to find another hotel for himself, but realised he would look all kinds of a prude and fool if he did so.

And so, with warning bells ringing in his ears, he signed his name next to that of Markie Kendall in the register.

*   *   *

They dined at the hotel on simple dishes that were well presented and cooked. Markie opted for the Caesar Salad and grilled trout, whilst Callum preferred the Herb and Stilton soup and baked Hake. Both of them declined dessert.

It was barely ten, but Markie said she was tired, and wanted to go up to her room. Her eyes flashed in amusement, as she looked

185

across the cleared table at him. 'And I daresay after all that driving, you're about ready to flake out too,' she said with a distinctly challenging tilt to her delightful chin.

Callum's lips twitched grimly. It was as if the little madam was well aware of how uncomfortable this whole situation was making him, and was laughing up her sleeve at him.

'Yes,' he said shortly, and got to his feet. They walked in silence up the single flight of stairs, Callum checking their room number on the key. 'This is us,' he said a moment later, and unlocked the door.

The room was charming—it was, thankfully, not particularly low-ceilinged, but some dark beams had Callum walking below them warily. His head cleared them with only an inch or two to spare. Big diamond-paned windows overlooked the square, and a large four-poster bed dominated the room.

It was also en suite, and Callum gallantly allowed her the use of it first.

Markie, with a cheeky half-curtsy in gratitude, swept up her case and disappeared from view.

Callum used the time to pull the curtains and take off his shoes and socks. He eyed the bed grimly. It was a monster bed all right, and ideal for someone of his size. The only other pieces of furniture in the room consisted of two armchairs and a low coffee table. He could, at a pinch, put the two chairs together, face to face, and spend the night in them. But he wouldn't get much sleep.

And suddenly he felt a shaft of anger lance through him. No! He'd be damned if he would! If Miss Marcheta Kendall thought he was going to pussy-foot around her, she could bloody well think again!

He unbuttoned his sports jacket and slung it across one of the chairs, and was unbuttoning his shirt when the bathroom door opened and she walked in.

His heartbeat ratcheted up and his breathing stuttered in his chest.

She was wearing a long, diaphanous white negligee and was barefoot. Her long black hair flowed freely down her back, and her face had been washed and cleansed free of make-up. Her natural beauty made her look younger and more vulnerable.

He swallowed hard.

'It's all yours,' Markie said brightly, indicating the room behind her. Her eyes, though, were on his hands, and the v-shaped triangle of skin on his bared chest. She could see silver-tinted chest hairs, and the broad, tanned expanse of his well-muscled chest. Her mouth went suddenly dry.

Callum nodded, and wordlessly moved past her.

In the bathroom he spent way too long brushing his teeth and shaving and washing. At last though, he could postpone it no longer, and walked back into the bedroom.

All the lights were out, but the street lamps outside shone through the lightweight curtains, bathing the room in an amber glow. From the monster four-poster he heard a slight rustle of movement. So she was already in bed and waiting for him.

He undressed wordlessly, slipping into the pyjama bottoms that were all that he wore in bed.

From the four-poster Markie watched, fascinated, as the huge shape of him loomed over her. He looked like a bronzed Adonis in the amber light, his silver-blond hair gleaming in the darkness. Her heart began to thump like a jack hammer.

What had she been thinking? Over Dinner she'd been able to airily assure him that it was possible for two rational human beings to be able to share a bed and do nothing but sleep. In an emergency, of course, what was wrong with that? She'd sounded insouciant and sophisticated enough then, she thought with a somewhat rueful grin.

But now, when she felt the man's weight and warmth beside her, and felt overwhelmed by the impressive latent power in his well-muscled physique, she felt suddenly, breathlessly, anxious.

She lay, tensed and ready for him to make his move.

Beside her, the psychologist in Callum

Fielding instantly sensed her sudden tension. And in the darkness he smiled broadly.

So the super-cool Marcheta wasn't quite the woman of the world she pretended to be.

Good.

And feeling infinitely happier, he turned over onto his side, and relaxed into sleep.

CHAPTER NINE

If Markie Kendall lay in bed that night wondering about an indifferent man who didn't seem to respond to her at all, several hours earlier, and back in Oxford, another young woman had exactly the opposite problem.

Namely, wondering how to cope with too much attention from a very forceful man indeed.

*   *   *

Nesta sighed resignedly, and got slowly to her feet from her hiding place beneath Sir Vivian's desk. 'Hello Lisle,' she said quietly.

Lisle stared at her, gimlet eyed. 'You've got some nerve,' he said at last, a trace of reluctant respect in his voice. 'I'll give you that.'

Nesta managed a rather unconvincing smile. 'Oh. Thanks.'

189

Lisle slowly shook his head. He took a further step into the room, turned, and quietly closed the door behind him. There was such an excruciatingly patient control in his every movement that Nesta felt the hairs rise on the back of her own neck.

He was furious.

She swallowed hard.

Just as well he hadn't caught her checking out Sir Vivian's home earlier. He'd really have hit the roof then! She'd gone there a few hours ago, remembering that Sir Vivian had kept a spare key to his back door in his rickety greenhouse. She'd gone whilst it was still dark, mindful of nosy neighbours, glad, for once, of the long, dark winter mornings.

But she had not found a trace of her father's papers at the house in Park End. She'd seen a lot of evidence of police forensic activity, though—the place had been covered with a shiny, black residue of dust that she assumed must have been used in checking for fingerprints. She'd been scrupulously careful to disturb nothing, and had read nothing of Sir Vivian's private papers at all. She'd felt enough like a grubby little spy as it was. Even though she was only trying to recover her property.

But, when the papers hadn't shown up in either Sir Vivian's study, the living room, or his bedside cabinet, she'd decided that either the police now had them, or that they were somewhere else. Working on the hypothesis that the police would not be interested in years old ex-students theses, she'd decided to check out his office. Just in case.

But, somehow, watching Lisle Jarvis turn and close the door and then lean against it, folding his arms across his impressive chest and staring at her like a starling inspects a particularly juicy worm, she somehow didn't think that now was the time to tell him what she'd been doing with her morning.

In fact . . .

'Tell me, Miss Aldernay,' Lisle said silkily, 'just where were you the night that Sir Vivian was killed?'

Nesta blinked at him. Then slowly smiled.

Did he seriously suspect her?

Yes, she thought, with mingled dismay and anger. He did.

'I was with friends. To be more accurate, with friends of my father. He was an undergraduate, then a graduate here, many years ago. I looked them up,' she told him, keeping her voice purely business-like and unafraid.

Lisle got out his notebook. 'Names please. And addresses.'

Nesta sighed wearily. 'I don't know all of their addresses. But I know the name and address of my father's old room mate. It was at his place where we all met up. And he lived in Wolvercote.'

She named the small village, right on the outskirts of the city. 'We met at the Trout, a pub in the village, and had a few drinks then, at closing time, we all moved to his place.'

She supplied the man's name and address, and a list of the rest of her father's friends. 'I'd called Roger Waring when I first came to Oxford, and told him who I was. He contacted the others, and invited them over. Most stayed in the area. Oxford, it seems, gets in your blood.'

Lisle ignored her more friendly tone. 'And your father? Did he come down from Durham to join in this little reunion?'

'My father died, here in Oxford. A traffic accident. He was knocked off his bike when he was 27.'

Lisle's face twisted briefly. 'I'm sorry. You must have been very young.'

Nesta shrugged. She didn't want to talk about it. Being in Oxford again was bad enough, and she was already about to dredge up the past enough to last her a lifetime.

Providing she could find her father's papers, that is.

For, even though she'd only arrived a few minutes ago, she'd already checked out the cupboards and Sir Vivian's desk, and there was no sign of them. Which meant, surely, that the police had them after all. Unless . . .

She went slightly pale. What if *she* had somehow learned what Sir Vivian was doing,

192

and had somehow got possession of them? Perhaps someone at the Bodleian had rung and told her that Sir Vivian, that great and eminent man, was interested in her old thesis. They might think it would thrill her.

But it would only terrify her.

What if she was too late? What if someone else had already got to Sir Vivian's home, or this office, ahead of her?

'What's wrong?' Lisle said sharply. Her skin was suddenly as pale as milk, her eyes as wide and tragic as an opera.

'What? Oh . . . nothing,' she said vaguely.

Lisle fought back the urge to walk up to her and give her a good shaking. It was obvious that something was very much wrong, and she seemed hell bent on keeping it from him. It made him want to kiss her stupid.

Aware that his thoughts were fast angling out of control, he forced himself to calm down. And pretend that thoughts of kissing a suspect hadn't even entered his head.

But it was vital he got whatever information from her that she was holding back. But what was he to do? Confront her? The way things kept getting so volatile whenever they met up warned him that he'd have to be careful.

Nesta's own thoughts were whirling.

If Naismith had got her father's and Sir Vivian's papers back in her possession, what could she do about it? Demand her father's papers back? But what good would that do? If she'd stolen them, they would have long since been burned by now. And if she didn't have them, she'd only be alerting the enemy that she was onto her. That she was being investigated.

She didn't know it, but her growing distress and dismay was clear on her face, and Lisle had finally had enough. Before she could draw breath, he was striding quickly across the room. And before he knew what he intended doing, he had her by the arms and was half-shaking her. 'Damn it, woman,' he all but shouted, 'I can almost hear the wheels turning in your head. Now tell me . . . what are you doing here?'

Nesta dragged in a ragged breath. She'd never been man-handled before. And she shouldn't be liking it, damn it! All her feminine instincts should be outraged. So why did the feel of his strong hands on her arms thrill her? Why did the scent of his aftershave, a clear, fresh, forest-like scent, make her head swim? Why could she feel his body heat through the thick layers of her clothes, setting her own flesh aflame?

She blinked. 'Let go of me!' She managed to invest her voice, at least, with a little backbone.

Lisle blinked, looked down at his own hands on her arms, and suddenly released her. He took a single backward step, and dragged in a huge breath. Hell! What was getting into him?

Shaken but carefully hiding it, he retreated back to the safety of the door and the familiarity of his police notebook. One look at the almost bare page showed him how unsuccessful he'd been in interrogating his suspect.

Suspect. She was still a suspect, remember, he reminded himself grimly.

'What time did you leave this Roger Waring's house?' he asked, his voice cold but still a little shaken.

Nesta rubbed her arms. He hadn't hurt her, she just wanted to capture the feel of his fingers against her flesh for ever and ever.

'I . . . er . . . it was late. Gone midnight. I'm not really sure. You'll have to ask him,' she murmured, every inch as shaken as he was. The atmosphere in the room was so fraught with various dangers that it was hard to breathe, let alone think clearly.

'I will, don't you worry about that,' Lisle said warningly. But if it was that late, she was in the frame for the Don's murder. He knew that to get to Wolvercote, she would have driven up the Woodstock Road to the roundabout at the top of it, the Wolvercote turn being the first exit. Which meant she could have stopped the car outside St Bede's, but the double yellow lines there might have attracted the attention of any late-night traffic wardens, and surely she wouldn't have risked getting a ticket?

But she could have parked on St Giles, and walked back easily enough. Carrying a bow and arrow? Even though it was night, there

195

were streetlights. And besides, even that late at night, someone would have been about. Perhaps she'd parked in St Bede's itself. The postern gate was unlocked.

But would she have known that?

Or, perhaps, he was looking at this the wrong way. Could she have *seen* the killer? Did she know him, or her. Was *that* why she was all so-fired interested in this case? Was she shielding someone?

A man.

Her lover.

He fought back a sick sensation of despair in the pit of his stomach. Damn it, he couldn't get personally involved here. He *couldn't*. What did it matter to him if Nesta Aldernay had a string of lovers?

'Did you see anyone entering or leaving the gates of St Bede's when you drove past?' he asked, trying to be fair, trying to be impartial and failing miserably. She was so lovely. He wanted her so much to be innocent of all this ugliness.

Nesta cocked her head partly to one side, frowning in thought. 'No, I don't think so. But then, I wouldn't have been looking would I? I didn't know where Sir Vivian was, or was likely to be, every minute of the day,' she pointed out, reasonably enough but with a sardonic twist to her tone.

And if she was being just a little bolshie, well, surely she was entitled. She was, after all,

196

just a little scared too. Just a little worried that she was becoming a prime suspect in a murder case!

Once again, she wondered if she should just tell him about her father's papers and get it over with. But if her enemy had them, what good would it do to tell the police? Even if they believed her, what could they do about it? Was it even illegal to steal someone else's academic work? Somehow, she doubted it.

Lisle narrowed his eyes. 'You're doing it again,' he growled softly.

Nesta looked at him quizzically. His hair was damp from the rain outside, and was drying into a slight wave against his scalp. It was such a rich, dark colour, the texture so thick and vibrant that she could almost imagine the feel of it under her fingertips. His nose, which had so obviously been broken at some point, lent his face a devil-may-care, he-man kind of look that, she felt instinctively, was not the whole picture. What secrets did that tough, grim exterior hide? What kind of music turned him on. Was he married? She paled. What a thought.

Grimly, she tried to drag herself back to reality. To concentrate on the matter in hand.

'Doing what?' she asked huskily.

'Turning over the cogs in your mind. If you know something about this case, I want to know what it is. If I have to drag you down to the station and keep you there, I can. And I will.'

'You can only keep me 48 hours,' Nesta guessed. 'I know my rights,' she added defiantly. Which was a lie. She'd never even contemplated being arrested before, but she could pretty quickly learn how she stood. 'And if you do, I'll squeal for my solicitor so fast, your ears will burn,' she snapped.

If she knew any solicitors, that is.

Lisle's lips twisted. 'Even so. You'd still be mine for 48 hours. I've got a nice little interview room all picked out for you. A wooden chair. A wooden table. A single light. It's real cosy.' His voice was strangely dreamy, almost hypnotic. Instead of being afraid of what he was describing, a vivid picture of the room flashed into her mind. A steel door. A bare and barren room, with just themselves, cocooned inside, the outside world forbidden to enter. He with his jacket off, his top two shirt buttons undone, his cuffs rolled back, revealing strong and hirsute arms. His eyes burning into hers . . .

She felt her nipples begin to tighten. She tried to drag in a deep breath.

'This is . . . this is . . . terrible,' she said at last.

Lisle too, seemed to be having trouble breathing. 'I agree,' he said flatly, his voice utterly bleak. 'So if you'll just tell me why you broke in past a police seal, and what you're doing in a murdered man's office, the better it

198

will be for both of us. Don't you think?'

Nesta wanted nothing more than to get out of that room. Get away from this man who seemed able, with the flick of his hazel eyes, to tie all her previously tightly-held principles and beliefs about herself into knots. 'I . . . I was looking for a pair of earrings,' she said, as surprised by her own subconscious choice of explanation as the policeman watching her.

'Really?' Lisle drawled. 'Do tell. I'm sure I'm going to find this fascinating,' he drawled, settling himself more comfortably, folding his arms ever more tightly against his chest.

If he only knew what his body language was saying, Nesta mused giddily, he'd have a fit. But if his body was screaming out self-protection, his eyes were openly mocking.

Nesta flushed. Damn him, did he have to disbelieve her so obviously?

'It might not sound much to you,' she began huffily, 'but they belonged to my mother,' she felt the lie running away with her. 'She died last year. They were her mother's before her, and they're the only family heirloom I have,' she finished miserably.

She lifted her chin, fighting a war within herself. One half was 'Appalled' and was battling to get her to tell the truth. The opposing side was 'Resolute', and was equally demanding that she stick with her original mission. Which was justice for her father. That was what she was there for, after all. And she'd better keep sight of it, or this man would quickly tie her up in knots.

Lisle was the man who was seeking Justice for Sir Vivian. Which was just as it should be. And it must still be for the best, surely, that she not interfere with that? Especially since she knew nothing that could help him with that.

'Look, I'm sorry Sir Vivian's dead. Really I am,' she said softly, earnestly. 'But I didn't see any mugger hanging around St Bede's that night. All right?'

Lisle grimaced. The papers were still touting the random mugging angle. And for that, he and his men were grateful. It kept the publicity down to a manageable level. He knew Lord St John James was behind that, of course, but for once he didn't care about the privileges of people who knew other people in high places.

But he also knew it couldn't last. Journalists had a way of worming out information. And once the news of the coroner's report leaked, as it inevitably would, they wouldn't only be making the front-page news in the local press, but the nationals would pick up on it too.

But for now he had a breathing space.

He looked at the woman in front of him. So beautiful and desirable. And so very dangerous.

He shook his head and ran a harassed hand through his hair. There was no point in telling her that this case was a long way from being a simple mugging. The less she knew, the more he might be able to trip her up.

Looking for earrings in a pig's eye.

But where did she fit in? Try as he might, he just couldn't picture her as a killer. And if he was right in his belief that the motive for the killing of the old man lay in Sir Vivian's belief that someone at that party was a cheat and an academic fraud, then it left this woman right out of it.

Nevertheless, he made a mental note to check out if any scandal hung over this young lady's head. Academic or otherwise.

'May I go now?' Nesta asked politely. She fidgeted beside the desk, looking more and more miserable with every moment that passed.

'Did you find them?' Lisle asked softly.

For a second, Nesta thought he meant her father's papers. She went white. Then she realised he was talking about the mythical earrings. Get a grip Nesta, she warned herself grimly. This man is running circles around you!

She shook her head. 'No. I must have lost them somewhere else.'

'Why are you looking for them here?' Lisle pounced, so softly, and with such finesse, that she didn't even see the trap.

'What?' she asked blankly.

'Why were you looking for them here?' he repeated relentlessly. 'You must have thought you could have lost them here, which means you must have been here before. So you've been to both Sir Vivian's house and his office here in College. Yes?'

Nesta flushed. Oh damn.

Lisle smiled in triumph. Didn't see that coming, did you, he mused grimly. 'Perhaps you'd better tell me why Sir Vivian brought you to this office? Was he getting worried that meeting you at his home was a little too public? Was it easier to sneak you into his office here in College? Where students would turn a grinning blind eye, and all his old colleagues would simply think what a dog he was?' He was taunting her ruthlessly, both because he felt his own, personal savage need to, and also because he wanted to see if he could goad her into betraying her secrets.

Nesta opened her mouth then closed it again helplessly.

What could she say? She'd neatly dug herself a nice little hole to fall into, and he'd so kindly given her a push. Bless him.

'These earrings,' Lisle said, pushing away from the door once more and walking towards her. 'Were they really your mother's? Or did Sir Vivian buy them for you. Expensive were they?' He watched her closely as he moved towards her.

Nesta began to back away. Lisle saw her confusion. A flush of resentment that crossed her face, and became a hint of pain. And suddenly, Lisle knew. This woman had no more been Sir Vivian's mistress than he was the Sultan of Brunei. Lady June had been right about her husband all along. He was not the philandering kind.

'Exactly what did you want from the old man, Nesta?' he asked quietly and much more gently now.

And because he caught her so unexpectedly on the raw, Nesta flinched. She had gone to that lovely old man demanding his help. She had hurt and upset him with her claims. She had made his last few days on earth miserable.

'If only I'd known he was going to die,' she mumbled . . . she'd never have done it. She'd have gone to someone else. Dr Callum Fielding perhaps. In her research on who was who at Oxford, Dr Fielding had been her second choice of possible helper. He was almost as well respected as Sir Vivian. He was younger, a member of a college that had nothing to do with either her father or the woman who had stolen his work, so he would be more inclined to be impartial. But she hadn't gone to him. She'd gone to an old man who'd loved Oxford, and had made him agree to hurt it. All for her.

A big fat tear slid down her cheek. She felt so guilty she could have screamed. She looked up at the tough-looking man who was standing so close to her again. She shook her head.

'Nothing,' she said. 'It's nothing that you'd be remotely interested in.'

203

She had no idea, then, of how wrong she was.

She felt his finger under her chin, lifting her head.

Lisle caught his breath. Her lovely emerald eyes were swimming in tears. The arrows of red hair, leading his gaze to her mouth, brushed the tops of his knuckles. He felt a tenderness he'd never known before flood into his mind. His heart. 'Oh, Nesta,' he said softly.

And lowered his head to kiss her.

Her lips were sweet, and tasting slightly of the salt from her tears. With a small murmured cry, she pushed against him, raising her arms to loop over his neck, turning into his warm embrace.

His tongue met hers. Duelled, caressed, promised . . .

Nesta felt her nipples harden into tight buds and was sure he must feel them pressing against his chest.

Lisle did. He dragged his mouth away. 'We can't,' he said thickly.

Nesta sighed. 'I know,' she agreed.

And they kissed again. And again. And again . . .

CHAPTER TEN

Sergeant Jim Neill walked into the incident room and slumped wearily down into a chair. He watched his superior's face as he listened to the speaker on the other end of the telephone. He had that long-suffering look of all good cops, when dealing with petty bureaucracy.

But Jim, who knew his boss well, also detected a certain look of, what—happiness— in his eyes? Had something broken on the case?

'Yes, Sir,' Lisle said flatly. His voice held that curiously neutral tone he used whenever speaking to one of the really big cheeses. Jim grinned.

'Yes, Sir,' Lisle said again.

Jim looked around the room. It bore the usual signs of any major incident room—a curious mixture of make do, and top-notch administrative work. In his time, he'd seen incident rooms set up in mills, theatres, church halls, even, once, in a sewerage plant. The idea was to stay as close to the scene of the crime as you could, space permitting. It was also a lot cheaper.

This room was a real prize, as far as such rooms went. Big, well ventilated and heated, and with adequate lighting. The room was lined with corkboards that bore information on all the latest results. Pictures from the crime lab, reports on alibi times, messages, little dots of yellow reminder paper, and many, many other bits and pieces. One desk was piled high with phones. Over in the corner, a WPC was hunched over a computer, her fingers flying over the keyboard. Uniformed men came and went, eating and drinking on the run, the room buzzing to the low-voiced backdrop of mumbled conversations. No doubt about it, this was a big operation. Jim was a bit surprised someone higher up the ladder hadn't stepped in before now.

Then he thought of all the possible ramifications of the case. Whoever was in charge would take a serious dent in their career prospects if they didn't solve it. And then there was the ever-present possibility of standing on some high up's toes. No, Jim grinned to himself, on second thoughts, perhaps it wasn't so surprising they'd left Lisle to run with the ball. Those who were opposed to him, (and in the upper echelons there were a few old-fashioned coppers who still were) were no doubt hoping he'd fall flat on his face. Whilst those who were in his camp had obviously decided that this was just the sort of high-profile case that could earn him his Chief Insepctorship.

If he could just pull it off.

Jim felt his shoulders tense. They were well

into the third day, and still no break. They still hadn't found the murder weapon. And although there was a sniff of a possible motive it was going to be very hard proving it. And apart from Dr Callum Fielding, they had no outstanding suspect.

Whichever way you looked at it, it was not looking good, and the pressure was on.

Lisle sighed, said a final 'Yes, Sir,' and hung up.

Jim glanced at him sympathetically. 'Fire from on high?'

Lisle grunted noncommittally. He was not the kind of man who passed his problems on to those working under him.

'Let's recap. Autopsy clear cut but of no particular use. Forensics?'

Jim handed over a large folder. 'You've already read all the relevant bits. The trouble is, the killer didn't get anywhere near the victim. You can fire a bolt from almost as far away as a gun, apparently. So there's no fibres from clothes, no fingerprints of course. Nothing.'

Lisle sighed. Wasn't that the truth? In a hand-to-hand situation, a criminal left all sorts of goodies for them to find. Hair follicles, with DNA nicely packaged at the end for testing. Blood, saliva, bite marks, you name it. But the area around Sir Vivian had been as barren as a desert.

'On the other hand,' Jim said with a more

up-beat note, 'we've finally finished collating our interviews with the party goers for that night.'

'At last!'

Jim grimaced. 'It's not so easy to track down, interview and compare over a hundred witnesses and their statements.'

'I know. I know, quit griping,' Lisle said with a grin. 'Just give me the relevant bits. Who do we have who *could* have done it?'

*　　　*　　　*

'Naismith. Rosemary. A very popular lady by all accounts. She was absent for about half an hour during the party after the sit-down Dinner. But, from what my various sources tell me, she's more likely to have been snogging some erstwhile suitor in one of the broom cupboards than anything else. She's a notorious flirt, and a bit of a man eater.'

His sergeant went on to list about ten others, including an Emeritus Professor of Classics, a local businessman who had deep pockets and an ambitious son, a timid and rather well-known poet, and a local GP. All were pillars of the community, and none, naturally, harboured a secret criminal history.

Lisle grimaced. 'A rather motley bunch, aren't they? What kind of dirt have you managed to dig up any of the other prize-winning wannabes? If we're right, and Sir

Vivian had found a skeleton in someone's cupboard, we should be able to rattle its bones a bit.'

Jim sighed. 'Nothing doing. Dr Ngabe is extremely well-respected. Several people have mentioned how hard-working she is. That's something of a rarity around here, I'm coming to think. Same goes for the others. The American contender is agitating to go back to the States, by the way. Apparently she has a long-standing commitment to lecture at Harvard and she's not happy. If you ask me, she's got a man over there—I can't see all this angst having to do with missing a few dates in the lecture halls.'

'Cynic,' Lisle grunted. 'And Naismith? She's in the frame—she have any interesting little quirks we should know about?'

'Nothing academic so far. She seems to be a pretty bog-standard sort of Don. No, all her juicy bits and pieces seem love-related. She's had some very strange partners over the years. Including somebody our friends over in CID were interested in.'

'Oh?' Lisle leaned forward.

Jim grinned and tossed his superior the file. Lisle read it with interest, but with no great hope. Apparently, some years ago, Dr Rosemary Naismith had had a live-in love affair with a Middle-East freedom fighter. No doubt he had terrorist connections, and had eventually been deported. Interesting, but hardly relevant. Sir Vivian had definitely hinted at some scholarship scandal before he'd been killed. He doubted the old man would have regarded anyone's love life as any of his business, no matter how risqué it might be. He sighed and tossed it to one side.

'What have we got on the victim?'

'Nothing. Semi-retired, no financial mess, can't even find an ex-mistress. No bad debts, nothing that smells even slighty off. Another paragon of virtue with not an enemy in the world.'

'My, my, we're just rolling along, aren't we?' Lisle said grimly. 'No murder weapon, no forensics, no witnesses, not much motive. Anything I missed?'

Jim paled slightly. 'Don't worry, sir. We'll get there. Something will break.'

Lisle wasn't so sure. He got up and grabbed his coat. 'Get those damned computers working. Hook up to the internet. See if you can get a line on that damned compound bow the experts reckon must have been used. He or she might have bought it online. And check the archery clubs or any internet games that have archery as a main theme. Perhaps our killer is a computer freak and we can track him down that way.'

'Right.'

'And re-interview Ollenback, Ngabe and Naismith. I want to know where they were during the time Sir Vivian died. Don't let up on them. Drag them down to the station if they look like playing it cute. And I want their statements in black and white and witnessed. Rattle a few cages. See if someone breaks.'

'Right.'

'And get me an appointment with our Lord St John James.'

'Right.'

Lisle was at the door now.

'Where'll you be?' Jim yelled above the hub-hub.

'I'll be back by six,' Lisle yelled back, unhelpfully.

He got into the car and drove towards Holywell. All the way over he told himself he was only following up a lead. As he parked and locked the car he told himself that, when you got to a dead end, you smashed a way through. As he mounted the steps and knocked at her door he reminded himself it was time he got some straight answers.

But when she opened the door, and looked at him with those big green eyes, he knew damned well he'd just spent fifteen minutes lying to himself.

It did not put him in a good mood.

'I want to speak to you, Miss Aldernay,' he said grimly, pushing open the door and forcing her to take a step back.

Nesta felt her heart leap. She swallowed hastily, and shut the door carefully behind him. Ever since first setting eyes on this man, she'd known, somehow, that she'd encountered, for the first time in her life, something inevitable. Something beyond her control, maybe even beyond psychological explanation. Something primal, and instinctive and utterly desirable.

She was very conscious of the quietness of the house. All the other tenants were at work, and at this hour, even her landlady was out shopping. 'Inspector Jarvis,' she managed to say drolly. 'How nice. Do come in.'

'None of that!' Lisle snapped, walking to the middle of the room, ramming his hands into his pockets, and turning to face her. 'Ever since we met, you've lied to me, distracted me, given me half-truths, and generally been a right royal pain in my neck. Now, I want some straight answers. Got it?' he thrust his chin out aggressively.

Nesta moved slowly over to the sofa. Her knees were weak, and her heart was pumping so much adrenaline through her body she needed to sit down. He looked so angry, and was all but pulsating with masculine energy. All her life, she'd played it according to the rules. Study. Go to college. Get her degree. Map out her career. Men had always been placed in a similar neat little box. Except this one. This one made his own space in her life, whether she wanted him there or not.

He watched her move to the sofa. She moved like a cat, he thought. All graceful indolence. She was wearing one of those deceptively simple 'granny-type' dresses. All demure tiny blue and red flowers, against a creamy backdrop. Simple shoulder straps. Almost no cut to it at all, just a straight swathe of material that fell modestly to just below her knees. Nothing about it should have been alluring or provocative, but it was, damn it. It was!

Her hair, he saw, had just been newly washed. It gleamed and glowed like it had a fiery life all of its own. As she moved, the demure dress hinted at the roundness of her breasts, moved across her hips, clung, briefly, to the movements of her legs. And then she folded herself down onto the sofa. Her eyes, somehow, had become greener. Softer.

'I've tracked down the men and women on that Dinner date list you gave me,' Lisle began grimly, but with that curious note of happiness that Jim Neill had spotted earlier. 'They confirm that you were at the Trout that night.'

'Were you surprised?' she asked mockingly. Now why, she thought, had she said that? Even she could hear the taunting and deliberately provocative tone in her voice. Where the hell had it come from? What did she think she was doing? Playing with this man was like poking a tiger with a stick.

Utter madness!

Except, some part of her *did* seem to know what she was doing. Some private, female, allbut ignored part of her that was now coming into its own. It was unusual. The psychologist in her couldn't help but be fascinated by her own behaviour. But she also knew, deep down, that it was dangerous. Taunting this man was so dangerous.

Lisle dragged in a ragged breath. 'Don't play games with me, Miss Aldernay,' he warned through gritted teeth. 'I'm just not in the mood for it.' His voice had the warning growl of a wolf in it.

Nesta felt herself flush. But it was not the heat of shame that was making her pale skin glow. It was something else altogether.

He was wearing a long black raincoat, and underneath, she could clearly see his rumpled white shirt and black trousers. He looked as if he hadn't slept in a week. There was a dark shadow of growth on his chin. His hair was tousled, untamed, like the look in his eyes.

All her life, she'd been used to so-called, civilised men. Fellow students, like herself, who could talk for hours and hours about the most convoluted and dull academic point. She'd always thought they were her 'type', those intellectual men of her own age. Men with their careers to forge, idealistic, liberated, careful men. People who thought just like herself.

Now, looking at this furious policeman, she wondered what the hell she'd been thinking of. Not one of her erstwhile suitors back at Durham had a tenth of this man's character.

Not one of them knew what life was really about. This man, she knew instinctively, could teach her more in a day than she'd learned in a year in the classroom.

She swallowed hard. Tried to control her body. Tried to remember what love could do to you. And suddenly realised that she couldn't even bring to mind the face of the man she'd thought she'd once loved. Couldn't even remember his name . . .

What was happening to her? She shouldn't be this far gone. Not so soon. She didn't even know this man. Didn't even know if he was married, had children. Didn't know his background, or his ambitions, or . . . She shifted uncomfortably on the sofa. She swallowed hard. She tried to get her breathing under control.

As if aware of the sudden heat and tension in the room, Lisle shrugged off his raincoat. Underneath, she saw that he'd long since discarded his tie, and the shirt was even more disreputable than she'd thought. A coffee stain trailed a biege path down the right hand side of his chest, and had gone unnoticed. Sartorial elegance, she could see, didn't hold a high place on his list of priorities.

'Now. According to them, you didn't leave Wolvercote until nearly 1.00 o'clock in the morning.' Which meant that the old man had been killed long before, and she was now, at last, truly and fully off the suspect list.

215

'Really?' Nesta said vaguely. 'I didn't think it was as late as that.'

'Well it was!' Lisle snapped, furious. 'And if you'd paid more attention, I would have known that you were in the free and clear long before now!' he almost shouted, goaded to the point of total exasperation.

Nesta dragged her eyes away from the coffee stain, and the outline of his hard male nipple beneath it, and lifted her eyes to his. There was a puzzled look in them. 'I'd have thought you wouldn't be this angry about it,' she said quietly. 'Wasn't I a prime suspect? Aren't you happy to eliminate one more dead end?'

'Damn you!' Lisle snarled. 'Of course I'm happy about it! It gives you an alibi for Sir Vivian's murder.'

Sir Vivian had definitely left the party at just before 12.30. Since he had gone not more than a few steps from the door, he must have been killed almost immediately.

He ran a hand through his hair, a man at the end of his tether, and watched her eyes suddenly widen. The green glow flared into an emerald blaze.

'You were scared,' she whispered with sudden understanding. Hardly able to believe what her singing heart was screaming at her, she mumbled joyfully, 'You didn't want it to be me.'

Lisle stared at her helplessly. 'Now where

216

did you get that . . . stupid . . . idea?' he asked, but all the strength had left his voice now.

Nesta slowly stood up. 'Are you married?' she asked quietly, walking towards him.

Lislc swallowed hard. 'I was. Divorced.'

Nesta kicked off her shoes. 'Do you have any children?'

Wordlessly, Lisle shook his head.

Nesta reached down and grabbed the bottom of her hem. In one fluid movement she lifted the dress over her head. She was wearing only a brief pair of pale pink panties underneath.

Lisle felt the sweat pop out on the back of his neck. Still, she was walking towards him, stalking him like a beautiful, sleek cheetah. His eyes feasted on the length of her body. Her slim flanks, the tiny waist, the rounded breasts with their cherry-pink tips.

'Is there anything you want to ask me?' Nesta asked, her voice husky.

'Were you and Sir Vivian lovers?' he croaked, suddenly needing to have it confirmed, in her own words.

'No.'

'Do you know who killed him?'

'No.'

'Can you tell me anything at all that could cast a light on his murder?'

'No.'

'All right.'

'All right?' she echoed huskily. 'Are you

sure? Is it all better now?'

Lisle nodded. She was no longer a suspect. She had an alibi. Independent inquiries had failed to connect Nesta Aldernay in any way with the victim, save for that one brief interview. He could now honourably touch her. Kiss her. Make love to her.

He groaned, and closed his eyes briefly. It was what he'd always wanted to do, from the very first moment. He just hadn't been able to admit it.

Nesta felt the sound rumble across the few inches separating them. The sound waves seemed to penetrate her abdomen, vibrating her insides, churning her into a molten mass of desire.

She reached for him blindly, pressing her palm against that coffee stain. Beneath the rumpled material, she felt his flesh leap at her touch. His eyes shot open.

'Nesta,' he said shakily.

'What is it?' she asked faintly, bending down to kiss the bare piece of skin, revealed at his throat as she undid the top two buttons of his shirt.

He swallowed hard at the touch of her tongue pressing against the pulse that was pumping there.

'I'm still not in the mood for games,' he warned her grimly.

'Neither am I.'

'You're so much younger than I am,' he

growled, half pushing her away. They had to restore some sanity. Quickly, before it was too late.

She immediately pushed back against him. 'Not that much younger,' she pointed out. Then, seeing the agony of uncertainty in his eyes, and understanding it at once, not through clever brain-power, but simple, straight forward feminine instinct, she smiled gently. And reassured him. 'I want a man, Lisle,' she said softly, listening to herself with wonderment. 'I want a man that I can marry. A man that I can have children with. A man who can support me for a little while, just until I'm a fully qualified psychologist.' Always before, that thought had been unthinkable. She was a modern woman. Modern women didn't need bread winning males. Except, now, she knew that she could depend on him. And neither of them would be diminished. She smiled, gathering in confidence as he continued to look at her, his hazel eyes flooding with hope with every word she said. 'I want a man who won't be in competition with me,' she carried on lovingly. 'A man who can give me a home, a start in life, a commitment.'

As she spoke, she knew how much she meant it all. Before, she'd only been playing with love. Playing at life. Suddenly, now, in this room, she realised that life wasn't a game at all. And her mother's house in Durham was just that. A house. What she needed, what she wanted, was a *home*.

A few days in this bedsit had taught her that!

And she wanted her children to have a mature and responsible father. She wanted a real man. A man who'd already forged his place in life. A man who had already achieved most of his goals and now needed other goals, goals that she could help him set.

'Oh Lisle,' she said. 'I want so much from you. Does it scare you?'

Lisle found himself looking into eyes that were all too human. Did it? Perhaps—a little. After all, he'd been burned once. This time, he had to get it right. Because Nesta Aldernay, he felt,—no, he *knew*—had the power to rip him apart.

'I'm not an academic,' he said huskily.

'Is that a crime?'

He bent and kissed her hard. 'I'm a hard-working copper. I've worked long and nasty hours. I'll have to work many more.'

'Is that supposed to scare me?'

'It's not easy. Being a copper's wife.'

Nesta became suddenly still. 'Are you asking me to marry you?'

For a second Lisle stared at her. Was he? Good grief, *was he?*

'I think so,' he said at last. 'But . . .'

Quickly she put a finger to his lips. 'Let's have a long engagement,' she said softly. 'That way, it'll give us time. Time to think. To get to know each other. It'll be . . .' Safer? Her lips twisted. This was really happening, she thought. Not a dream, although the last few minutes had had a dreamlike quality.

Then he reached for her, and all sense of fantasy faded. Suddenly they were on fire.

Her hands dragged his shirt apart, and her lips quickly conquered the territory it gave up. She kissed the ridges of his ribs and nibbled and pulled on the two dark turgid nipples as his own fingers plunged into the back of her panties.

She felt his palms cup her buttocks and felt her knees weaken and give way. He went down with her, and they collapsed onto the floor. The floorboards were cold to her back, and she made a little mewl of protest.

Without pausing, and without taking his lips off hers, Lisle lifted her, carrying her to the rickety bed, and laying her down in the centre. His hands pulled off her panties, and for a second he moved away from her. But only so that he could strip himself naked.

Nesta just had time to catch a brief glimpse of strong legs, with a long jagged scar in one thigh. An old knife wound?

And then he was with her on the bed.

She felt the dark soft hairs of his chest move across her sensitive breasts, and gasped. His knees nudged her own apart with an urgency that was not gentle, but not brutal either.

She felt herself being opened to him, drew

in a ragged breath, and then he plunged into her. She bucked, gasped, and then groaned as the long, hot, hard length of him seemed to overwhelm her.

He made love to her as if he meant it, as if it had been a long time for him. As it had. He made love to her as if he'd lost his mind, as if his life depended on it. Which it did. And when it was over, when they lay together, satiated, stunned, throbbing, a little appalled, a little triumphant, Nesta began to cry.

He held her, saying nothing, just staring bleakly at the ceiling.

He knew this had been a mistake. Already she was regretting it . . . As she sobbed in his arms, he began to feel guilty. He should have known better. She was little more than a kid.

Finally, her tears spent, Nesta gave a little frown of puzzlement, and wondered what she'd cried for. And then she knew that it didn't have any dire, psychological meaning. She'd cried just because she'd wanted to.

Life was good. She'd grown up, truly grown up, in just a matter of minutes. And she liked adulthood.

It was getting dark outside now. For a long while, Lisle held her in his arms and stared at the ceiling. He had to do the right thing. It would kill him to let her go. He was going to pay for those wonderful, agonising, ecstatic moments of bliss. Perhaps he could just pretend that she was really his for a few minutes longer . . .

Finally, though, he spoke.

'I won't hold you to it, you know,' he said, his voice determined and as bleak as the moors in January. 'What we talked about before. About marriage. We were both acting out of character. We let ourselves get caught up in the moment. You can just get up and walk away and I'll understand.' He fumbled for the words, but could only come up with trite clichés. 'You have a glittering life ahead of you. You're young and beautiful and you don't even have to explain . . .'

'Lisle, shut up,' Nesta said softly.

She turned and snuggled into his armpit. She kissed his salty flesh and sighed in contentment. 'What do you think about a Spring wedding?'

CHAPTER ELEVEN

Markie slowly opened her eyes, aware at once that something was different. She felt warm, and safe and comfortable. And under her ear there was a strange, wonderful drum beat. She blinked, then slowly raised her head, and stared down at an expanse of broad, muscular and very male chest.

Memory came flooding back. Slowly, cautiously, she began to lever herself away from Callum Fielding. How had she come to be snuggled up against him like this? Hadn't they just spent the night lying rigidly apart?

But somewhere in the cold dark early hours, she had snuggled over to his side of the bed, and now she gingerly lifted his arm from her shoulder. He turned on the mattress, muttering sleepily, and his arm tightened instinctively around her.

Markie froze as she felt her own heart beat drum louder. With a small sigh of satisfied resignation, she let her face back down to press against his naked skin, and contemplated his nipple.

Idly, she let her fingertip touch it in the most feather-light of caresses.

Callum Fielding sighed deeply in his sleep, and underneath her fingertip, the button of his flesh began to harden.

Markie grinned in satisfaction and triumph. His conscious mind might be made of unbending iron, but at least his subconscious mind wasn't hell-bent on rejecting her!

She gently let her fingertips march across the expanse of his chest to his other nipple. His skin was slightly golden, retaining the last vestiges of a summer tan, and a few silver-golden hairs tickled the sensitive pads of her fingers as they marched.

Callum muttered something indistinct and half-lifted his head from the pillow. Her fingers froze, and his leonine head settled back

224

against the pillows once more. Markie gazed at his face, mesmerised. The sharp planes of his cheekbones really made him devastatingly attractive. And with the beginnings of a golden stubble on his chin, he looked almost rakish. Vastly different from the buttoned-up, tightly controlled doctor of psychology that she knew and was beginning to love-hate.

She played with his nipple again, watching his face closely. His hand beside his face on the pillow jerked reflexively, and she watched it, fascinated.

Would he wake if she just lowered her head down a little and sucked on . . .

Callum shot upright in bed, and Markie sprang back feigning a surprised yawn. 'Good grief, you scared me,' she said accusingly. 'Do you always wake up with a leap like that? What time is it anyway?' she shot the questions at him rapidly.

Callum shot her a suspicious look in return. Slowly, he eased himself upright to lean against the headboard. He was tingling pleasantly from head to foot and . . . yes. He was hard. He drew up his legs to hide his condition from her and let his forearms rest against his knees, his large sensitive hands dangling down.

'Were you just touching me?' he asked suspiciously.

Markie looked at him with wide-eyed innocence. 'Me? I was asleep, until you scared me half to death by leaping out of your skin like that. Were you having a bad dream?' she asked guilelessly.

Callum's stormy grey-green eyes narrowed on her. 'Hardly,' he said flatly. Then glanced at his watch. 'We'd better get up if you want breakfast. The hotel probably stops serving at ten.'

Markie give a little yelp. 'It's as late as that? I'm nearly always up by seven at the latest.' And, when she had a photoshoot, she could be up with the larks.

Callum looked at her sardonically. 'Yeah, right.'

Markie, on the verge of wriggling out of the embrace of the monster four-poster, caught his disbelieving tone and turned to look at him.

'Yeah, exactly right, buster,' she said flatly. 'A lot of photographers doing an outdoor shoot like the early morning light. You're like everyone else—you think the life of a model is all wine and roses. We work bloody hard, let me tell you.'

Callum, somewhat taken aback by her ferocity, found himself apologising.

Markie left him with a flounce and hogged the bathroom.

*   *   *

The car wasn't ready until nearly lunchtime, so they decided to have lunch in town before

226

setting off for Sir Vivian's Cornish hideaway.

They found a small restaurant in the centre of the little market town, and ordered the day's special—which wasn't particularly special, but which was at least well cooked and warming.

But as they ate, Callum slowly became aware that his companion was attracting attention. It wasn't anything she did exactly, for she ate and talked with her usual mix of simple pleasure and surprising erudition, but he became aware that more and more people in the restaurant were looking their way. And an excited buzz, like a roused wasps' nest, began to permeate the atmosphere.

Eventually, one of the waitresses approached them with trepidation, egged on by a waiter and the manager, who stood on the sidelines, watching avidly.

'Er, excuse me. But you are Marcheta, aren't you?' the young girl said tentatively. She was about twenty, with rather too much weight about her middle and a mass of rather badly-dyed blonde hair. Her face was just slightly awe struck.

Markie smiled at her brightly. 'Yes, I am. Thank you for noticing.'

The waitress half-laughed and half-gushed at this ingenuous response and held out her order pad. 'Could I please have your autograph?'

This, of course, opened the floodgates for all the others, and Callum watched in amused exasperation as she quickly became surrounded by admirers. He let himself be willingly pushed to the sidelines, and watched her work.

Such attention would have driven him mad within moments, but she dealt with them all kindly, and with patience. One of the older men she even kissed on the cheek and allowed his almost incoherent daughter to take their picture thus. She flirted with the young men, but never let them get out of hand, and won over the slightly-jealous women with her easy-going friendliness, handling them with an ease that an experienced psychologist could only admire and marvel at.

After twenty minutes or so, she graciously extracted herself, and they walked out to the car park.

Callum got behind the wheel and drove out of town. Beside him, Markie Kendall used her compact to artfully repair her make-up. It should have only confirmed her image to him of a bubble-headed shallow woman who earned too much money for doing something utterly ridiculous.

But it didn't.

'Tell me about your new perfume,' he heard himself asking. 'I heard someone say you were in Oxford to check out the labs who are making it?'

Markie nodded, and told him about choosing the kind of fragrance she wanted.

From that, he skilfully segued into getting her talking about her long-term plans.

Although he was no genius when it came to finance, as like with most very clever men, he tended to live and breathe only in his own area of expertise, it quickly became apparent to him that this young woman had a remarkable grasp of both reality, finance and business.

In fact, by the time they came within sight of the sea, and he turned off into the small hamlet where Sir Vivian kept his holiday cottage, Callum Fielding was rapidly revising a lot of his misconceptions about Miss Marcheta Kendall.

*　　　*　　　*

'Here it is,' he said, pulling up outside a small, stone-built cottage with a grey slate roof. Beyond it was a panoramic view of the sea, and gulls wheeled noisily overhead.

'Vivian said he always liked this garden,' he mused.

Markie looked at the cottage bemused. 'But it hasn't got one. It's just wild flowers and grassland right up to the front door.'

Callum smiled wryly. 'Exactly. He said he could escape the tyranny of weeding here.'

Markie laughed, then quickly sobered. 'I'm sorry. You really miss him, don't you?'

Callum got out of the car and stretched his long legs with a sigh. 'Let's just say that I'm

229

really angry about what's been done to him and leave it at that, shall we?' he said grimly.

Markie nodded wordlessly, and followed him as they approached the front door. The cottage looked to be the only habitation for miles, and when he used one of the keys on his keyring to let them in, the cottage had the echoing, empty sound of an abandoned building.

'I always think that houses somehow know when their owners have truly left them,' she said quietly. They were standing in a tiny hallway, with a set of steep stairs leading off one side, and two doors opening out into rooms on the other.

Callum, who'd been thinking much the same thing, glanced at her quickly. He hadn't expected her to be so sensitive to atmosphere. 'Yes, I know what you mean,' he said softly.

For a moment, the two of them simply stood in the quiet cottage in silence. Then Callum shrugged his broad shoulders, and said briskly, 'Right, let's get searching. I'll take his study area, through here in the living room,' he indicated one of the doors. 'You take the bedroom upstairs. See if you can find any diaries, personal papers, anything that might give us a clue as to who might have wanted him dead.'

'Right,' Markie agreed just as resolutely, heading for the stairs and sprinting up them with the grace of a gazelle. She was wearing a plain stone-coloured skirt, with a deep rust top. Her hair was held back in a ponytail, and tied with a chiffon silk scarf of the same rust colour. With the minimum of make-up and flat rust-coloured shoes, Callum thought that she couldn't look more strikingly perfect if she'd been wearing Dior and diamonds.

He pushed open the nearest door and found himself in the familiar living room. In one corner, bookcases lined the walls at a forty-five degree angle and a small kneehole desk housed a simple computer. It was where he'd done his own work whenever he came down here to write some papers in peace, and now he made his way over to it and sat down in the old-fashioned swivel chair.

He offered up a brief prayer of regret to his old mentor and asked his forgiveness in desecrating his privacy in this way, and then with a stiffening of his spine he opened the first drawer and began to take out the folders he found there.

It didn't take him long to find what he was looking for, and he soon found himself looking down at what was obviously a photocopy of an old thesis. The name of the author, Brian Aldernay, was unfamiliar to him, but when he began to read it, he found that the contents of the work most definitely were not.

He felt a cold chill creep down his spine as he continued to read.

Upstairs, Markie was sitting on the edge of a double bed and was reading just as intently. But she had in *her* hands an old fashioned, leather-bound journal, and she was reading Sir Vivian's own handwriting as he described his first meeting with a young woman called Nesta Aldernay.

She read it all—feeling every emotion that the old psychology Don must have felt as she read his account of Nesta's story. She understood at once why he'd been so appalled and hardly able to believe or credit her story.

She could see instantly, from his words of pain and regret, how much it hurt him, when he began to do his own research into the matter and slowly, inexorably, came to the heart-breaking conclusion that she was right.

'Oh you poor old soul,' Markie said, closing the journal and unable to read on any further. She needed to get this to Callum.

But when she went downstairs, she saw him hunched over at the desk, reading something with such a ferocious scowl on his face that any words died in her throat. Every now and then he would stop and stare unseeingly out of the window, obviously deep in thought, then he'd bend his head once more to the pages in his hand.

He was so deeply absorbed that she made her way, as quietly as a mouse, to the sofa opposite him, and curled up on it, watching him silently, Sir Vivian's journal placed carefully on the floor in front of her.

With his mind so fully occupied elsewhere, she was able to study him and think. And she had plenty to think about.

Why was she so deeply attracted to this man? Because she most definitely was! Their first meeting couldn't have been less auspicious, and since then, it seemed to her, he'd done nothing but rebuff every attempt she'd made to get closer to him.

OK, she sort of got the whole Oxford thing. He was an old-fashioned man, with a brilliant mind, who was into living life in the ivory towers of academe. But did that have to mean he lived life like a monk?

Her lips twisted into a grim smile as she remembered the blonde woman who'd been all over him back in his College rooms. Obviously not!

So he had a love life. He was not so crusty and staid that he was gathering dust, like some of the books on his shelves. So was it just that he didn't fancy her in particular?

The thought made her smile ruefully. For all the adoring fan mail she got, and all the proposals of marriage from moon-struck men, she didn't regard herself as irresistible.

Let's face it, she told herself, some men just preferred blondes!

But for all that, she didn't think it was the

case here. For once or twice she'd caught that unmistakable gleam of desire in his stormy eyes. He might not *want* to, but Dr Callum Fielding desired her all right.

The thought gave her some comfort.

She sighed and stretched, and suddenly the sun came out and shone through the window directly onto his face, highlighting his classic features and turning his hair into the colour of old-gold.

Good grief, he was gorgeous. Big, brainy, brawny, and determined to keep her at arms length.

Take last night. How many men, given the opportunity to spend the night in a four-poster bed with 'Marcheta' would do absolutely nothing about it? Markie almost laughed out loud as she remembered her own chagrin when she realised he actually had fallen asleep.

Still, the question remained, why? Why hadn't he even made the most basic attempt at seduction?

And she could only conclude that it had to be because he wasn't interested in having a relationship with her. Was it intellectual snobbery that was the problem? Did the great man think she was beneath him?

If so, she had the feeling that he was beginning to realise there was far more to her than just a pretty face. But to be fair to him, she didn't think that he was that arrogant.

No, she was more and more convinced that

Callum was determined to remain cold and aloof as a form of self-defence. Which was flattering, since it meant that he saw her as a distinct threat to his way of life.

Her mind turned back to her first view of his rooms at College. So masculine and academic. So lifeless. And she realised that he was right to be afraid. She *did* want to shake him up a bit. He wasn't getting any younger, and the thought of him becoming middle-aged and then old and alone, still stuck in those rooms like a fly in amber, made her want to cry out in anger and denial. He was a deeply attractive and intelligent man. And, she felt sure, beneath that carefully controlled exterior, lurked a vibrant and passionate man.

It gave her a peculiarly feminine ache, deep inside, that insisted she be the one to rouse the male animal in him.

She simply wasn't going to give up. No matter what it took, no matter how prickly he got or standoffish. She was going to find a way under his guard and under his skin if it was the last thing she did!

At that moment, Callum turned the last page of Brian Aldernay's thesis and shut the folder with a precise neatness that underlined, rather than concealed, the cold anger he felt.

He'd been skim-reading it of course. He'd need to study it in far more detail before he was sure, but he'd read enough to get the gist of it.

And recognise it.

He should. After all, he'd read the same thesis, published under the name of Rosemary Naismith, whilst she had been his tutor.

He sensed movement, and his head shot around in alarm, but it was only Markie. She was curled up on the sofa opposite, looking at him curiously. He felt the tension in his shoulders instantly ease.

'You were so intent on what you were doing, I didn't like to disturb you,' she said gently.

Callum nodded wordlessly.

'Found anything?' she persisted.

'Yes. A thesis from a student called Brian Aldernay.'

'That ties in with the journal of Sir Vivian that I found upstairs,' Markie said, and, reaching down, she retrieved the volume and got lithely to her feet, walking over to him and handing it across. 'Start here,' she said, finding the entry where Sir Vivian first met the young woman from Durham.

As he read, Markie stood beside him, and slowly raised her hand to touch his hair. When he made no demur, she slowly ran her fingers through the thick silver/gold mane, his scalp feeling warm beneath her fingers.

Callum found the words in front of him beginning to blur. It was almost impossible to concentrate when she was touching him.

'The thesis was stolen, wasn't it?' Markie

236

said softly. 'At least, that's what Sir Vivian thought. I read enough of his journal to find that out. He was researching it at the rary. He came to the conclusion that someone called Dr Naismith had stolen it and taken the credit for the work someone else had done. That's, like, the worst thing that someone in your world can do, isn't it?'

Callum nodded, again wordlessly.

Slowly, Markie slid down to kneel beside him and put her hand comfortingly on his arm. 'Are you all right?' she asked softly.

Callum smiled grimly. 'Not really, no.'

Markie looked down at his big hands, cradling the old man's journal. 'Do you know who they're talking about? Nesta Aldernay and Sir Vivian—do you know who this Dr Naismith is?'

Callum slowly closed the journal and turned to look at her bleakly. 'Yes. And so do you. You met, briefly, in my room.'

For a second, Markie couldn't think what he was talking about. She certainly couldn't remember being introduced to any Dr Naismith. And then she realised the mistake she was making. She was assuming that Dr Naismith was a man.

But he wasn't.

'The blonde woman who was kissing you,' Markie whispered, appalled. Her face went pale with distress for him.

'Oh Callum! They were talking about your

237

lover.'

'No!' Callum denied fiercely. 'Rosemary and I are not lovers. We never were lovers. She was my supervisor, when I was doing my own thesis, that's all. We were never that close.'

'And does she know that, I wonder?' Markie asked darkly, unable to help feeling jealous. 'From the way she was all over you, you seemed pretty close to me.'

Callum got up and walked restlessly to the window to look outside. It had begun to rain fitfully. Showers and sunshine. A perfect metaphor for life.

He sighed heavily. 'Rosemary is . . . complicated. I think she's having problems. She was always volatile, always a bit of a compulsive, obsessive personality. She drinks too much, and always seemed to need the approbation of men—and the more dangerous the men, the worse for her they were, the better she liked it. Looking back, I suppose I've always felt that she seemed hell-bent on self-destruction, and could never understand why.'

'And you think maybe this explains it?' Markie said quietly. 'She had this big dark secret hanging over her?'

At least she now knew that there was nothing going on between them. He sounded sincerely bewildered and wary when talking about Naismith. With relief, she felt the green-eyed monster within her retreat, appeased.

Callum turned and looked at her and spread his hands. 'Maybe. Who knows what Rosemary is thinking? I've never pretended to understand the woman. But that's not the question, is it?'

Markie looked at him for a moment in puzzlement, then went even more pale than before. 'You mean, did she know that Sir Vivian was on to her,' Markie asked breathlessly.

Callum nodded, stony-faced. 'And if she did know, did she kill him to keep him quiet?'

＊　　　＊　　　＊

Lisle wearily collected his coat, gave a few words of encouragement for his flagging team, and headed for home. He pulled up at a set of traffic lights and tapped the wheel impatiently. He'd be better off buying a house here, in Kidlington, he mused. It would save the short but traffic-jammed commute into Oxford itself.

Perhaps he and Nesta should start looking for one.

He found himself grinning again.

Nesta.

It was madness. She'd been a suspect in a case. He'd known her only a few days. She was so much younger, so much smarter, so much out of his class, it was ridiculous to even think of marrying her. And if someone had told him just two weeks ago that he'd be engaged to be married to a woman with all those credentials, he'd have laughed himself sick.

It was so fraught with possible dangers.

But then, he thought soberly, the first time around, he'd done it all by the book. He'd known Marie, his first wife, since school. They'd gone out for two years. Had a proper engagement party. Put a deposit down on their first starter-home. Had the white wedding, and all the rest of it.

And *that* hadn't worked out.

For all he'd thought that she'd been prepared for life as a copper's wife, and for all Marie had thought so too, they had just been proved wrong. It had been as simple as that. The missed Dinners, parties, birthdays, had become more and more aggravating. The long hours, the odd hours, the lack of status in being a cop's wife, the pity of friends, it had all undermined them. The times she'd had to go to hospital, after being told he'd been wounded in the course of duty. The tension it had caused for months afterwards. Eventually, there had just been no escape, except divorce. Now he was glad they hadn't had children. He was also genuinely glad that Marie had found someone else—a dentist, with a good income, steady hours, and a nice detached house in the village of Yarnton.

Just what Marie should have had in the beginning, if they'd only known.

But with Nesta, Lisle just knew it was going

to be different. Not just because, as a soon-to-be practising psychologist, she'd be better able to cope with the stresses that came with the job of being Mrs Lisle Jarvis. And not just because things were better, now that Lisle had earned his last promotion, which meant that there would be a lot less likelihood of him being stabbed by a drug-crazed suspect on the streets now that he was no longer in the front line. The hours were not quite so crazy, except when he had a big case on like this. And he was well and truly on the ladder to promotion—provided he could just solve this damned case.

No, even with all those improvements, he knew that wasn't why he felt so outlandishly confident that this time, with this woman, it would all work out. It was something more nebulous. Just something he felt deep inside that he'd never felt with Marie. Something he'd never even known that he *should* be feeling.

He got home to find all his lights on. Inside, a Dinner was cooking. Not one of those candlelight meals like Marie had prepared for them, during their first year of marriage. Oddly, if it had been, alarm bells would have started ringing.

He could smell that this was nothing that had taken painstaking hours to cook. Just a simple shop-bought meal.

Chicken Kiev, by the smell of garlic.

As he walked into the door, he could see that the table was set, just with his ordinary odds-and-ends, and a sauce bottle. Nesta was sat on his sofa, books and papers scattered all around her. She was looking over the photocopies of her father's thesis, and she hastily gathered them together when she saw him walk in. He'd given her a key to his flat yesterday, and her bedsit was looking more and more like a no-go area.

She'd spent the day at his place, going over her options. With Sir Vivian gone, she had to decide how to proceed.

She'd almost decided that a direct approach to the woman concerned was the only way, but right now she had better things on her mind. Her face lit up into a welcoming smile, with not a trace of unease or reproach for the lateness of the hour.

'Lisle!' She thrust the papers into her battered briefcase and uncurled herself from the sofa. She wore no make-up, and was dressed in a faded pair of jeans and a rumpled thick-knit sweater.

She looked gorgeous.

She walked into his arms and kissed him. 'Hungry?'

'Starving.'

'For food first? Or for me?' she asked huskily.

'What do you think?'

She led him to the bed, watching him as

242

he shrugged off his shirt. Mimicking him, she pulled the sweater over her own head and matched him, stripping herself article of clothing, for article of clothing, both of them feasting their eyes on the other, until they were naked.

When he joined her on the bed, she was breathing rapidly, her eyes as large as a cat's at night. The moment he touched her, she moaned, her skin tingling with goose bumps that had nothing to do with the cold.

Lisle reached for her, all his cares simply slipping away . . .

CHAPTER TWELVE

'Who are you calling?' Markie asked. It was getting dark, and they'd decided to spend the evening at the cottage, before heading back to Oxford. Now she watched Callum as he used the landline and dialled a familiar number.

He glanced at her, ready to speak, then heard the voice in his ear instead and half-turned away from her. 'Hello, Sin Jun. Yes, me, Callum. Look, do you have the number for Inspector Jarvis?'

As Markie made a face, Callum looked back at her and shrugged. Putting his hand over the receiver, he said softly, 'He's got to know what we found out.'

Markie sighed. She still hadn't really forgiven the policeman for treating Callum as a suspect. 'If you say so,' she muttered darkly.

Callum made a note of the number, and reached for the phone. At the incident room, he learned that Inpsector Jarvis had just left for the day.

'All right, but can you give him a message please. It's important. Can you tell him that Dr Fielding called. I'm at Sir Vivian's country cottage, and I've found his journal, and papers relating to the person he suspected of cheating. Have you got all that?'

He listened as the constable on the other end repeated his words back at him and sighed. 'No, I'm not in Oxford, so I can't come in first thing. I'll be starting out from Cornwall some time in the morning. But I will go and see the inspector as soon as I can. Yes? Fine, that's right.' He listened for a few moments longer, then rang off.

'You must feel really strange about all this,' Markie said thoughtfully, coming to stand beside him. 'Is that why you didn't actually give him Dr Naismith's name?'

'Partly,' Callum agreed. 'But mostly because I need to read the results of all of Vivian's research first. It's possible he could have made some errors.' His lips twisted as she gave him a knowing look. 'Yes, I know, it's unlikely. But damn it, Markie, you don't just accuse a colleague of theft and plagiarism without being absolutely sure of your facts first. Besides, one of the first rules is always check your data. Not that I don't trust Sir Vivian to have done his homework, but still, I have to check it out for myself as well.'

'So once we're back at Oxford, you want to hit the libraries, right?'

'Right.'

Markie nodded. 'OK. You carry on reading, and I'll make us some Dinner.'

Callum looked at her surprised. 'You can cook?'

Markie put her hands on her hips and glared at him. 'Of course I can cook,' she scoffed.

She didn't, however, tell him that she could cook particularly well.

*   *   *

Considering she had recourse only to the tins and dried staples with which the tiny cottage kitchen was stocked, she thought she hadn't done too badly. A few hours later, they sat down to the first course, tinned soup and herb bread croutons. Callum ate with a mechanical air that told her he was not really tasting the food, which was probably just as well, she thought wryly.

'So, you've never been married?' she said artlessly, making him nearly choke.

He patted his mouth with a paper napkin

and shook his head. 'No. You?'

'Not so far,' she said gaily. 'But it's not as if I'm anti-marriage or anything. If the right man came along, I suppose I'd consider it.'

'Very magnanimous of you.'

'I thought so.' She cleared away the soup bowls, and came back with a makeshift stew of tinned stewed beef, tinned carrots and tomatoes, with a scattering of dried herbs for flavouring. Without a word, Callum began stoically eating again.

Markie grinned. Just wait until he realised what she had planned for dessert!

*   *   *

It was nearly midnight before Callum had finished reading the last of Sir Vivian's notes, and feeling tired, depressed and heartsick, he turned off the downstairs lights and climbed the steep wooden stairs.

Markie had gone to bed an hour ago, saying she was sleepy, and he'd barely muttered a vague 'goodnight' in her direction. Now he was careful not to turn on the landing lights as he made his way to the biggest of the two bedrooms, determined not to disturb her. He trod lightly, and opened the bedroom door with a silent snick. The curtains inside were drawn, and as he shucked off his clothes, he reflected that tomorrow was going to be a grim day.

246

Once Lisle Jarvis was presented with Rosemary's name as the one Sir Vivian was going to denounce, her movements on the night of the Prize-giving party were going to be put under a microscope. He could only hope that they'd stand up to such scrutiny.

But deep inside he had the sick feeling of dread that they would not. And the thought of what would happen then made his head ache. The scandal for the city, and the university in particular, wasn't even the worst of it. There were June Dalrymple's feelings to consider, when it all came out, as well as the tragedy for Rosemary Naismith. How would a woman like that take to being sent to prison?

He pulled back the blankets and slid his naked form into the bed, then jumped as a warm hand and knowing fingers slipped up his back, and hooked over one broad shoulder.

'I thought you were never coming up,' Markie complained softly.

'Sorry. I thought we'd agreed you were having the smaller room,' he said stiffly, putting one foot on the floor, preparatory to leaving.

For a slightly built woman, Markie Kendall's grip was remarkably firm as she pulled him back down onto the mattress. '*You* agreed that I'd be sleeping in a different bedroom,' she corrected huskily. 'I just never put you right.'

In the darkness, Callum tensed. 'I don't think this is a good idea.'

'No?'

'No,' he said resolutely.

A pair of soft lips brushed the column of his neck. 'No?'

He swallowed hard. 'No.'

Her hand moved down his shoulder, across his chest, and began to dance over one hard, male nipple. She pinched it hard, just short of pain, making his muscles clench in exquisite anticipation.

'No?' she whispered.

He tried to speak, but found he couldn't, and merely shook his head instead. In the darkness, she interpreted the movement and smiled.

She bent her head, and began nibbling on one earlobe. Then she let her tongue dart into his sensitive ear, and sighed softly.

'No?' she murmured. 'Really?'

Callum groaned.

She pressed herself against his back, her tender naked breasts pressing into the hollows of his shoulderblades.

'No?'

Callum turned onto his side and wordlessly reached for her. For all that he was so much bigger than her, he was a remarkably tender lover, careful, considerate and consummate. Markie soon found that she couldn't speak either, but her cries grew from soft, whispering endearments, to sharper, higher, moaning cries as he nudged her legs apart and with a sure, firm and conquering thrust, entered her. Her fingernails raked his back, and her heart hammered as she heard him moan in response.

Years spent keeping fit in the gym lent her shapely legs a surprising strength, as she hooked them over his hips and her hands on his firm masculine buttocks pulled him ever more deeply into the core of her femininity.

The slow, sensual dance became faster, more urgent, and soon Markie could only scream his name as she felt her body shudder and spasm beneath his heavy, comforting weight.

Later, in the darkness of the night, as Markie Kendall slept happily in his arms, Callum Fielding lay awake, cursing his stupidity.

Because it was impossible. Their pairing was simply doomed to failure. And he would have to tell her soon. Tomorrow maybe. No, perhaps not tomorrow. There was so much to do tomorrow. But the day after, perhaps.

The grim decision made, Callum nodded in the darkness. Yes, it had to be done soon. Because he had the feeling that if it wasn't done soon, hearts might be broken.

*   *   *

The next morning, Lisle was pacing up and down in Nesta's bedsit. She'd insisted on not spending the night at his place, and had been

249

out when he arrived at her digs. And since he had no way of knowing where she was, he was forced to pace and wait.

It was not yet mid-day, but he could feel the morning ticking away. Once again, the sensation of time running out became stronger and stronger. With every moment that passed, the chances of finding Sir Vivian's killer were getting more and more remote. Which meant that he felt more and more guilty at being here at all. He cursed and paced some more.

He tensed as he heard a sound outside, and suddenly Nesta was in the room. She brought with her a sense of fresh air, of real life, of vibrancy and passion. She saw him, and beamed. 'Lisle! You'll have to stop sneaking these odd hours to be with me,' she teased. 'You'll get the sack.'

'I want to know exactly why you went to see Sir Vivian,' he said curtly. 'I've had enough of pretend mistress, pretend would-be student, pretend lost earrings. I want to know the whole story, here and now.'

His voice was as hard as diamonds.

Nesta stared at him in blank amazement. 'I thought we had this all sorted out?' she said, a worried frown crossing her brows. 'I don't know who killed him. We both know that I had nothing to do with that.'

'Why did you come to Oxford, Nesta?' he asked, more calmly this time, hating to see the look of hurt in her big green eyes. And hating even more the fact that he had put it there.

Nesta blinked. She could lie to him no longer. 'It was something to do with my father. He was a student here, many years ago. He'd got a B.A. in Experimental psychology. He died, like I think I told you, when his push-bike was hit by a lorry.'

Lisle shook his head. She was so obviously telling him the truth that he felt sick to his stomach. Why had he suspected that she knew something? That she might somehow be the key to this damned case? He was so crazy-much in love with her, he was letting it distort his whole method of thinking!

And all she'd been doing was catching up on old times, for pity's sake! A natural enough thing to do, considering she'd just got her own B.A.

'Oh, Nesta!' he said tiredly, holding out his arms to her. 'Come here.'

Nesta needed no second bidding. She held him to her, stroking his hair, sensing some kind of crisis, and determined to deal with it. 'This case is getting to you, isn't it?' she murmured quietly. 'Come here.' She led him to the sofa, and sat him down on it. Overwork, stress, she could see it all. And she knew only too well where that could lead. To burn out, or even worse—a coronary! And it was not going to happen to him!

'Let me kiss it better,' she offered huskily. Her lips met his, then slid down the side of

251

his neck. He smelt of aftershave, and car-leather. She kissed his throat, tracing the rise and fall of his Adam's apple as he swallowed compulsively. Her hands went to his chest, pushing aside his jacket to run across his rib cage.

He sighed. 'I have to get back,' he muttered, but without any real enthusiasm. 'I left Jim . . .'

'Hmm, poor Jim,' Nesta sighed, and opened two buttons to give her access to his sternum. She kissed him softly, square in the middle of his chest.

Lisle sighed. The clock was still ticking. From what he'd intimated last night, Callum Fielding might be putting himself in danger. He had to concentrate on what he'd say at the interview, when the psychology Don got back from Cornwall.

But Nesta was unbuckling his belt now, and he told himself that he could do nothing until they found out what Callum and Markie Kendall had discovered at Sir Vivian's country place. He sighed, and then gasped, as her knowing fingers slipped down between his trousers and underwear, her knuckles massaging the growing hardness she found there.

He stretched on the sofa, allowing her rubbing hands more freedom.

Nesta smiled, loving the way the tension eased from his face. 'You like that?' she asked huskily.

Slowly she slipped to the floor, pulling down his trousers, having to wrest off his shoes before freeing him. She kissed the sides of his knees, then moved higher, kissing his trembling thighs, then higher, pressing her tongue against the clean white cotton of his briefs, feeling the hot, pulsating flesh jump beneath her tongue.

Lisle groaned, shrugged himself naked, slipped off the sofa, and rolled her beneath him. The floorboards gave a protesting squeak.

Nesta giggled, then lifted her hips to slip off her own panties.

Soon they came together, Nesta giving a gasp of satisfaction as his long hot length filled her. She clamped her legs around him, holding him against her breast as they moved together in a dance as old as time. For long, long minutes, the pleasure built, the power, passion and urgency of love, ebbing and flowing around them, building in one, then the other, then together, always together, harder, faster, deeper, harder, until they were moaning together, their cries timed to the thrust of their bodies.

A single moment of universe-shattering importance. Then the slow, languorous, sweet slide back to earth.

Afterwards, Lisle dressed almost immediately. He still felt guilty for even taking these few stolen minutes with her.

253

Nesta watched him dress and straightened her own clothes. She didn't even think of protesting. He obviously had something breaking in the case, and finding the killer of that lovely old man was more important, at the moment, than anything else. And she had no problem with that.

Lisle finger-brushed his hair, and walked to the door. At the door he turned and looked at her.

'Did Sir Vivian tell you what you wanted to know? About your father?' he asked softly.

He assumed that Sir Vivian had been her father's supervisor. He supposed, as D.Phil. theses could take as much as 15 years to complete, that a supervisor and his student could grow into good friends over the years.

Nesta's face clouded a little. 'I don't know,' she said honestly. 'He never got the chance to tell me.'

If Lisle hadn't been so anxious to get back to the office and check on their progress, he might have asked her what she meant by that.

And Nesta, unable to deny him anything, would have told him all about her suspicions of her father's supervisor, Rosemary Naismith, stealing his thesis.

But, as they were both to learn much later, that day was going to be a day choc-a-block with such ironies.

And danger beyond their wildest dreams.

CHAPTER THIRTEEN

It was nearly eleven o'clock the next morning before Callum and Markie finally set out from Cornwall for Oxford. He'd intended to get an early start, but had got rather distracted.

Markie was very good at that.

Now as they drove towards Oxford, she leaned back in her seat and stretched like a cat that had fed well on cream and canaries.

'When we get back to the city, I need to do some work at the Bodleian, before we take what we know to Inspector Jarvis,' he said, trying to keep his eyes firmly on the twisting road ahead, and not on the way her breasts strained against her blouse.

'OK. You can drop me off at the hotel, and we'll meet up—say about fiveish, at St Bede's?' she replied.

Callum nodded. 'That sounds good.'

'Then we'll go and speak to that wretched policeman together,' she said with satisfaction.

Callum's smile widened. 'What have you got against poor Inspector Jarvis? He struck me as being an honest man, doing a good job.'

'He had you in his sights, that's what I've got against him,' Markie grumbled. 'And anyone who's against my man has got me to contend with as well.'

Callum felt himself go hot, then cold, at her

255

words.

Her man.

But he wasn't her man. And he could never *be* her man. It was just impossible. Their worlds were too vastly different. Their personalities too mismatched. They didn't think the same, and surely couldn't want the same things.

Callum knew himself well enough to know that if he ever did give his heart and love unstintingly to any woman, he would at some point want marriage and kids. And what supermodel would ruin her figure with childbearing? Or give up her jet-setting, glamorous life to live in Oxford?

He drove in silence, unaware that he'd tensed in his seat, or that his lips were pulled in a tight line, or that Markie Kendall had seen and noted all these tell-tale little signs.

And when he did turn to glance at her, she was looking out of the window, her face turned away, so that he couldn't see the pain in her eyes.

*   *   *

Rosemary Naismith left her flat and drove towards the suburb of Headington. She parked her car down one of the many little cul-de-sacs, filled with small, boxy housing, and walked down several more little narrow streets and mini-housing estates. She looked over her shoulder several times, but was sure she wasn't being followed.

Ever since Sir Vivian had cornered her at that damned party, and told her he knew her thesis had been stolen work, she'd never felt totally safe. As the street lamps came on, and the day around her darkened ever further, she picked up her pace.

But her mind kept going back to the night of the Prize-giving Dinner.

It had started so well. Even though she knew things were over with Pete, her current partner, and half-suspected that he'd use the time she was out to pack more of his things, she'd been in a good mood. After all, she might just win the Prize—or, perhaps, and far more likely, she still might be able to sell a sob-story to Callum Fielding and get him to share a little largesse if *he* won it. Ever since she'd tutored him as a young man, she'd always suspected that Callum Fielding had a compassionate heart, beneath that buttoned-down exterior he showed to the world. Which made him eminently exploitable. Or so she'd thought, until she'd quickly realised that getting him into her bed wasn't going to be as easy as she'd expected. Still, that was then, and this was now, and she had never been one for giving up!

So she'd dressed well and gone to St Bede's, flirted, and had dined (for once) on reasonable food, and been looking forward to the announcement. Of course Callum snaffled the Prize. It had annoyed her to be right, and of course she was disappointed not to have got it herself, but it was nothing she couldn't handle.

Just another day at the office.

And then that stupid old man had made that first crack. About someone not deserving their reputation. For a second or two it had paralysed her. But then she'd forced herself to relax. There was no reason, after all, to suspect that the old fool had a bee in his bonnet about *her*, specifically. He could have picked up on anybody's skeleton in the closet. She'd told herself that she was just being ultra sensitive, when it came to *that* subject.

But then came the after-Dinner party in the SCR. The old man had become even more drunk and yet more voluble. But he had never come out and actually mentioned a name. And so she'd allowed herself to hope that whatever it was that had the stupid old man in such an indignant lather didn't have anything to do with her own shameful secret.

Until, fortified on his wine and brandy and sherry, he'd finally cornered her, and, thankfully keeping his voice low, had told her that he knew what she'd done.

At first she'd tried to bluff it out, keeping a wary eye on all the other guests, in case they were being overheard. But everyone just gave her sympathetic looks, no doubt thinking that Sir Vivian was making a fool of himself with her, now.

And then he'd mentioned *that* name. The name she'd never allowed herself to even think of, over the last ten years or so.

Aldernay. Brian Aldernay.

And she knew it was all up.

After Sir Vivian had stumbled off, after giving her a slurred and rather jumbled speech about honour, and doing the right thing, and resigning, thus saving Oxford from a scandal, and all that other guff, she'd wandered around the room, stunned, but smiling and flirting in all the right places.

At first, she'd felt nothing but fear. It was all over. She'd be shunned and ruined. Then came anger. Why did this have to happen now, after so many years of silence? Then began her self-justification stint. After all, what had she done that was really so bad? She hadn't killed that brilliant young man, Brian Aldernay. She had, in fact, been a genuine admirer of his. She'd been his supervisor for two years, taking over after his old one had died of a coronary. She had been sad when she'd learned that he'd died in such a senseless and wasteful way. But she was hardly to blame for fate, was she? And besides, why should all that brilliant work go to waste?

She'd known for some time that the thesis he'd been researching and writing was a far superior work to her own. And so the idea had just naturally come to her. They were researching in very similar fields. Few people knew of her exact thesis composition—like all academics, she kept her cards close to her chest, always worried that someone might steal her ideas.

In the darkened streets of Headington, all these years later, Rosemary Naismith paused to laugh grimly at her thoughts.

Then she continued her torturous path through the maze of houses, her thoughts still on that fatal night, and on Brian Aldernay.

After his death in that biking accident, she'd quickly come to realise that Brian too, had kept his cards very close to his chest. Only she really knew the full extent, knowledge, and the brilliant theorising that epitomised his work. And, really, it had all been so absurdly simple. His wife had had no idea what he'd been working on. Didn't even express an interest. She'd only wanted to take his work back home north with her because it was a reminder, a keepsake of him. A keepsake! That brilliant, original theory?

She'd made an excuse to keep it for a while, and had feverishly photocopied every chapter. Every reference. Every scrap of notes, before handing it back. And then began the slow turn around of her own fortune. She began to discuss her work a little here and there, dropping it in the right ears, preparing the ground. Her college came to learn that their Research Fellow was rumoured to be getting ready to hand over a blinder of a D.Phil.

It had taken her barely six months to refine and complete Brian's original theory. At first, when it had been so well received, and had earned her a full Fellowship of her college, she'd been scared, sure that someone would crawl out of the woodwork and expose her. An old room mate of Brian's, perhaps, who might have been allowed to read a few bits and pieces, just enough to piece it all together. Or another psychology Don that Brian might have consulted.

Looking back on it, it had really been quite a gamble.

But it had paid off, she thought proudly. For years, it had paid off. Her future was secure. Her reputation, on that one thesis alone, had been made. It was as she'd always thought— fortune favours the bold.

And then, all those years later, at a Prize-giving Dinner, a boozy old fool had brought her world crashing down around her ears.

For half an hour she'd toured the party, her mind in turmoil. She tried to think up a convincing excuse for resigning from her college and from academic life, but couldn't think of one. Besides, she didn't *want* to. She loved it at Oxford. Loved having men fear and respect her because of her awesome brain power, as well as her sexy ways. She enjoyed the privileges, status and lifestyle that went along with being an Oxford Fellow.

And, at some instant during that evening, she knew that she simply could never give it up. But how to keep it, that was the question. Sir Vivian, she knew, was not the kind of man she could seduce. Which was a shame. A quick affair, then a threat to tell the ill wife, and he'd have been forced to keep quiet, and none of this need ever have happened. Nor was he a man who was likely to respond to tearful pleas. He had too much love for Oxford to allow her to continue to teach in his beloved University. And she knew he'd hardly be open to a financial bribe, even if she had been in a position to offer a substantial one—which she wasn't. He was already far more wealthy than she'd ever be.

And so he had to die.

Rosemary paused in the dark streets now, looking around her at the mostly dark houses. People wouldn't be coming home from work until at least five o'clock.

When the thought had first come to her—that she must kill Sir Vivian Dalrymple—she'd been sipping sherry and talking to one St Bede's many theologians. A man of God.

It had made her feel slightly sick.

But it hadn't stopped her thinking.

How to kill a man? A woman couldn't do it physically—not even the fittest of women could reasonably expect to be able to strangle even an older, drunken man. They just had too much superior upper-body strength.

She needed a weapon then.

A knife? There were plenty at the party of course, on the meat trolley. But a knife was too messy. It left too much blood, too much of a forensic trail. She'd be bound to get caught. And then, barely a few seconds after making the decision to become a killer, Rosemary remembered Pete.

And his compound bow.

Pete had bought the newest bow about a month ago. He'd been so pleased with it and eager to show it off that he'd taken her out into the woods to demonstrate it. He didn't want to take it to his usual archery club until he'd mastered it. His professional pride wouldn't let him be seen with such a wonderful masterpiece until he could use it like a maestro. Which meant top-secret practising.

And Rosemary, always intrigued by the unusual and the exciting, had gone with him. And learned how to use it right along beside him. For Pete had been only too pleased to show off his prowess, and to be the teacher for once. Usually it was Rosemary who held the upper hand. Having her in the role of learner, for once, had been irresistible to him. He was just a jock—true, an Olympic jock, but nothing more, and Rosemary knew he'd always felt secretly inferior to her. It had always amused her and allowed her to keep the upper hand.

And that night, she'd almost gloated at the way her luck always held. Even when life dealt her a blow, she didn't sit still for it, but would always meet it head on.

So now she had the perfect weapon all ready and waiting. And she knew how to use it.

The decision made, she'd left the party, racing to Pete's home in her car, and furiously thinking up some excuse to borrow the bow. In the event she hadn't had to bother. She got back there to find half his bags packed, and Pete himself missing.

She knew where he'd be of course. In the pub or at a party somewhere, getting drunk and telling some beautiful girl that he was an Olympic champion. She didn't care. She'd taken the bow from the cabinet he'd cleared out and used especially to house his archery equipment, selected some bolts, and returned to the party.

And there she'd waited in the car park for Sir Vivian to make his way from the party to his room.

Then she'd followed him in the shadows until he was about to enter his residence block.

And then she'd killed Sir Vivian Dalrymple.

She'd put the bow back in her car and slipped away. Only to realise, before she'd gone a hundred yards, that she was being incredibly stupid. Shock, she supposed, had numbed her brain for a few minutes. She'd re-parked the car and returned briefly to the party. Laughed. Drank a bit, making sure several people would remember her and note the time, and then drove herself, and the compound bow, safely home.

Once there, she'd returned the bow to the cupboard and waited up for Pete to return home, all the while feeling curiously calm.

And since then Pete had packed up the remainder of his gear and had left, taking his bow with him. He was, she knew, on his way to America, where he did his serious training. The world championships were coming up. Which meant that he'd taken the murder weapon with him, all honest and above-board. It would travel overseas with its own licence, all legal and untraceable. The police would never find the murder weapon here now, no matter how much they tore Oxford apart looking for it, and she was free and clear.

Sir Vivian was dead.

But it hadn't ended there. On no. If only it had!

Instead, she'd begun to hear rumours that Callum Fielding was asking questions, as was that media-bitch, Marcheta Kendall. Apparently, the police had Callum in their sights as a main suspect—which was sort of funny in its own right, when you came to think about it, she mused now grimly.

Unfortunately, it had probably scared Callum into doing some serious thinking. And worst of all, he'd been at the party that night as well, and had heard Sir Vivian spouting off about how someone had been a cheat and a liar. Which had given him a starting point. He also knew the old man very well, which would give him an advantage over the police.

And with the supermodel egging him on, who knew how long it would be before he finally found out what Sir Vivian knew? The librarians at the Bodleian and other places would be only too happy to let him know just what Sir Vivian had been researching lately. And just one little thread leading back to Brian Aldernay's thesis, and she'd be on the hook again.

Rosemary, rather short-sightedly, didn't fear the police. She was positive she hadn't left any forensic evidence behind her on the night of the murder, and didn't believe they'd ever catch her, let alone convict her. But Callum's brains, and Marcheta's money and clout, were something else again.

She needed an out. Just in case.

Which was what she was doing in that particular cul-de-sac, walking cautiously up to the door of that particular house, in the late autumn afternoon.

She rang the door bell and glanced yet again over her shoulder. She must stop doing that! There was no one there and nothing to see.

She saw the little glass spy-hole in the door darken briefly, and knew she was being scrutinised.

A moment later the door opened and a short, dark, swarthy face appeared around the crack. He beckoned her in silently.

Rosemary quickly walked inside. The door was closed rapidly behind her.

The house was uncarpeted. She was led into a living room, where the furniture was cheap, and the whole room had the look of a place that was a temporary stop only. Which is what it was.

Seated at a table, rising and looking at her suspiciously was a man she'd never seen before. Young, and incredibly good-looking, with the raven black hair and soulful black eyes of a true Arab. She turned around, eyeing the man who'd let her in with a warm smile. 'Hello, Faisal.'

The swarthy man didn't smile back. He nodded stiffly. 'Dr Naismith.'

'Please, call me Rosemary. Can't you do that, Faisal? For Ahmed's sake?'

Faisal's lips twisted grimly. 'Rosemary.' He said it with forced politeness.

Rosemary knew Faisal had never liked her. He had a typical misogynist's attitude to women. Keep them veiled, pregnant, and out of men's business.

She knew that, as an Oxford Fellow, Faisal resented her even more. She was living proof that women were capable of rising to the top in any field, given the social opportunity to do so. And since he was fanatically loyal to Ahmed, and had always been deeply jealous of her hold over him, Rosemary realised she was

267

in the presence of a man who probably hated her guts.

She smiled. 'I need a favour, Faisal.'

The stocky man stiffened. A look of disbelief settled over his face. Then a smile. A rather nasty smile.

'So, even in the west, women still need men, Dr Naismith?' he said, his voice thickly accented.

Rosemary shrugged one shoulder, and decided it was time to capitalise on her connections. 'Have you heard from Ahmed recently?'

Faisal's face fell. 'No. We think he has been captured by the authorities.'

Rosemary felt genuinely sorry. She knew what happened to freedom fighters (or, as the government preferred to call them, terrorists) in Ahmed's country.

Death.

'I'm sorry to hear that, Faisal. Truly.'

Faisal inclined his head stiffly once more. 'What is it you want, Dr Naismith?'

Rosemary smiled again. 'I want a bomb, Faisal,' she said softly.

The stranger behind her suddenly shifted, no doubt in stunned surprise. He didn't altogether share Faisal's distaste for western women, and had been running his eye appreciatively over the blonde woman's body. A bit long in the tooth for him, of course, but then it was said older women were more inventive. And needy.

Now he felt shocked to the core.

Faisal, however, merely smiled crookedly. 'Oh? Any particular sort?'

Rosemary shrugged. 'A car bomb?'

When she'd first met Ahmed, he'd been wary of telling her what he did. But, over the months, as he came to realise that Rosemary's gypsy soul would thrill, rather than shrink, from his world of violence and politics, he'd gradually introduced her into his world. Soon, she could talk of guns and hostage taking and death, as easily as she could talk of Freud versus Jung.

Faisal looked at her steadily for a few moments, then nodded his head towards the kitchen area.

'Follow me.'

The younger man suddenly let rip in a burst of agitated Arabic. Faisal curtly shut him up.

In the kitchen, Faisal lifted up a hidden trap door in the floor, disappeared for a few minutes, and then returned. During that time, the stranger prowled and scowled. When he saw what Faisal was bringing back up from the hollowed-out cellar, he once more broke into a rapid spate of Arabic.

Faisal continued to ignore him.

He closed the trap door, re-covered it with the dirty square of linoleum that had covered it, and placed on the well-scrubbed kitchen table a small, rectangular box. It was about the size of an old video cassette. There were two buttons, one red, one green, on the right-hand side.

Rosemary looked at it with avid interest. 'This is it?'

Faisal nodded. 'Simply push the green button. The red button will come on. Exactly five minutes after that . . . boom!' He waved his hands in a big circle in the air.

Rosemary nodded, reached for it gingerly, and put it in her bag, careful that nothing pressed against the buttons.

She turned to look at Faisal. 'Faisal, I could kiss you.'

The older man took a quick step back, an appalled look on his face. Rosemary laughed, and walked to the door. 'Don't worry. I'll see myself out.'

She was going to go straight to St Bede's, and have a quiet chat with Callum and see if she could gauge just how much he'd learned.

When she was gone, the young handsome Arab turned to Faisal, a look of amazement on his face. He would never normally even think of questioning his cell leader, but he couldn't help but satisfy his curiosity.

'Why did you give her that bomb, Faisal?' he stuttered, his eyes round as saucers.

Faisal shrugged. 'For Ahmed. He loved her. And she never betrayed us,' he added grudgingly.

The younger man shook his head. 'No,

Faisal. I mean, why did you give her *that* particular bomb? Farquar said he wasn't sure that it would work properly. It was a new design. It hasn't even been tested.'

Slowly Faisal began to smile. 'That was why I gave her that particular bomb, my little pomegranate!' he laughed, turning to caress the handsome man's cheek gently. 'Now it will have its field test. And if it doesn't work and explodes when she sets it, well, none of us need get hurt. And if it doesn't perform as it should . . .' he shrugged. 'Well, it will be no skin off our noses, will it? Hum?'

And he leaned forward and kissed the younger man on the lips.

He took this politely, but when his cell leader moved away, he surreptitiously rubbed his mouth with the back of his hands.

But he knew he would die for Faisal. Because Faisal had just shown why he was a cell leader. He was clever, and unscrupulous, and could turn any situation into their advantage.

The cause was lucky to have him.

*   *   *

Outside, in the darkness, the car bomb in her handbag, Rosemary drove towards St Bede's.

CHAPTER FOURTEEN

Nesta stretched on the uncomfortable couch, and reached for her notebook. Outside it was fully dark, and the orange streetlights filtered through her thin curtains, casting an eerie orange glow around the shabby room.

She tucked her legs more comfortably beneath her, and shivered a little. She looked around her for her coat, then shook her head. Shivering a little in her cold bedsit was one thing—just a trifle sad. But hunched up in a coat in her bedsit was bordering on the pathetic! She laughed, but only, she admitted to herself with scrupulous honesty, because she had a way out. Soon, she knew, Lisle was going to ask her to move in with him permanently. Or perhaps suggest that they go house-hunting together.

She'd never been so sure of anything in her life.

She tapped her pen thoughtfully against her notebook, but thoughts of her father, and his cheating supervisor were, for once, a long way off.

Lisle.

To think that one man could change your life forever, and with just—what? A look? A word? She didn't know. She only knew she was no longer the same person who'd left Durham just a few weeks ago. Then she'd been this young girl who knew nothing of life. She'd just graduated with a B.A. in psychology, but what did she really know about herself?

She thought she'd been given a raw deal, a man who'd cheated on her. But people often said that first love was the hardest. Except, of course, she knew now that it hadn't been love. Or at least, not the same kind of love as the love she'd found with an Oxfordshire copper.

She thought then that she'd been alone. Now, she knew she would never be alone again. First there would be Lisle. Then, a few years down the road, children. Then, decades later, when the children had left, it would be just Lisle and herself. Then, after that grandchildren. Then old age, together. What more could she ask for?

Two weeks ago the thought of all that would have seemed as alien to her as living on the moon. Now she knew that it was really going to happen. Here, in her cold old besit, she could see her future as clearly as she could see her own reflection in a mirror.

She sighed blissfully, and settled down to think about Lisle. And she couldn't think of a better way to pass a dark winter afternoon. She hoped this rosy first glow of new love would last for a good long while, but she was not afraid of the day when it would eventually fade, because she knew that what would replace it would be stronger, more enduring.

She remembered walking in and finding him, pacing about, a ferocious look on his face. Why had he demanded to know, *again,* about her relationship with Sir Vivian? Obviously, something more must have happened in the murder case. Frowning thoughtfully, she got up to check the downstairs hall. Sure enough, a local paper had been delivered. As far as she could tell, her fellow tenants treated the papers that were delivered more or less as communal property. First to get them read them, then put them back on the table in the hall for the others to grab.

She glanced at her watch and saw it was barely twenty to five. The others wouldn't start straggling in from work for another half hour. So she didn't feel too guilty about snaffling a quick peek. She skipped lightly down the uneven stairs and gathered up the *Oxford Mail.* Back in her room, she settled back in her sofa, and unfolded it.

As expected, Sir Vivian's murder was still the top story, and the first page screamed the progress, setback, and fortunes of the case. Apparently, one of the psychology Dons at St Bede's, a Dr Callum Fielding, had been questioned and released.

Nesta frowned, and quickly she read the front page blurb.

Dr Callum Fielding, (pictured right) was unavailable for comment this morning, when we went to his College to ask him about the events concerning Sir Vivian Dalrymple's death.

Mystery still surrounds his five-hour long interview at Kidlington Police Headquarters with Detective Inspector Lisle Jarvis and another police officer.

A spokesman for the Kendall family has made it clear that the Kendall Prize, awarded to Dr Fielding at the Dinner which the murder victim attended, is in no way linked to the tragic events of later that night.

Dr Fielding is a well-known friend and colleague of the murder victim, Sir Vivian Dalrymple, who was killed on the night of the 4th, after leaving a Dinner held in St Bede's. He was on the short-list for the Kendall in psychology, along with others, including Dr Julie Ngabe, and Dr. Felicity Ollenbach. Dr Fielding was named as the winner of the Prize at a special announcement at Dinner at High Table in Hall.

This was followed by the fateful cocktail party in the SCR. It was just after leaving this prestigious affair, hosted by the famous supermodel Marcheta, that Sir Vivian was attacked and killed. So far, the police have made no arrests, although a rival paper mistakenly printed that Dr Fielding had been arrested for the crime.

In fact, we can confirm that Dr Fielding was released, after questioning, without charge.

This did not stop Marcheta (pictured below) from issuing a statement to the Press via her PR

Company, the moment the false reports of his arrest had been printed.

However, we have heard from several sources that Marcheta was outraged at the police treatment of Dr Fielding, and threatened to bring her considerable clout to bear, and prosecute the Thames Valley Police Force for malicious arrest.

So far, the man in charge of the case, Detective Inspector Lisle Jarvis, an ex Blackbird-Leys resident, has had little comment to make.

Lord Saint-John James, Principal of St Bede's, has also been most reticent, merely stating that the college was doing everything it could to help the police, and sincerely regretted that such an atrocious act could take place on College grounds.

More intriguing still is the fact that unsubstantiated rumours are beginning to filter through that the method of Sir Vivian's demise is NOT consistent with a routine mugging after all, and security at the coroner's office is unduly tight.

The questioning of a man of Dr Fielding's reputation and standing also seems to suggest that the police are not only following up the idea of a random slaying, but that Sir Vivian was murdered by someone he knew, perhaps even someone at the prize party.

An anonymous source close to the police investigation said this morning that the police had been searching for a certain weapon connected with archery.

Is it possible Sir Vivian was killed with a bow and arrow?

Dr Fielding, as any follower of the sport will know, is an accomplished archer, as are many of St Bede's illustrious graduates. They boast three Olympic medal winners in the last 35 years. The thing that really puzzles this newspaper, however, is what possible motive there could be for one of Sir Vivian's friends or colleagues to murder him?

Please turn to page 4.

But Nesta didn't bother to turn to page four. Instead she felt the paper slip numbly from her hands, but made no attempt to stop it falling to the floor. She stared blankly at the wall for a long, long time, her mind whirling. She felt sick. Giddy. Like she'd just witnessed something horrific—like a plane crash.

She had to struggle to re-arrange all her preconceived ideas. Sir Vivian had been attending a fancy Dinner at St Bede's. As a psychology student herself, Nesta knew all about the prestigious Kendall Prize. And any winner of it was set for life! And Dr Fielding had won it. But, more importantly, at that same Dinner, Rosemary Naismith had been in attendance. She'd have been bound to be.

Why oh why hadn't any of the papers thought to print this piece of information before? Her lips twisted grimly. Obviously because it was not spicy enough. Wasn't interesting enough to help them sell more papers! She felt like screaming in frustration! All this time she'd been thinking it was just a sad case of random violence.

She forced herself to calm down, to think rationally.

Was it just a coincidence? Could it possibly be just a weird twist of fate, that Rosemary Naismith and Sir Vivian had been thrust together, under such tension-making circumstances?

Nesta, without realising it, was suddenly on her feet.

She shook her head, to try and clear it.

Coincidence? How could it be? She just didn't believe it. And now they were saying that the police suspected someone at the party. And she knew someone at that party had a perfect motive for killing Sir Vivian. And it wasn't Dr Fielding!

Nesta had her coat in her hand, and for a moment she stared at it blankly. She realised she was colder now, and it had nothing to do with the inadequate radiators. Shock. She was in shock. She'd had vital evidence all along and never known it . . .

Lisle. Of course. She must talk to Lisle.

She walked to the door and clumped down the stairs, all her previous light-hearted skipping totally gone. She felt old, and curiously numb.

She'd never once thought that Rosemary Naismith could be responsible for murdering

Sir Vivian. Why should she? Even now the thought was so hideous. Stealing a dead person's work was surely a long way from committing cold-blooded murder.

And yet . . .

With one newspaper article, Nesta's whole world seemed to have been set on its head.

If only Lisle had told her about that Dinner and its true importance! And if only she'd realised that Naismith was present when Sir Vivian had been killed! She'd have told him instantly about her father's thesis. When she thought of all the times they'd been together, and he'd been keeping his police secrets so close to his chest, sweating his guts out trying to solve the mystery, when all the time, the one person who could crack his case for him was right under his nose.

If only he'd trusted her. If he'd told her everything, she could have helped him.

Once again, she felt like screaming at the cruel tricks life could play. She only hoped, now that fate had had its little joke on them, that it would leave them alone in peace in the future, and let them live a relatively care-free life!

As she walked to the end of the road, and the public telephone booth, Nesta quickly began to piece it all together, and as she did so, some of the shock began to wear off. With the resilience of youth, and her psychological training, she began to accept the fact that she was on the trail of a murderer.

Sir Vivian must have cornered Naismith and told her what he knew. She could well understand how Rosemary being at the Dinner when she had no right even to be in Oxford, must have really aroused Sir Vivian's sense of outrage.

But had nobody heard him accuse her?

No, she thought, opening the door to the phone booth and shutting it behind her. No, Sir Vivian would not make a scene in public. He would want Naismith to go in as quiet and dignified a manner as possible. For the University's sake more than anything.

She rang Directory Enquiries for the Kidlington Police number, but when she got through there, she was told that Inspector Jarvis was not in the building.

A pleasant-voiced WPC asked if she could take a message.

Nesta hesitated. She really needed to speak to Lisle. On the other hand, she couldn't keep information like she had to herself for any longer.

'Do you know where Detective Inspector Jarvis is, please? It's really urgent.'

'I'm sorry, I can't give out that information. If you have any knowledge of a crime, however . . .' the pleasant voice became just a touch sharper, and before she knew what she was doing, Nesta had put the phone down. She stared at the instrument for a while, torn

280

between a desire to pick it back up and another, slightly stronger desire, to go and find Lisle for herself.

She backed out of the telephone booth and stood looking around her. Oxford was choc-a-block with commuters now. The streetlights bounced light off ancient stone walls. The domes of the Sheldonian and the Bodleian library stood out against an inky black, starlit sky. It was all so beautiful, but Nesta had never felt so suddenly alone. Or so laden with troubles.

She walked back to her car and got inside. Her car keys were in her coat pocket and she put them in the ignition and turned on the engine, hearing the little car roar into life.

But where could she go?

'Damn it, Nesta, think will you?' she muttered to herself. Where was Lisle likely to be, if not at Headquarters? There was a police station in the city, but she didn't think he'd be there.

St Bede's?

Suddenly, Nesta realised that they must have set up an 'incident' room. And didn't they usually do that as near to the scene of the crime as possible? And St Bede's was a college, which meant it was bound to have a room to spare to lend to the police investigation team.

With a small grunt of relief, she turned the car around, and headed as quickly towards St Bede's as the traffic would let her.

*   *   *

As Nesta pulled into the car park of St Bede's, Rosemary Naismith pulled into what had once been the old Radcliffe Hospital next door to the college, and parked her car. She got out, holding her bag ultra-carefully by her side. She didn't dare leave it in the car, just in case some car thief took it, or her car got towed.

By rights, if she had any sense, she'd take it home and then come on to St Bede's, but she had a desperate feeling that she had no time to waste. She needed to see Callum. She just *had* to know how much he knew. How much he'd learned.

As she walked through the front gates and past the porters' lodge, Nesta Aldernay cut through Wallace quad, and headed for the lodge from the opposite direction.

Rosemary, who was heading for Callum's rooms at the far end of the college in Wolsey passed her. The two women, in the dark, barely glanced at each other.

Nesta knew only Rosemary's name—it was in fact, burned into her soul—but she had no idea what she actually looked like. Why should she? She'd never so much as seen a picture of her.

But both women, on reaching their destinations, found themselves disappointed.

Rosemary knocked and knocked on

Callum's door, reluctant to leave and not wanting to acknowledge that he was out. It was such an anti-climax that she wanted to lean against his door and cry.

Nesta learned from the porter that the police incident room was in the theatre in Webster, but when she went there and stood quietly in the doorway, she could see for herself that Lisle was not inside. So she walked slowly back through Wallace quad, towards her parked car, wondering what she should do next.

At that moment, Rosemary walked under Becket Arch and began to make her way back to the main gates. She'd have to take the bomb back to her house after all, and come back later. Callum, unless he was dining out, would be back to dine in Hall by six, at the latest.

Had not Marcheta also arrived at that moment, what happened next would never have happened at all. Nesta would have gone back to her cold bedsit, to spend miserable hours waiting for Lisle to get in touch with her, and Rosemary would have been arrested. But Marcheta, who'd just come from the Randolph, now stepped out of a taxi and walked through the main gates, quickly heading for Wolsey.

She wanted to see if Callum was back from the Bodleian.

Opposite the entrance to the car park, Rosemary saw the unmistakable tall and leggy figure of the supermodel and hesitated. The woman's long flowing black hair was a dead give away, and in the well-lit quad, Rosemary had no trouble spotting and identifying her.

And Rosemary instinctively knew that she didn't want Marcheta Kendall to see her. The tall cross of the War Memorial provided an ideal hiding place, and with a quick side step, she flattened herself against it, becoming all but invisible in the cold night.

At the same time, Nesta, coming out of Webster, also spotted the tall, unmistakable figure of the beautiful woman. She looked just like her photograph in that evening's edition of the *Oxford Mail*. She was glad that the poor, beleaguered and unquestionably innocent Dr Fielding had someone fighting his corner.

She was just a second too late, however, to see the furtive figure of the other, blonde woman in the quad slip behind the dark shadowy War Memorial.

Nesta quickened her pace. 'Miss Kendall?' she called, and only then wondered what she was doing.

Markie stopped and looked around. She saw a woman with a bell-shaped cap of lovely red hair hurrying towards her. As she stopped and waited for her to reach her, (somewhat impatiently as she was dying to talk to Callum) she saw that the woman's face was pinched pale with worry. Even in the artificial electric light streaming from the various college windows, she looked haggard and upset.

As she got within a few feet, Markie could see that her big green eyes were large with worry. In the deserted quad, their words carried clearly in the night air, echoing off the ancient walls of the buildings.

'You are Marcheta Kendall, aren't you? The one who's friends with Dr Fielding?' Nesta asked a trifle breathlessly.

'Yes. That's me,' Markie said, intrigued now.

Nesta came to a halt, and once again wondered why she'd attracted this woman's attention. She smiled grimly.

'I don't suppose you know where Inspector Jarvis is, do you?' Nesta asked. 'He's not in the incident room.'

Had she known it, she'd only missed him by a matter of twenty minutes or so. And right at that moment, he and Jim Neill were frantically searching Rosemary Naismith's College rooms. For Callum Fielding had telephoned them from the Bodleian not half an hour ago, and had told them everything that he'd discovered.

It was yet more irony piled upon irony.

But now, Markie shrugged and smiled a little grimly. 'Unless he's out trying to harass Callum again, I have no idea, sorry,' she drawled.

Nesta went, if possible, even paler. 'I'm sorry. You and Dr Fielding must be having a hard time of it, and it's all my fault.'

Behind the War Memorial Rosemary, who had been waiting impatiently for the two women to move away, suddenly stiffened. Her ears pricked.

The quad was still deserted. At this time of day most students coming back to the college to dine, entered by the many side and postern gates, nearest to their Houses. Those that did come in through the main gates ignored the women, uninterested in them or their conversation. And all of them missed seeing Rosemary, huddled deep as she was in the shadows.

Markie frowned. 'Your fault? I don't understand.'

Nesta sighed wearily. 'It's a long story, and rather complicated. And, oh Hell, I need to see Lisle. Where is he?' she all but wailed.

Markie smiled. 'You know Inspector Jarvis?'

Nesta flushed tellingly, and Markie felt herself grinning. So, the dour, handsome, gruff policeman had a lover did he? Good for him! It was about time some woman took him in hand. And this woman with the fiery red hair and flashing green eyes looked like she could handle such a man all right. But right now, such speculations, interesting though they were, had to take second place.

'I still don't understand,' Markie persisted, 'why you should think that any of this is your fault?'

Which was a sentiment, had she but known it, that was being echoed most fervently by Rosemary Naismith in her hiding place.

Nesta sighed. 'I'm sorry, I haven't even introduced myself. I'm Nesta Aldernay.'

Both Markie and Rosemary gasped.

Markie stared at the woman in front of her, unable to make the leap. 'Aldernay you say? You're not a relation of Brian Aldernay are you?'

Behind the War Memorial Rosemary's heart seemed to stop beating.

'Yes!' Nesta said, stunned. 'But how do you know my father's name?'

Rosemary felt sick. Her father!

Of course, she remembered now, Brian had had an infant daughter. But what was she doing here? She clutched her bag tighter to her in unconscious worry, then realised what she was doing. She broke into a sweat and forced herself to relax, frantically checking that neither of the lights on the side of the bomb were lit up.

They weren't.

Had Rosemary known it, she wouldn't have felt quite so relieved. That bomb might not be ticking, but, less than a quarter of a mile away, another bomb was. For Lisle and Jim, in her rooms, were bagging the photograph of her Olympic archer friend and, the search over, were heading towards the door.

287

In the deserted and dark quad, however, Markie and Nesta still stared at one another in equal amazement.

'But Callum and I have just found your father's papers in Sir Vivian's country cottage,' Markie said.

Rosemary gasped again. Luckily for her, against the sound of traffic roaring up the Woodstock Road just a few yards away, neither of the other women heard it.

'So that's where it was!' Nesta said, momentarily distracted. 'I searched everywhere for it! Lisle was so cross with me!'

Markie couldn't help but laugh at that. She'd just bet he was! But how had Nesta Aldernay and Lisle got together and why hadn't they pieced it together and . . . No, she gave herself a mental shake. All that could wait.

'But how did Sir Vivian come to have your father's papers?' she asked, dying of curiosity now.

'Because I gave them to him,' Nesta said, with earth shaking simplicity. 'I was an undergraduate at Durham,' she carried on, trying to keep the explanations short. 'I found my father's thesis in the attic, after my mother died. Because I was studying psychology too, I understood what I'd read. And, as luck would have it, I'd also studied Dr Naismith's thesis as part of a summer course I did a year ago. I recognised the similarities. Then I did some digging, and found out that Rosemary Naismith had been my father's supervisor.'

'And you put it all together?' Markie finished. 'Wow. So all this time you knew. Why the hell didn't you come forward?' she asked angrily. All this time and effort she and Callum had been putting into it, when all the time, this woman knew . . .

'But the papers said Sir Vivian had been mugged!' Nesta groaned. 'I thought it was a random act of violence. It wasn't until I read the papers tonight that I put it all together! Part of me still can't believe that Dr Naismtih killed him. It still seems so extreme!'

Markie shook her head, not in denial, but with the same sense of disbelief that she could sense in the redhead. It did seem bizarre. But she knew that Callum believed it, even if he'd never said so. And he knew the woman better than either herself or Nesta Aldernay.

Behind the War Memorial, Rosemary started to shake. She could feel herself begin to collapse. This was so much worse than she'd expected. It was a catastrophe. Brian Aldernay's daughter! And Marcheta Kendall. They both knew now, and soon, that damned copper was going to come back and they'd tell him and it would all be over.

Rosemary reeled against the cold stone cross, feeling herself disintegrate. She could see years in prison stretching ahead of her. The disgrace and ignominy.

'We have to tell Lisle,' Nesta's clear voice echoed around the quad.

In her hiding place, Rosemary fought back a sob of panic.

'We'll have to wait for him to get back,' Markie agreed.

'My car's parked in the car park,' Nesta said. 'A VW Beetle. Shouldn't we go to the Kidlington Police Station? We can't sit on this any longer.'

But Markie hesitated. 'Callum should be back by now—I was just on my way to his room to see. He's got your father's papers. He's been at the Bodleian all afternoon checking it out. It makes sense for us all to go together,' she pointed out with perfect logic. 'Between us, we've got all the pieces of the puzzle now.'

'OK. But let's hurry!'

Rosemary shrank back even further against the stone cross, but she needn't have worried. Nesta and Markie were walking so fast when they passed by the War Memorial that they were almost running.

But as Rosemary watched them disappear through Becket Arch, she began to function again. She had to kill them! All of them.

She pushed away from the War Memorial and headed quickly to the car park.

A Beetle. She saw it immediately. It was the only Volkswagen in the car park.

Luckily it was an old model, one whose boot could be opened from the outside without the use of a key. As in all the Beetles, the engine was in the back, so she walked to the front of the car to open the boot. Looking around furtively, she opened her bag, took out the cassette-shaped bomb and put it into the dark boot. She glanced at the buttons and hesitated.

Five minutes, Faisal had said.

She knew that Callum was not in his room, but for how long would the two women wait for him? Not more than five minutes surely? But then they had to walk back.

She decided to wait. She glanced at her watch, her finger hovering over the red button. As soon as she heard them coming, she'd set the bomb going.

*   *   *

In their car, Lisle and Jim headed back towards the incident room. Lisle wanted to get an APB out on Rosemary Naismith as soon as possible.

But it was the rush hour, and progress towards the college seemed so slow.

*   *   *

Nesta hurried back into the car park, her heels clicking. Rosemary Naismith heard her clearly.

Unaware of the danger she was in, she pressed the red button on the unstable, untested bomb. There was a slight click and

291

then the green light came on. Rosemary closed the boot and quickly raced towards the main lodge gates. She was so far gone in panic and bloodlust now that she was no longer thinking straight.

But she felt in perfect control.

As she stepped out of the main gate, her face was resolute.

Back in St Bede's car park Nesta got into the booby-trapped Beetle.

CHAPTER FIFTEEN

Lisle walked forward quickly, ready to pounce in the unlikely event that the tall blonde giant should make a dash for it. 'Hello, Dr Fielding,' he said grimly. 'I've been wanting to catch up with you all day,' he added, with biting sarcasm. 'Fancy seeing you here.' His lips twisted grimly.

Beside him, Jim grinned wolfishly.

'I want to know just what's been going on,' Lisle demanded ominously.

Simultaneously, Callum said 'Inspector Jarvis, I have that evidence I promised you.'

Both men broke off and looked at one another.

Oblivious to the passing traffic and pedestrians, Lisle sighed heavily. 'What exactly did you find?' Lisle snapped again, in no mood to play forty questions. 'And I want details this time, not the bare minimum that you gave me before.'

Callum held up his battered leather briefcase. 'As I told you on the phone a while ago, I found out why Sir Vivian was killed,' he said simply. 'And I think I know who did it as well.'

Lisle nodded. 'Yes I know, you said. Dr Naismith. Yes, I agree. Did you know her current partner is an Olympic champion archer with a crossbow? It's not too great a leap to suppose that the lady herself is conversant with how it works.'

Both men seemed unaware that they were stood in the middle of the pavement outside the entrance to St Bede's, beside a busy street, where anyone could overhear them. Now that he'd finally met up with Lisle, Callum wanted nothing more than to unload his burden onto the police, get back to Markie, and put this whole sorry episode behind him.

He suddenly realised how natural the thought of going back to Markie had been. Already, it seemed, his subconscious was beginning to think of her as someone permanent in his life. He felt himself tense as he thought of what he'd have to do tomorrow. Breaking up with someone was never easy—especially when you knew how special they could be to you. But that was just the trouble—he couldn't afford for Markie Kendall to mean so much to him.

Luckily for the three men, the commuters milling around them were too busy trying to get home, walk to bus queues or get to their parked cars to bother with the huddle of men blocking the stream of pedestrian traffic.

As people dodged around them, Callum began to explain his day's activities.

'As I told you, I found a fifteen year old thesis in Sir Vivian's study in his cottage,' he began crisply. 'It was by a man named Brian Aldernay, and . . .'

'*Aldernay!*' Lisle all but shrieked.

Both Jim and Callum stared at him in blank amazement. Lisle quickly snapped his mouth shut, and took several deep, calming breaths.

*   *   *

Unaware of the nearness of their men, in the car park and sitting in Nesta's car, Markie and Nesta began to fasten their safety belts.

It was exactly two minutes and twenty-one seconds since Rosemary Naismith had armed the bomb.

*   *   *

'Forget it,' Lisle said gruffly, suddenly aware that the two men were gaping at him, as well they might. 'I just recognised the name, that's all,' he explained feebly. 'Please, carry on.'

Callum nodded uncertainly. How had the policeman come across the name of Aldernay before? Did he know more than he was letting on? 'The thesis was a brilliant one, and nearly completed. From Sir Vivian's notes on it, I knew that the student concerned had been a graduate here, and had been killed in a bicycle accident before he'd had the chance to present his D.Phil.'

Lisle's eyes narrowed. 'Which added up to what, exactly?' he asked ominously. Just wait until he got back home to Nesta . . . .

*   *   *

At that moment, Nesta was reaching for the car keys, about to turn the ignition. It was now two minutes and fifty-eight seconds since the bomb had been armed.

*   *   *

'I also found out that Brian Aldernay's supervisor at the time of his death was . . .' Callum began, but Lisle was not about to be robbed of his moment.

'Rosemary Naismith,' he said flatly.

'Yes! Did you know this all the time?'

Lisle shrugged, not about to divulge to a member of the public what the police did, or didn't know. 'This thesis. I take it that it's relevant?'

Lisle was enjoying himself enormously. He wouldn't have been human if he didn't enjoy besting one of the best brains in Oxford—in the country, even.

Callum found himself smiling slightly. It was never a good idea to underestimate the police, it seemed.

Blissfully unaware of the drama taking place in car park just a few hundred yards away, neither men would have been so happy if they'd known how Rosemary Naismith had spent her afternoon.

*   *   *

In the Volkswagen Beetle, Nesta turned the ignition and revved the engine.

They now had less than two mintues to live.

*   *   *

'Yes, it's relevant,' Callum said firmly, and was bumped from behind when a secretary leaving the college, and hurrying to catch her bus, failed to see him in time and jogged his elbow in passing. Callum instinctively half turned, and began to walk slowly down the alleyway, towards the college car park, and Lisle and Jim fell into step beside him.

They could hear the sound of a car revving in the car park now, but none of them paid much attention, save to step to the side of the alleyway to make room for it when it happened to pass by them.

'This thesis was, save from a few finishing bits and pieces, the same thesis that Rosemary presented as her own D.Phil, about nine months after Aldernay's death,' Callum explained bleakly. His words echoed off the narrow walls of the alley. Apart from a dim streetlight it was dark and eerie in the narrow passageway.

Lisle suddenly shivered. For some reason he felt a grim, dark, nasty sensation of impending disaster. It was a repetition of what he'd been feeling all day, only stronger. More urgent. He couldn't understand it. He was not used to 'feelings' like this. His career had been based on good old-fashioned foot work, research and logic.

He tried to shrug it off.

*　　　*　　　*

In the car park, Nesta put on the headlights and the heater. 'You don't mind if we wait a minute for the old buggy to heat up, do you?' she asked Markie, who was also shivering.

She glanced ruefully at the windscreen, which was fast misting up, and shook her head. 'No, not at all.'

Outside, the three men were only a few yards from the postern gates that led to the car park.

'So you're saying that she stole this chap's work?' Jim Neill said, picking up the thread of Callum's argument.

Callum nodded. 'Yes.' Catching Lisle's look of disbelief, he shrugged and smiled sadly. 'It's not as hard as you might think. Brian and Rosemary were researching in the same field. Everyone who mattered would have known that. And every serious academic I've ever known keeps his work and research and theories top secret. Sometimes even from their supervisor. I doubt Rosemary's own supervisor knew much about her original work for instance.'

'They're so close-mouthed and possessive, I suppose, 'cause they're scared someone's gonna pinch their ideas?' Jim guessed sardonically.

Callum sighed and nodded. 'You know,' he said wearily, 'I'm getting really fed up with research. With teaching even. With Oxford. All the academic in-fighting and back-biting is getting me down.'

Lisle and Jim exchanged glances, eyebrows raised. That was quite some admission for a University Don to make!

'But what I don't understand,' Callum carried on, as the three men stepped through the postern gates and into the car park, 'is how Sir Vivian got onto it all in the first place. All this happened years ago.'

Lisle snorted. 'I think I can answer that . . .'

In the Beetle, Nesta turned on the windscreen wipers in a bid to clear the glass. She saw three men in the beam of her headlights.

Callum, being so toweringly tall and fair, was instantly recognisable, and was the first man that both the women instinctively looked at. As they did so, the bomb in the front of the car had been ticking away for four minutes and forty-two seconds.

Markie gave a short yip of surprise and fumbled for the window lever. 'That's Callum!' she crowed, as Nesta looked across at her questioningly.

Looking out of the cleared windscreen, Nesta's eyes moved to the other two men with him, and instantly recognised Lisle.

'And Lisle!' she breathed, a great smile of relief and welcome spreading across her heart-shaped face.

The three men glanced across as they heard the squeak of a window being lowered. Lisle recognised the comical little Beetle at once. He took a step towards it.

As he did so, Callum saw a dark head emerge from the window. A pair of dark blue eyes, and a wide smiling mouth. For a moment, his heart lifted, and all doubts and worries seemed to run screaming into the night. It was Markie. And he loved her. Nothing else mattered. All this heart-searching he'd been doing, trying to convince himself it could never work between them, as just the action of a coward. He hadn't wanted to fall in love. He hadn't trusted his feelings. Now, in a fraction of time, he saw it all so completely clearly.

All he had to do was trust her. To trust what they had together. It was just a matter of trust, that was all.

His heart soared. 'Markie,' he said softly, joyously.

Their eyes met . . .

And the car exploded.

Or at least, it seemed to.

Everything happened so fast, and yet in amazing slowness, that it was only later that the police bomb disposal experts were able to put all the pieces together and say what must have happened.

To the two women sitting in the car, though, everything changed in a heart-wrenching instant.

One second they were each looking at the men they loved, and in the next instant, at a wall of flame.

There was a 'crummppph' of sound, a tearing, squealing, rending sound, like a pig in pain. It was in fact the bonnet of the car being blown off its hinges and into the air by the force of the explosion. Although the experimental bomb had gone off according to schedule, it had not gone off as it was supposed to, in one single devastating blast.

Instead, there was this first, primary explosion, which had only a fraction of the force it was capable of. It did, however, send a wall of flame shooting up in front of the windscreen, and a rising, bilious cloud of curiously white and pale smoke engulfed the car.

Inside, the two women were thrust back by the force of the airwave deep into their seats.

Markie, with a scream of surprise, instinctively flung up her hand in front of her face, as a scorching wall of heat shattered the windscreen. Beside her, Nesta did the same. Simultaneously, they felt their arms sting to the laceration of a hundred tiny cuts.

Markie felt her chin and the top of her forhead flinch with tiny pinpricks of pain.

Nesta felt her right cheek tingle in sudden cold-hot numbness.

Luckily, both women's cuts were superficial, and would heal quickly and without any scarring, but right at that moment, they weren't even thinking about that. They didn't have time to think about anything. The stench of burning metal and rubber assailed their noses as the spare wheel in the boot caught fire. The smoke went from white, to choking, foul black.

It seemed to envelop the car in a shroud of darkness.

'Get out, Nesta! Get out!' Markie heard a voice screaming in the darkness, choking in the smoke, and realised that it was her own.

She tried to reach for the door, but something seemed to stop her.

Beside her, Nesta fumbled for the catch of her seatbelt, and Markie suddenly realised that it wasn't a huge, death loving beast that was determined to keep locked in place, but only her own humble seatbelt. She too fumbled for the catch to free herself.

In the boot of the car, the main set of explosives in the bomb began to heat towards detonation point . . .

The three men outside the car seemed rooted to the spot forever, but it was, in fact, less than a second. Even so, it was hard to believe what they were seeing. Callum and Lisle screamed a horrified 'NO!' at precisely the same moment.

They both darted heroically forward as the car disappeared into a pall of black, evil-smelling smoke.

The fierceness of the fire, though, pushed them back in a wall of blazing heat that seared their faces, singeing their eyebrows and burning off the moisture on their lips in a matter of seconds.

Markie felt her door pop open and literally fell onto the hard wet tarmac. She was coughing so hard and her eyes were watering so badly she could see and hear nothing.

She felt the car rock slightly, and realised that Nesta, too, must have got free, and gave a groaning sob of relief. Then she scrambled to her knees, instinct screaming at her to *run, run, run* . . . to get as far from the car as she possibly could. But she could only seem to crawl.

Jim Neill screamed at the two men to get back, but his voice was drowned out by an almighty crack.

Instinctively, Lisle threw himself to the left, and Callum to the right, as the main part of the bomb exploded.

Luckily for everyone, with the bonnet of the car gone, the force of the bomb exploded mostly upwards, harmlessly erupting its fury in a straight line up to the sky.

Nesta, who'd managed to get to her feet, nevertheless felt herself catapulted forward by the shock wave.

She hit the wall of the car park with a 'whoomp' and crumpled to the ground. Lisle, who'd thrown himself to the side of the driver's door, saw her slender figure fly through the air as the explosion seemed to batter his eardrums, threatening to burst them.

He cried out in anguish, and before the sound had even died down to a mere ominous echo, he was on his feet and running towards her inert figure, his heart racing sickeningly, his soul cringing in fear.

'Nesta!'

Markie, who'd still been on her hands and knees when the bomb detonated for the second, more devastating time, felt herself being flattened to the ground. Her cheek scraped painfully against the tarmac, and suddenly she was aware of a heavy weight pressing against her, shielding her, as bits of car fell down all around her head.

'Markie! Darling, are you alright?'

Her ears were still tingling from the huge crack of the explosion, but, nevertheless, she heard his voice clearly. It was the most beautiful thing she'd ever heard.

She felt herself being rolled tenderly onto her back. Over Callum's shoulder she vaguely saw Jim Neill's face, a picture of shock and worry, glance down at them.

He must have seen that she was still alive, though, for he quickly disappeared.

But Markie barely acknowledged his existence. Her whole vision was filled with the sight of two icy-blue eyes blazing down at her with more heat than even the bomb had been able to generate. He shook her, gently but frenziedly. 'Speak to me, damn you,' he husked, pausing to cough in the pall of smoke that hung around them.

He had a huge black streak down one side of his face, and his eyebrows were singed brown, but he was the most beautiful sight she'd ever seen.

She smiled. 'Not much of a cold-blooded academic now, are you?' she murmured, giddily.

Callum knew the words didn't make sense,

but they *were* words, and she was speaking, breathing, smiling . . .

She was *alive*.

'Oh, Markie,' he choked. 'Don't ever do that to me again!' he sobbed. 'I love you so much.'

And he bent down and kissed her.

Markie's arms curled hard and possessively around him, and as she held on to him, hugging him close, they both knew that she was never going to let him go.

And they were both more than happy with that.

People, alerted by the awful sound of the bomb, began to stream into the car park now. One of the more level-headed of the students' ran for the lodge to telephone for the fire brigade—for the Beetle was still on fire—and an ambulance.

Callum, oblivious to their goggle-eyed audience, slowly lifted his head. His eyes glowed liked banked blue fire. His lips had tasted of charcoal, but Markie had never enjoyed a kiss more in her life!

She watched his lovely and loving face, only vaguely realising how close she had come to death. Just slightly hysterically, she began to laugh.

Callum, still lying protectively on top of her, his elbows bent either side of her head, began to laugh too.

'What?' he demanded.

Markie shook her head. 'Nothing. Nothing

my lovely aloof academic. Nothing.'

Callum's eyes glowed. 'Aloof, am I?' he said huskily, and lowered his lips to hover just above hers. 'We'll see about that!' he whispered, and kissed her passionately, holding nothing back.

It made her see stars.

Over against the wall, Lisle wasn't faring so well.

He'd reached Nesta, his mind an agonised mass of fear, and very gingerly turned her over. As gently as he could, he cradled her in his arms. With a shaking hand he pushed a swathe of dark red hair away from her cut cheek and tenderly kissed her temples.

'Don't be dead,' Lisle whispered against her unresponsive face. 'Please, don't be dead. Oh God, please, don't let her be dead . . .'

He was still repeating this litany, over and over again, when Jim Neill knelt beside him. For a stunned second, he realised that his superior was totally out of his mind. It was the first time ever that Jim could recall, when Lisle had been anything but clear-headed in a crisis.

He swallowed hard, as he realised what this woman must mean to his boss. Fighting back his own sense of fear, he reached for the woman's wrist and felt her pulse.

It was strong and sure and steady.

Jim let out a huge breath of relief. Then, his policeman's training taking over, he gently ran his hand over the redhead's scalp and felt a bump on the back of her head.

He laid a comforting hand on Lisle's shoulder.

'It's all right, Lisle,' he said quietly, but firmly. 'She's just been knocked out, sir,' he added gently. 'She'll be all right. You'll see.'

And as the smoke crept up into the night sky, and Lisle and Callum held on tightly to the women they'd loved and had so nearly lost, one of Oxford's many clocks began to chime the hour of five.

*   *   *

Six months later, Nesta and Lisle were married in Durham, with the supermodel Marcheta in attendance as Chief Bridesmaid. They honeymooned in Hawaii.

Dr Callum Fielding bought his first house just twenty miles from the city of London, where he regularly spent most of his time with a beautiful woman, rumoured to be a supermodel.

Dr Rosemary Naismith stood trial almost a year to the day after Sir Vivian Dalrymple was murdered. She was charged not only with his murder, but with the attempted murder of Miss Nesta Aldernay and Miss Marcheta Kendall.

She was found guilty on all counts, and sentenced to life imprisonment.